CONFINED BY LOVE

A TAIT BROTHERS STANDALONE

JAS B.

WANT TO BE A PART OF THE GRAND PENZ FAMILY?

To submit your manuscript to Grand Penz Publications, please send the first three chapters and synopsis to info@grandpenz.com

SYNOPSIS

Confined by Love

Ambiguous is the only term suitable when it comes to the Tait brothers. The saying, "Things aren't always what they seem," rings true with Apollo, Zeus, and Nyx.

Apollo is a paramedic who's also holding down his family's business. That same business lands love right in his lap. Hazel Cox was everything Apollo felt he needed. She just wasn't aware of it quite yet.

Hazel is a rising marketing agent on a personal healing journey. That journey soon reveals its own set of mysteries. Mysteries that, unbeknownst to Hazel, can only be unlocked by Apollo.

Zeus is a middle school science teacher passionate about kids and a thrill for chemical explosions. After helping his brother out, he's faced with the thrill of his

life—saving Mocha Cox from the biggest mistake of her life.

Mocha is a scorned woman trying to find her way back to herself. She's discovering her passion and the fact that she never really felt what it meant to be loved unconditionally until she met Zeus.

Nyx is a medical examiner and mortician. Let anyone tell it, Nyx was an introvert, mean, and closed off. And Nyx would agree. He preferred being alone. Especially since he wanted to keep his personal flaws under wraps. That was until Braiza made him consider changing his ways.

Braiza felt like her biological clock was ticking. Looking to settle down and start a family, something about Nyx Tait made her feel like he was just the person for the job. However, breaking down his barriers had her ready to call it quits.

But there was something about the love of a Tait that wouldn't let these women go. They were in too deep... They were lost without them... They were—confined by love.

ONE
HAZEL COX

"You're free to go, Ms. Cox," Detective Drescher came into the cold, gray room and announced. I'd been sitting there, going through a series of questions with different people, and I was ready to get the hell out of this police station.

The chair scratched the floor as I pushed away from the table. I couldn't breathe inside of there and the gasp of air I sucked in once I plowed through the station, bumping into multiple people to get through the front door, felt like a lifesaver.

"Hazel!" Mocha rushed toward me. She was the only person I thought to call when I found my fiancé's body. I ran into her arms. My sister hugged me like everything in the world was going to be OK. "What the hell did they have you in there for twelve hours for?"

"Murder."

The vibration from my phone woke me up from the nightmare of reality.

"Hey, Mocha," I croaked.

"Don't hey me. I've been calling you all morning. Do you see what time it is?"

I pulled the phone away from my ear to look at the time and jumped up.

"Shit, I didn't hear my alarm. I'm supposed to be at the shelter in ten minutes," I grumbled.

"Well, that's not going to happen, look outside."

I walked to my window and was met with the sun's brightness bouncing off a thick blanket of snow.

"I'll call you back. This shit is going to take me at least an hour to shovel," I told Mocha, as I stood in front of my glass door, looking at the mess this year's snowstorm had made.

"I don't know why you won't just call Von. He would probably take about an hour to get to you," Mocha responded.

"That's what he said when I needed a jump, and he ended up taking three hours. Ain't nobody got time for that." I looked into the camera with a serious look. She wanted me to be with her husband's cousin, Von, so badly that she expected me to excuse all the red flags. It was not happening. I wasn't down with the swirl. I preferred my meat to be a little seasoned.

"You're just impatient."

"I'm not impatient. The quicker I get this done, the faster I can leave. Majic is probably running around like a chicken with her head cut off. Bye."

Not giving her a chance to debate, I hit the end button. After showering and getting dressed, I sat at the bottom of my staircase to pull on my snow boots. Mocha knew how vital my community work was to me. Her dismissing it only aggravated me more than Mother Nature already had.

I grabbed my thick winter coat and pulled my hat and gloves out of the sleeve. This was how my mother made sure I didn't lose them as a kid, and at my big age, I still needed to do it. I would lose shit in a heartbeat.

I went through my garage door to grab my shovel and got to work on my driveway and walkway. Thank God for my garage; I wouldn't have to clean my car off. These were the moments where I hated being single; however, one thing Hazel Cox was, was an independent woman. After my last relationship, I vowed I would never place myself in a position to need a man for anything.

Backaches from bending over and lifting the heavy snow to toss it to the side caused me to pause here and there, but I finally finished the driveway after an hour. I was standing there, holding on to the top of the shovel, staring at my walkway I had yet to touch, and wondering how the hell I was sweating in twenty-degree weather when the snow crunching behind me turned my attention.

"You need some help?" a guy that was just as bundled up as I was asked. A winter hat and face mask left nothing but his dark brown eyes visible. I instantly got lost in his gaze. Men always had the best natural lashes. Breaking eye contact, I looked around trying to figure out where the hell he'd come from and why he didn't show up sooner before my eyes fell back on the stranger. His deep, dark eyes consumed me, and I could not speak immediately. "I'm sorry for sneaking up on you. We haven't met yet, but I just moved in across the street."

"Ohh, that was you?" I recalled seeing a moving van earlier this week parked on the street, but I hadn't laid eyes on my new neighbor.

"Yea, I'm Apollo." He extended his gloved hand, and I shook it. "I can knock this out for you if you'd like."

"Thank you! That would be great." I sighed in relief and handed my shovel over to him. Something about him seemed familiar. Especially when I shook his hand. As he'd stated, I knew for a fact I hadn't met this man a day in my life, but those deep eyes seemed to look right through me. It was hard to decipher what I was feeling, but it was like his presence made me comfortable and shy at the same time.

"Go in out of the cold and I'll come let you know when I'm through," Apollo suggested. He didn't have to tell me twice. I trudged slowly through the snow that was still on my walkway. I'd never been clumsy, but Apollo also had my knees feeling unstable.

"Shit!" My boot got stuck in a pile of snow and I almost fell forward. Strong arms caught me mid-way, sending electrical waves through my body.

"I saw that coming the moment you went to yank your boot. Next time, just slightly pull upward, not forward, until you feel your foot loosen enough to yank with a little more force. Are you stable enough for me to let go?"

I nodded, giving Apollo the green light to let go, and went inside. "Woo!" The heat hit me immediately, equivalent to how my damn body felt enflamed when this stranger touched me. I pulled off my gloves and fanned myself, standing in the foyer, deciding not to get comfortable since I had to leave right back out.

I was busy trying to contact Majiq at the center and hadn't noticed that Apollo finished shoveling until he tapped on the glass door. I got up off the steps and opened the door for him to join me out of the cold.

"Thank you, again. I would offer you some hot chocolate or some-thing, but I really have to get going," I told him, taking the wet shovel from his hands.

"It's all good, we'll have plenty of time for that. I'm right across the street. You're driving to work in this mess?" he asked, looking back outside for a second.

"No. My office is closed for the day. I volunteer at the community center down on Jefferson."

"Impressive." He nodded. I looked over and grabbed my coat. "Eau de Parfum."

"Excuse me?"

"Your perfume." Apollo looked like he was in a daze.

"You're familiar with fragrances? Nice," I complimented.

"Somewhat." He shrugged. "I'll let you go, though."

I couldn't help but watch Apollo walk back across to his place. I had so many questions. It was rare that a man bought a property alone and offered help without wanting something in return. However, he didn't even hit on me. But who was I to complain or pry?

I returned the shovel to its original storage place and prayed that the center wasn't in disarray due to my tardiness.

"Where have you been?" Majiq, a dear friend of the family asked when I came in from the back entrance. As expected, we were packed wall to wall with people just trying to get out of the cold and get a meal.

"Uhh, it is six feet of snow out there," I pointed out. I was being a bit dramatic, but hey.

"It is not six feet!" She laughed. "I've been bouncing around between soup and sandwiches. Take your pick."

"Soup," I chose. We were past capacity, and I was fine with that due to the weather, but there was no way we could fit anyone else. Majiq and I made sure everyone was fed and warm before preparing for the next meal.

———

CHRISTMAS WAS APPROACHING FAST, and so was the deadline for my advertisement pitch for a company's new candle brand. It sounded so simple, but coming up with new and innovative ideas wasn't simple at all. I rubbed my temples while trying to figure out the best way to draw attention to the collection of aromas.

"Knock, knock," Mocha announced herself with a few taps on my door before entering my office. The interruption caused me to jump a little. "Yo' ass always jumpy. Somebody after you?"

Little sisters sure knew how to work a nerve. She knew I was in the middle of a brainstorming session with myself. I don't know what I was thinking when I convinced my boss to hire her as my assistant, but my sister was also my best friend and I understood her need to shift her life as a stay-at-home wife. Mocha sat on the couch I had against the large skyline window that stretched across my office. "Come up with anything?"

"Still putting things together in my head." My tone reflected my mood, and I hoped she got the hint.

"Oh, it'll come to you. It always does." She dismissed the fact that I was frustrated at the moment.

"Do you have any suggestions?" I inquired. She shook her head. "Did you need anything regarding your job?" Again, she shook her head. "OK. Please go back to your desk so I can focus."

"Fine," she snapped. "If you don't want any of Mama's gumbo, I'll keep it all to myself."

"Wait, wait, wait! Bring it on in." I dramatically waved her back inside. My mama's gumbo was on another level. Mocha and I grew up in a two-parent household where my southern mother put her foot in every meal she made.

"That's what I thought," she hissed. Mocha disappeared for a few moments and returned with Tupperware filled with gumbo. Then, it hit me. I pulled up the emails that contained everything I needed for this campaign, and all the colors somehow matched the idea that had just sparked.

"Why didn't I think of this?" I thought aloud.

"I assume you came up with an idea, and something is telling me that your brilliant little sister had something to do with it without even trying." Mocha sat back in her seat grinning and moving gumbo around in her bowl.

"Yep. I'm going to pitch these candles to be marketed using winter comfort foods. Like gumbo." I did a presentation wave over my bowl.

"I like it!" Mocha expressed. "Now you can take a break without chewing my damn head off. Have you seen your mystery neighbor again?"

"Every damn morning," I confessed. "It's like we leave out at the same time every morning since I leave early to stop at the center, and all he does is stare." My body shook in my chair, thinking of the deep pools that Apollo called eyes. I still hadn't seen his entire face up close, and it was weird because my instinct was telling me he was too fine for his own damn good.

"I think you should speak. It doesn't have to be awkward Haze.

At least you know he's a gentleman, and if he was going to bite, he already had the opportunity to do so."

"I think it's time to go back to work," I suggested.

"I'm sure it is." Mocha took her things and went back to her desk. The man only shoveled my damn walkway, but the way he continued to look at me from across the street made me uneasy—in a good way.

I'd completed most of my presentation by the end of the day and began to pack up when I heard a thud. Looking up from my briefcase, I noticed everyone rushing in my direction. The only desk near my office belonged to Mocha, so immediately, I rushed out there.

"I'm calling 9-1-1!" Zoey, another marketing agent, shouted before going to the closest phone.

My chest tightened witnessing Mocha unconscious on the floor. I tried talking to her, pushing her to keep breathing until the paramedics arrived. Minutes later, two men rushed off the elevator. We cleared the space and allowed them to work. I heard them speaking to one another and his voice momentarily took my attention off my sister.

Then, he looked up.

Soft caramel skin, a full beard, nice full lips, and deep, thick eyebrows that gave him that natural menacing look. But it was the eyes that got me. *Apollo.*

TWO
APOLLO TAIT
THAT MORNING

The crimson-red blood seeped into the fresh white snow as the mouth wound leaked rapidly. What was supposed to be a simple hit had turned into an all-out brawl, and I'd finally knocked this mother-fucker out. I stuck Moses Edwards in his arm through his clothing and injected him with Fentanyl. Backing away from the body, which had made its own indentation in the snow, I turned to exit the dark alley. The blown streetlights and heavy snowfall helped me blend in as I hit the sidewalk and began to remove articles of clothing.

I slowly discarded the gloves, jacket, and snow pants I wore into three random sewers along the side of the street for six blocks. Pulling the hoodie I wore underneath the jacket over my head, I revealed my complete work uniform and had to thug it out in the brutal cold until I made it to the noisy, and most ironically joyful area during the holidays.

Stanton Memorial Hospital had decoration lights, multiple Christmas trees, and donation stations throughout the building. A building where life, death, and all things in between occurred, did its best to make sure the patients and staff are happy during the holiday season. No matter what took place in the neighborhoods surrounding it.

Walking into the front of the hospital, I pulled out a few bucks and tossed it into the bucket sitting next to a Santa that stood there ringing a bell. Making my way to the employee entrance, I went to my locker to get out of the boots and hoodie that I still sported and changed into my uniform shoes.

"Tait! We just got a call. A man was found a couple of miles from here. Last shift ain't trying to take it, so we're up!" My coworker, Gavin, ran out of the locker room toward the ambulance bay. I quickly grabbed my coat and headed out without even clocking in. Yeah, I was a paramedic by day and the Angel of Death by night.

I SAT BACK for the short ride and allowed Gavin and the driver, Eddie, to jump out first. They rushed to the body while I took my time behind them, careful to make my own set of footprints. I'd changed my shoes so there was no way that the earlier footprints would directly match mine except for size. I made a mental note to burn them.

"I wonder what happened here." Gavin shook his head at the middle-aged man lying in the snow.

"Probably a drug thing that went wrong." I shrugged.

"You always say that."

"And I'm almost always right," I replied. They turned him over and, sure enough, his eyes were glossed over. Gavin looked back at me like he was tired of me being correct, and I simply shrugged.

Regardless of my satisfaction, I get that it wasn't the ideal start to their workday, but hey, one job often ran into the other, given the fact I was on the six to four shift.

LATER THAT DAY.

I was shocked and low-key happy to see her too after the day I'd had. However, now wasn't the time for shorty to freeze up.

A lady next to her shook her shoulder and repeated, "Hazel! Is she allergic to anything?"

"N-no, not that we're aware of," she stuttered.

"She's for sure having an allergic reaction," Gavin said. "Her airway is almost closed, and hives are beginning to form."

I went inside our bag and pulled out an EpiPen. I plunged it into her thigh, releasing the medication.

"OK, the airway is opening," Gavin announced. The young lady's eyes shot open, and she inhaled deeply. Sitting her up, we asked her the typical questions before advising her to go see her physician for an allergy test immediately.

I finally realized how much she and Hazel looked alike, Hazel was just a little lighter. I diverted my attention to Hazel. "Y'all related?"

"Sisters," she confirmed. I stood and faced her fully.

"Well, your sister will be just fine," I assured her. Hazel was bundled up during our first encounter and every morning when she left out for work. But observing her now, she was even more stunning than I recalled. Hazel had the most beautiful and unique skin tone. She had a soft caramel tone and her skin seemed to have a natural bronze to it. Hazel's skin was blemish-free, paired with a button nose, small lips with a deep cupid's bow, and almond-shaped eyes.

Blonde curls fell down her shoulders and the green slacks she wore with the cream blouse all composed a masterpiece.

"Thank you!" she said sweetly. "You've just become my personal hero lately, huh?"

"If that's what you wanna call it, I'm here for it." I smiled.

"Tait! We gotta go, she doesn't want to go to the hospital." Gavin was headed for the elevator.

"I'll see you later, neighbor." I winked at her and headed out. I prayed we were on our last call for the evening; I was ready to go home.

"IS IT DONE?" my father said from the other end of the phone.

"Yes, it was the first stop of the morning the other day. I'm sure Nyx has everything covered by now," I confirmed, mentioning my baby brother. My pops had been in prison for almost two years; however, he made sure that his business kept running. His trial extended over a year, and the detective on his case was a bitch who acted as if her husband left her for a man or some shit. She had a stick up her ass and wasn't letting up on the Tait name. Not even for the money we offered her to make the charges disappear. She made sure Alonzo Tait was locked away for the next ten years on an attempted murder charge.

"What was that about?" I was curious about the last kill. I'd caught him coming out of his home, dressed for work.

"You know not to ask for details. I give you a target, and you do the job," he expressed. All I knew about the jobs given to me was that the targets were predators in one way or another. We talked about my mother and brothers for a while and then ended the call.

On the outside, Alonzo was the man to go to when you had a problem, and the way he was still making shit shake behind those walls proved why. What started as just a hit-for-hire thing in the streets where we were just sure to cover our tracks, had now become a structured organization.

My father had a run-in with the law before his current conviction, which made him switch shit up. To this day, I wondered, with everything we had set in place, how he still ended up behind bars. I had my speculations after the first go around, and I knew it had to be someone close.

Unlike other organizations, my father had a strict no-Fed policy, so we didn't believe in having them in our pockets. We were Taits, and the streets knew who to fuck with and who not to fuck with. So, the fact that my father's name was thrown into the mix of a murder investigation was suspect as hell. He beat it, but to then have the hit behind his incarceration interrupted mid-job, wasn't a coincidence.

I never mentioned who my eyes were on as the snitch to my brothers or my father. I just knew that once I had concrete proof, I was going to kill their ass brutally.

It was six in the evening, and because the last call took longer than expected, my shift ended an hour ago. I watched Hazel move around her living room, making sure gift bags had what they needed and prepared food baskets. I felt like a stalker but didn't give a damn. Since shawty had turned around to greet me when I offered to shovel her snow, those sexy ass doll eyes of hers and pouty lips stayed in my thoughts even more than before. I could even see myself combing my fingers through those blonde curls as she ate my dick up.

Today, she wore a red sweater, light blue jeans, a brown peacoat, and furry boots that stopped at her ankles. She'd avoided me the last few days and I think it was time I stopped stalking her through my living room window and let it be known I was interested. I'd always been a nigga who got what I wanted. My interest had been there since before I moved, and I typically would've snagged her by now. The circumstances in this matter had me moving differently, though. I gave myself this speech daily about remembering who the fuck I was. I knew where she lived, worked, and volunteered. Yet, I still stood back, watching her like a creep, studying her every move; simply because I knew I had to handle her with care.

Hazel made a trip to her car carrying bags with the phone pressed to her ear. She glanced my way as I stood in the window, sipping coffee. Yes, I was drinking coffee in the evening. My jobs began right before the crack of dawn, and if I didn't stay up now, I would sleep the day away and I would be up hours before it was time to work.

Closing her car door, she returned to grab another handful of gifts. Then it dawned on me. *Go help, nigga!*

I threw on some Timberlands and a coat and walked across the street. Hazel was wrestling with the door handle when I made it to her.

"Let me help with that." I grabbed the bags out of her hand.

"Oh, thank you!" She pulled the door open and adjusted the phone that was also about to slip from between her face and shoulders. "I have one more load. Do you mind?"

I shook my head and followed her inside. As I walked past her in the doorway, I heard a woman asking through the speaker, "Girl, is that him?"

I heard her mumble something, and I could only chuckle at what may have been talked about once I fully stepped inside.

I took the last load out and she placed her hand over the speaker to thank me.

"Again, it's not a problem. While I have you here, I was wondering what day would be good to take you out?"

"And who said you could even take me out?" she asked. The person on the other end of the phone yelled, *"You better let him!"*

She hung the phone up and tossed it onto the front seat. "I'll think about it. Right now, I have to get down to the center."

I watched her get comfortable in her car and pull off. I had an idea.

THREE
MOCHA SAPORA

Looking myself over in the mirror, my body looked amazing in the beautiful gold sequined, long-sleeved gown I wore. My smooth, coffee-colored skin popped against the fabric. I was glad my hives had cleared up quickly or this dress would be out of the question. Thanks to my newly developed allergy to shellfish, I had now cut my favorite foods out of my diet.

My husband, Pierre, walked up behind me and placed a diamond necklace around my neck. I gasped and turned to look at him.

"Pierre, this is gorgeous. All those stuck up bitches will envy the fuck out of me tonight!" We were on our way to Pierre's parents' annual holiday gala. An event I dreaded going to every single year. But if I had to go, I was going to be the baddest in the room. We had been married for three years and those snooty ass rich people always came looking down their noses with their smart remarks.

"Be sure not to call them stuck up in their face this time," Pierre told me sternly. This was the side of him that made me resent him. Being as though Pierre was biracial, Hispanic, and white, we had it tough enough as an interracial couple. Yet, he still expected me to hide who I was, and take all the shots his family and their friends threw my way. But the one time I called out his blonde, airhead ass cousin for what she was, I was wrong.

"Someone comes at me wrong again, then it will happen again," I told him as we made our way downstairs. I was his wife and he was supposed to defend me at all costs, but he was too busy trying to uphold an image for everyone else.

"Mocha, if you can't behave yourself, then you can sit this one out. There will be major business deals in the building and I don't need you tarnishing any relationships before they even start!"

"Oh, trust me, you don't have to tell me twice. Talking about behaving myself. I am not your daughter. Fuck you and those business deals!" I kicked my heels off so damn fast and was about to take my ass right back up the stairs.

"It's those business deals that have you sitting pretty in this house my son pays for." Ivory, Pierre's mother, came around the corner from the dining room area, holding a champagne flute with the tip of her fingers.

"Why is she in my house?" I questioned Pierre. He scratched his head and looked away. This was the shit I was talking about.

"This is my son's home, and I'll be here whenever I please."

"Ivory, I don't give a fuck if Pierre pays the majority of the bills. I hold more than my weight around here and that shit ain't light. Your silspoon-fed fed ass wouldn't know anything about taking care of a household." I looked back at my husband. "Get her out of here."

Again, I took a lot on the chin when we got married because I knew what I was getting into when I said my vows. I'd dealt with disrespect and degrading comments from every direction and they would not be thrown around in my own home.

"Mocha, I didn't mean that when I said you didn't have to come tonight. I just didn't want any drama. I'm sorry." He tried to rectify the situation, but I was out of my dress before he could blink again.

"I'm good. I have better things to do with my night." I picked up my phone and went to my sister's contact.

"Come on, babe, the car is already outside."

"Well, looks like you should make your way out there. You don't want to be late, you might tarnish a few business relationships," I mocked him. Pierre knew that when my mind was made up, it would be a waste of time and breath trying to change it. Call it what you wanted. Fuck that gala. I didn't feel like dealing with the rest of his family, anyway.

He kissed my forehead and walked out, shaking his head. His lips made me cringe. Even after the quickie we'd had before getting dressed. I'd only participated in that because I wouldn't dare step out on my marriage. Some shit needed to change, though, or that mindset would.

Flopping down on the bed, I tapped the screen where my sister's number was displayed and listened to the ring.

"Hey, Cha!" Haze answered. Cha had become a nickname since my mother said that Hazel was unable to say my name properly when they brought me home. The only people to call me Cha were Hazel and my stepdaughter, Nina. "Ain't you supposed to be at that thing with my brother?"

See, my family and friends never treated Pierre wrong. Yes, everybody joked about him being the white boy, but it was always good vibes. After eight years of being together, I was never able to receive that kind of love on his side of the family.

"Fuck him and that event. What you doing tonight? My hair and makeup is slayed and I need to get out of this house."

"I'm getting these bags together for the center. We're giving out gifts and dinner. I'm also trying to ignore the burning feeling of someone watching me from across the street."

"He still hasn't spoken?" I asked. That fine ass paramedic who saved my life would be perfect for Hazel. Maybe he could revive her rusty ass pussy.

"No. I wish he would already so I can turn him down gracefully." I heard the ruffling of bags being grabbed seconds before her alarm announced that her front door had been opened.

"Hazel, you know damn well you're not turning that man down."
I rolled my eyes. She was about to debate when I heard his deep,
husky voice. "Girl, is that him?"

The phone went quiet and I knew that heifer had put me on
mute.

"I'm sure he heard your loud ass," she mumbled when she came
back to the phone.

"My bad, I thought I was whispering." I laughed.

The phone muffled for a second, but if she thought she had hit
mute again, she was wrong. Apollo asked her out, and of course, my
stubborn sister gave him a hard time.

"You better let him!" I yelled before the phone call ended.

Laughing, I went to my closet to find something to wear. Hazel
could hang up all she wanted. I knew where to find her. Plus, it had
been a while since I'd helped her down at the center. She swore I
didn't care about her passion and today, I knew it would excite her if I
showed up.

I decided on a simple pair of dark Fashion Nova jeans and a red,
off-the-shoulder sweater. I unpinned my hair and let my curls fall
down my back. I finished my look with thigh-high boots and a
Versace coat. Pierre kept a bitch laced in the finest, I just wish he'd
put that energy into our marriage.

On the ride to meet Hazel, I thought about my marriage again.
Pierre and I met in college. Those days were the best of our relationship. Pierre wasn't the saint his parents thought he was. He was literally my partner in crime in college. We partied and snuck alcohol and
weed into my dorm room. Might I add, the dorms were not co-ed. But
what attracted us the most about each other was when it was time to
refocus and get schoolwork done, we were always able to reel each
other back in.

After graduation, we both found jobs and he introduced me to his
family. We had become used to the controversy that our relationship
came with, so his family being hesitant to accept us, didn't bother me

at first. We chose to elope to avoid all negativity on our special day, and Pierre asked me to quit my job.

I obliged, but since then, blending into his world had been an issue. Since then, it had been one thing after another. In the beginning, Pierre never allowed it into our relationship. I soon realized that it was only that way as long as I rolled with the punches. The moment I defended myself, my husband looked at me differently. I loved Pierre, and I couldn't say that everything was bad. He had me sitting in our huge ass house, I had three closets of top-of-the-line designer clothing, and four cars in our driveway.

None of the material things made up for the displacement I felt in marriage. Me, my feelings and dreams came after everything else. *When will you get tired of taking this shit, Mocha?* Enduring disrespect on top of the pain caused by an affair. An affair that resulted in a stepdaughter I had to obtain legal guardianship over since her mother wasn't shit, and constant disrespect was not what I envisioned when I said *I do.* But it was what Pierre had delivered.

Getting a job with Hazel helped me overcome it all since I had something else to focus on throughout the day. But hell, it wasn't like I could see myself in a real interview, anyway. Four years in college as a communication major and I would freeze up the moment someone asked, "So, who is Mocha?"

I'd been lost on that answer for quite some time now. I had one foot out the door and needed that extra push. A push that never seemed to come along.

No matter how she'd gotten here, Nina had become the light of my household and we'd created a special bond. She was diagnosed with dyslexia at four. Since the diagnosis, I'd been sure to let her know she was just as special as any other kid. I even bought us matching eagle pendants as a reminder that no matter how challenging it may be, she will always soar. My nickname for her was even Bird. I loved that brown-skinned, blue-eyed little girl more than life itself, and she was all there was to appreciate at this point.

Needless to say, I was ready to bounce. For now, I was playing the part and plotting. Getting a job with Hazel was a part of that plot. If my mama, Chai, taught us anything, it was to always be able to survive without a man. I was making my own bag, and soon, I would file for divorce.

I pulled up to the community center and the place had me in awe. Hazel and Majiq had it decorated beautifully and for the first time since the holiday season began, I was in the Christmas spirit. I didn't have to worry about galas or company Christmas parties. Just laughs and fun with my sister and friend.

I found Hazel posted up on one of her stations, shouting out directions. I laughed at the fact that we damn near had on the same outfit. She was so busy that she didn't notice me walk up on her. "Where do you need me?"

"Oh my goodness! What are you doing here?" she squealed and hugged my neck so tight. This place was her baby, so the hug she delivered showed her gratitude.

"First off, heffa, you hung up on me." She laughed. "But then, I thought about the fact that I haven't supported you fully in your community work. So, here I am."

"That's sweet, Cha. You can help the kids with arts and crafts. Everything else is covered." Hazel giddily squeezed my hands and went back to shouting out directions. I blew a kiss to Majiq, who was handing things out as well.

I had to admit, I missed this environment. The genuineness in the building had the energy at another level. Being with Pierre would have been fake and boring. I was 100 percent certain I made the right choice by coming here.

The evening carried on, and just as we were about to clean up the stations to sit and eat, we heard the sounds of caroling out front.

This was a community center for families and children, and I rushed to the door because curiosity had me by my edges, wondering who would be singing "Let it Snow" by Boyz II Men.

Hazel caught up with me and a crowd formed behind us to enjoy the entertainment.

"Oh, my God!" Hazel gasped. I looked at the three men who stood on the curb and it was my personal savior himself, Apollo. I could feel the heat coming off Hazel's cheeks as she blushed at him singing to her. I glanced back and forth at the other two men and they all favored.

I locked eyes with one. He was tall, not too bulky but not scrawny, and had the same menacing eyebrows as Apollo, but his eyes were softer and framed by designer glasses. They were all light in skin tone. What got me was the fresh braids at the top of his head that was surrounded by a crisp fade, and a freshly shaped goatee rounded his full lips.

I wanna wrap you up baby, then you'll see you're the only present I need! he sang. His singing voice was husky and I felt tingly in places my husband had been unable to activate in quite some time. They finished the song and the third of the group immediately went back to a vehicle and peeled off. Hazel was all in Apollo's face and Mr. Braids still had his eyes trained on me.

I flashed a smile and returned to the kids. Moments later, I felt a presence standing over me. It was him, I just knew it. I tucked my left hand underneath my right arm and looked up. This man lifted his leg and propped himself on the side of the table.

"Why'd you run?" he asked. I looked up and he pushed his glasses up his narrow nose.

I tilted my head in confusion. "I didn't run. I'm sorry I didn't catch your name."

"Zeus," he replied, extending his right hand. I noticed a few burn marks that only added to his masculinity.

My tucked left hand went into my lap so I could shake his hand.

"I'm Mocha." I used my manners and returned the introduction. "Well, Zeus it would be great if you stood up from the kids' artwork and allowed us to get back to work. It was nice meeting you, though." I flashed him an innocent smile, even though my panties were getting moist.

He let out a hearty chuckle and stood, exposing his full six-foot frame again. Zeus began to walk away, but a shiver traveled down my spine when he leaned over and whispered into my ear.

"I see that ring, too. Shit don't mean nothing. It only tells me you made a mistake somewhere down the road. I'll see you soon."

He stalked away like he hadn't just opened my damn floodgates. I was about to say fuck this ring, too.

FOUR
ZEUS TAIT

"What are we doing today?" Tina asked as she ran her fingers through my freshly washed hair.

"Just give me a few of those stitch braids you be doing and touch up my temp," I responded. No other hands had graced my head in almost a decade, and Tina never disappointed. I sat back and let her work her simple magic until I was satisfied with the four braids that fell past the middle of my back.

Tina faded my sides like I liked them and shaped up my hairline and beard.

"The mamas probably be drooling all over yo' ass at that school," Tina smirked.

"Of course. I'm the finest teacher they know." Turning my head from side to side, I caressed my beard and admired the overall look.

"Cockiest one too," Tina debated. I stood and grabbed the crotch of my jeans and took a quick dip.

"You should know," I smirked at her.

"Whatever! Let me get out of here!" She laughed and began to clean up her things. I was able to persuade her to stop by before going to the shop because my house was closer to the school. Tina and I dabbled from time to time, but through it all, she remained the homie.

"My bad, ol' boy must be hiding in my bushes or something," I teased her about her on-and-off-again boyfriend.

"Nah, he is stopping by the shop for breakfast, though. Don't you have to get to work?"

"Don't worry. I ain't the sneaky link that wants more. I know how to play my position. I'ma let you go." I laughed. "Thanks for stopping by, for real, I appreciate it."

I squeezed her tightly before walking her out. All I had time for was a quick ten-minute shower, then I needed to hit the road. I was a seventh-grade science teacher and loved what I did. Chemical reactions fascinated me in every sense. Teaching it only made sense, until moments like today.

"Mr. Tait!" the principal, Ms. Daniels, yelled down the hallway as I made my way to my classroom. Beside her stood one of my students, Xavier, and his mother, who seemed pissed off. "Can you join us for a quick meeting before the first bell rings?"

I was a little annoyed because she could've sent me a message or some shit. But her old, pressed ass was yelling down the hallway. I thought they made principals older so they had a little class. Ms. Daniels was bad as hell, but she was loud and sarcastic as fuck.

I groaned and followed everyone into her office. Xavier and his mother took a seat in front of Ms. Daniels's desk and I opted to stand by the door. Ms. Daniels leaned against her desk, facing me, and folded her arms.

"It seems as though Xavier decided to go home and repeat a science experiment that was done in your class and caused a house fire, Mr. Tait," Ms. Daniels stated.

"That's a damn lie."

"Mr. Tait!" Ms. Daniels yelled, acting like she was appalled.

"My bad. But, that's not true," I corrected her. "Any experiment done in my classroom is completely safe."

Xavier turned around in his seat. "But Mr. Tait, you said—"

"Exactly! I said. The kids often ask about the reactions between two substances and I'll occasionally let them know. I also emphasize that they shouldn't try them at home." I shot a hard look at Xavier to emphasize my point.

"Well, how about we stick to the curriculum and not give these children any ideas that may cost them their lives? I believe Xavier has your class first period. The bell is about to ring, so you guys can get to class." Ms. Daniels called herself dismissing us. If it was after 3:00 p.m., I would've told her about herself.

Xavier grabbed his backpack and dapped me up.

"Bring yo' snitching ass on," I mumbled and discreetly pushed him into the hallway.

"Oh, Mr. Tait!" Xavier's mother called after us. She pulled Ms. Daniels's door closed behind her and leaned into my space. "I was wondering if you'd like to come over to tutor Xavier sometime during the weekend since he's struggling so much with science."

"Ma!" Xavier shouted. "That's some thirsty shit."

I hit him upside the head and told him to go inside the classroom. His mama was definitely thirsty as fuck, but he wasn't about to disrespect her in front of me.

"Ms. Carson, your son has one of the highest grades in my class. I'm flattered, but have a nice day."

This was the shit I went through, being a fine ass specimen like myself. However, after meeting Mocha, I vowed to save myself. I snickered to myself as students began arriving, knowing good and got damn well I was lying to myself. Shawty was going to be my future wife, though. She just gotta get rid of what she should now know as her biggest mistake. If she didn't, I would surely make it crystal clear for her.

Classes went by with a breeze and I was now sitting at my desk, grading papers before meeting up with my brothers. It was a week before Christmas break and I always took it easy on my students before the holidays. However, finals were a must and I was proud to see they did not put me through the wringer. Their grades were looking good. There were only a few low scores, but I would take that out of four different classes.

"I'm here!" My loud ass busted through Apollo's front door. I set my briefcase down and walked toward the aroma that had my stomach growling already. "Nyx isn't here yet?"

"Nah," Apollo said. He was cutting some shit up on one of those wooden boards. "He shouldn't be too far behind you, though."

I threw my coat on the back of one of his bar stools and washed my hands before lifting the lid of one of the pots on the stove. "Jambalaya?"

"Yea," he answered, spinning around and gesturing for me to move out of the way so he could get to the pot. "The shrimp is the last to go in. We can eat once that's done. It won't be long."

People didn't know that Apollo had a love for cooking. His choice to become a paramedic still annoyed the fuck out of me because I knew it wasn't his choice, and it allowed cooking to come second to his hits.

"You talked to Dad today?" I asked, going back around to sit at the table.

"Yeah, I'm glad you asked about him because I almost forgot." The front door opened again and our youngest brother, Nyx, strolled in. Per usual, he didn't speak. A simple head nod was all he offered as he sat adjacent to me and turned his attention to Apollo as mine had been before he walked in. "He wants all of us to come see him in a few weeks."

Nyx let out a groan that matched my confusion.

"Why a few weeks?" I inquired.

"Something about the timing of the next job. I'm assuming he needs you both in on this one if he's specifically asking for all of us." He stirred the pot of Jambalaya like it was nothing.

The family business was something I always knew we were expected to be a part of. Apollo loved the shit. The thrill of taking job after job festered on his humanity sometimes and I didn't even think he knew it.

I mean, don't get me wrong, the three of us all had our hands in this shit, and as teenagers, it excited us. Our first job had all of us stimulated, but something in Apollo ignited. It was the same thing that had been aflame in my father for years, and it connected them on a different level than Nyx and I. It became somewhat of an obsessive connection for Alonzo, to the point where Apollo was all he knew until he needed Nyx and me.

That shit tainted the family dynamic and shifted how we saw one another. The lifestyle ultimately affected us all differently. But, Apollo was savage with the shit. Nyx, on the other hand, had become a mean ass shell. Let him tell it, it had nothing to do with the business. We never knew what he was thinking half the time unless it was a rude thought or if he was shit talking. He also only gave us access to the bare minimum when it came to his personal life.

Me? My students were my safe space. It gave me peace knowing I had a hand in molding them to not be like the motherfuckers we were paid to get rid of.

"Aight, I guess just let us know when y'all schedule it." I shrugged. I looked over at Nyx, whose face was buried in his phone. "Was everything smooth in the office today, Nyx?"

"Yea. Same ol' shit," he casually answered. "I didn't get to the body you sent in the other day yet, Apollo. But, I'll go back in after dinner."

Apollo turned from the stove with a wild look in his eyes. "So who the fuck is there with the body? Since when do you slip up like this? Shit gotta be done right or the cops will—"

"Nigga, I know! Karmen is there. She knows what's what and she can handle it. I'll go behind her after I eat. Damn!" Nyx yelled, cutting Apollo off. Nyx was quiet, but anyone would be a fool to piss that nigga off. "I know how to do my fucking job. No one is there. Unfortunately, other niggas like you exist and we got backed up. Ain't nobody slipping, nigga. I'm hungry! Now turn the stove off before you burn my fucking food!"

The three of us fell out laughing. This was what I loved about our brotherhood. The family business got hectic at times and we were dysfunctional, for sure, but we vowed that the love we had for one another would never waver. The problem was out of the picture for now, so we were able to stand on that. Apollo's cooking always had a part in it too.

We grabbed bowls and crowded around the stove to fill them, reaching over one another like savages.

"Mama would be disappointed in y'all moving around this kitchen like this," I joked as we uncoordinatedly moved around, grabbing utensils and drinks.

"Too bad Mama ain't here," Apollo said, taking his seat. Our mama was a photographer. Her lifelong dream was to travel the world to "capture its essence" as she would put it. The moment Pops got his bid, that was exactly what she did.

"Apollo, what's up with ol' girl you had us singing for the other day? I need to get back in touch with her sister," I asked. I only really gave a damn about Mocha.

"By the way, I ain't doing soft ass shit like that again," Nyx chimed in, not looking up from his bowl.

Apollo waved him off. "She's still playing hard to get, but she did agree to come over for breakfast the day after tomorrow. I'm sure I'll get her."

"Annndd her sister?" This nigga still hadn't answered the question I wanted to know.

"I mean, I know where they work." He shrugged. "Shawty almost died last week from an allergic reaction. I'll shoot you the address. I know that's coming next."

"Lemme find out your crazy ass actually does real work on the job," Nyx stated, causing Apollo to flip him off.

"You may know where it is without the address. They work at that marketing firm over on Benson," he said.

"Say less."

PERSISTENCE WAS one of my best qualities. Especially when I saw something I wanted, and Mocha was a must-have. Whatever nigga slipped that ring on her finger had a Tait coming their way. The way Mocha's eyes lit up when we locked eyes outside of that community center told me that whoever the mistake was, wasn't hitting or loving her right. When you take care of your woman, ain't shit another nigga can do for her.

The elevator dinged and I stepped off onto a busy ass floor. People were walking in every direction, either speaking to someone else, going over files, or sipping coffee while typing away on their phones.

Scanning the area, I spotted her. Mocha's hair was pulled up into a curly bun. Those slanted eyes moved around a computer screen as she clicked away at the keyboard with a phone pressed between her shoulder and face. Approaching her desk, I set down the bouquet I was carrying.

It took her a second to look up, and the double take sealed the recognition of who was standing before her. Mocha physically became unsettled in her seat. I chuckled at how she stuttered and shifted while confirming an eleven o'clock meeting for Hazel.

She hung the phone up and cleared her throat. My smile grew as she took a deep breath to regain her composure before addressing me.

"I assume your brother told you where I worked?" she queried.

"Is that an issue?" I replied.

"Depends on what you're here for. Who are the flowers for?" Mocha's head tilted to the side as she waited for me to answer her.

"If I got your work address from my brother, who the hell else would I be bringing flowers for?" I responded. The flirtatious, back-and-forth thing was cute, but I didn't do games.

She rolled her eyes and reached for the roses. Pulling out the envelope attached, Mocha slid out two tickets to the late showing of a play that was in town on Christmas Eve.

"Before you ask me another question you know the answer to, there's no pressure for you to say yes. If you're interested, we can start the day at Apollo's for breakfast in the morning and I'll just hope that you show up that night. And if not, just know I'll be back for you," I informed her.

"Zeus's, my hus—"

"Life allows you to make up for your mistakes. This is your chance. Now, don't bring that nigga up again."

I walked away from her desk, and back toward the elevator.

"For future reference, I like tulips!" she shouted.

I laughed and nodded in acknowledgment as I pushed the elevator button. A smirk was on her face as the doors closed.

Sexy ass. I brought my wrist up and checked the time. I had just enough time to make it back to the school before the bell. I did not feel like hearing Ms. Daniels's shit.

FIVE

NYX

As I closed the drawer, pushing the body into the freezer, I thought about the whys regarding the bodies that ended up on this metal table. The hows were always reported and I observed all kinds of shit before putting them on ice. This place, the cold and dark morgue, had consumed me over the years. All I knew these days were these walls filled with bodies, and at least three cases a week were at the hands of my oldest brother, Apollo.

We all played our part and mine ensured that the cause of death on the death certificate aligned with what Apollo needed it to. My cousin Karmen, Uncle Ace's daughter, both secured jobs at the morgue. The family also owned our own mortuary, with a crematorium on the property. I had to say, being at the mortuary was one of my favorite occupations. We had staff at the mortuary since we were most needed at the morgue, but stitching up an open corpse had become a satisfying talent over the years.

Since I was a kid, I noticed I was different from my brothers. I was less expressive, however, my thoughts never stopped. They were jumbled and out of place sometimes thanks to my hidden dyslexia, but they never stopped. An introvert is what most would use to describe me, which in turn made it easy for me to take my place in the family business and hide my learning disability. Death intrigued me, but only to the point where I found it somewhat easy to be myself. No judgment, just me and my thoughts. No one is bugging me to step outside of my character or pushing me over my limit to complete the paperwork.

Judgment was never received with anything when it came to my brothers but my parents hated the fact that I was never as open and expressive as Apollo and Zeus. Even before my dyslexia diagnosis, I knew I was different. It sounded weird, but I couldn't trust my parents with my flaws. Especially when they were always fighting with one another about who they thought we should be. Their feud made them make their own speculations about who and what they thought I was. Now, my relationship with Alonzo was damn near non-existent. But our mother, Venus, at least tried. Therefore, our relationship was rocky.

She and Apollo never really spoke because of Venus's dismay at Alonzo's hold on him. Zeus was a mama's boy if you asked me, and lil ol' me dangled in the wind.

After a long fight, I closed my last file and tossed it on top of the stack to my right. Wiping my hands down my face, I let out a sigh.

I heard the large metal doors open behind me and was glad to know my relief was here. I sat in silence for a few minutes before making sure there was nothing else for me to do tonight. I leaned into the door frame two doors down as I left. "Karmen, I'm gone. You think you can hold it down till the morning?"

Karmen waved me off over her shoulder and continued to work. Karmen was Uncle Ace's daughter and she and I were alike, but if you think I didn't like people, Karmen was on a whole other level with it. Neither of us liked social settings, which was why working around ones that couldn't speak was sometimes a plus. Karmen, however, hadn't uttered a word around the family for a few years now. It wasn't that she couldn't speak, she was just so fucking intro-verted, she wanted to keep her thoughts private.

I hit the fob to unlock my car and immediately hit my favorite playlist. *Musiq Soulchild* blared through the speakers, and I sang along. Just like my brothers, my voice was amazing. I loved to sing but the world would never know. That was why I got the fuck out of dodge when Apollo asked us to serenade his new piece. Shit was soft as hell, and he knew damn well I didn't sing in public.

The music paused so that my notification could sound, and I picked up my phone. It was Apollo in the group chat, letting Zeus and me know the day and time our father wanted to meet up. My attitude went from zero to one hundred. Why Zeus and I needed to be present for this nigga to address and praise Apollo the entire time was some bullshit. As of right now, it was up in the air about whether I was going.

It was then that I realized I needed a few more moments to wind down. I cruised and listened to some music, ending up at a cliff over-looking the Chesapeake River.

The winter was brutal, but my need for tranquility had me bundling up, leaning against the front of my car. I had an audiobook blasting from my speakers and a blunt in my hand. An extra set of headlights approached, causing me to go for my waistline. I recog-nized the car and relaxed a little.

I turned around to continue soaking in the view of the city and soon felt the hands of my somewhat girlfriend Braiza wrap around my arm.

"I knew I'd find you here." She beamed, walking around me and leaning her body against mine. Braiza was the only person who knew about this place, along with my brothers.

"I thought I was meeting you at my place." I pulled out my phone and paused the audiobook.

"Well, this place was on the way, and I just thought I'd stop by to see you since I wasn't sure of what time you'd be home. Karmen shooed me away, so I knew that I'd just missed you. Was that the book I sent you?"

"Yea, it's slow but it's getting crazy," I responded. Thanks to Braiza, I developed a thing for true crime audiobooks.

"I just started it. I missed you today, though." Brai lifted onto her toes and tried to kiss me. I swiftly moved my face and shot her a look that told her to back up. I didn't kiss.

"It's been six months, Nyx. When are you going to stop this childish shit?" she spat, standing up.

"I'll see you soon," I replied dryly.

"Whatever." I waited until I heard her pull off before letting out the groan that fought to express the disdain of Braiza's attempt to make me do something I wasn't comfortable with. I fucked with Brai hard; shit, she even had a key to my place. However, she knew that that type of intimacy wasn't my thing. Distance was my fortress. The more I cut off access to the real me, the safer I felt.

I finished my blunt and headed home. My peace was disrupted, so I was hoping to at least fall into some pussy. I turned into my driveway and shifted the car into park. The light in my room was on, so it was evident Brai was still up. She hadn't moved in and that wasn't even part of the plan, but it was easier when I gained her trust to have her go to the house when I had to work late.

Upstairs, she had some music playing softly. I pushed the bedroom door open and my dick bricked up immediately. Brai was sprawled out across my king-sized bed with a red lace bralette and thong set on. I took off my shirt and tossed it to the side, stepping up to the foot of the bed. Braiza seductively crawled toward me, unfastened my belt, and relieved my hard dick.

She looked good as fuck as she gripped my dick with her French manicured nails. Her full lips kissed the tip before her tongue circled the tip. Braiza snaked that motherfucker down and around the shaft and then swallowed me whole, making my grown ass moan.

I slipped my fingers through her box braids and guided her as she bobbed up and down. She was trying to take me out quick as hell. I had to pull back. She grinned, knowing she had me where she wanted me. She kissed around the outside of my shaft and made her way down to my balls, licking them softly.

Shawty had my fucking knees buckling, so I added pressure to the grip I had on her braids and pulled her up. Just as Brai always did, she planted trails of kisses on my chest and neck. Without giving her the opportunity to piss me off by making her way to my face, I roughly turned her around. The sounds of her sucking her teeth ain't mean shit to me. She assumed the position as I knew she would.

I grabbed a condom out of my wallet and ripped the lace thong and bit my bottom lip. The sight of her fat pussy glistening from behind was mesmerizing. Braiza had that mature pussy and every time I slid up in that motherfucker, it gripped my shit like one of those Chinese finger trap toys we all used to play with as kids.

Gripping her hips, I positioned myself and rubbed the tip of my dick at her opening. She was about to get all the frustrations of my day and ain't even know it. Sliding in slowly, I gave her a few soft strokes so that we could both catch a rhythm. Braiza loved this position, so I allowed her to throw it back to get her nut before I went in on her.

At the same time, I admired the dimples and tiger stripes that graced her ass and hips. I loved me a natural ass, and the way it jiggled with each thrust had my shit thumping. I felt her walls tightening, letting me know she was about to cum, and I tightened my grip on her hip. I felt her explode and I waited until I felt the peak of her orgasm to start hammering her shit.

"Oh my God, Nyx!"

"Damn that old ass pussy tight as hell!"

"Fuck you!" she shouted, with her face buried into the bed. I smacked her ass hard as hell and it felt like another wave came over her. Braiza's shit was coating my dick and I felt my nut building up.

Braiza slid back, putting her chest closer to her knees and that was all she wrote. I felt like I was about to fall in her pussy but her walls were keeping where I needed to be. I emptied my seeds into the condom and stayed there until my dick stopped twitching.

Pulling out, I walked to the bathroom to discard the condom. Turning the shower knob to the red side, I began taking off the rest of my clothes when there was a light tap on the door.

"What's up?" I cracked the door open to see what Braiza wanted. I didn't do that sappy ass after-sex shit.

"Can I at least get a towel, Nyx?" She sighed. I turned and opened the linen closet inside the spacious bathroom and tossed her a hand towel. Sucking her teeth, she returned to the room.

The bathroom was getting steamy as I looked myself over in the long, rectangular mirror over my double sink. I stood at six feet two inches, and tattoos covered most of my light skin. My thick eyebrows furrowed over my dark, slanted eyes. It was the one thing we all inherited from our mother. Those and my round nose. My full beard lined my small lips, and my semi-crooked smile held a gold tooth with a diamond in the center.

I pulled my locs up into a bun and showered. When I returned to my room with a towel wrapped around my waist, Braiza was gone. I didn't know what her problem was, but I hoped she didn't think I was about to blow her phone up about it. An empty bed meant a better night's sleep for me.

IT WAS FINALLY Christmas Eve and breakfast at Apollo's was always the tradition since my mama left on her little adventure. Women's voices were heard when I entered the foyer and I immediately got annoyed. I'd forgotten that Apollo said that he invited shorty from across the street to breakfast. I tuned these niggas out so much that when I heard it, it didn't even dawn on me he meant Christmas Eve.

I walked into the kitchen to everyone sitting around Apollo's island, sipping on those Mimosa drinks. I nodded and took my seat at the end. Scanning the room, it seemed as though my unspoken presence made the women uncomfortable.

Zeus must have felt it too. "Mocha, Hazel, this is our little brother, Nyx."

Still, I remained silent. But the Mocha girl seemed like the type who didn't like silence. She cocked her head to the side before proceeding to piss me off.

"Wait! So you have Apollo, Zeus, and Nyx. I know Apollo and Zeus are Greek gods, but wasn't Nyx a goddess?"

"I can lay my dick on this counter to assure you I ain't a goddess," I said seriously.

"Bruh! You gotta chill." Zeus shoved my shoulder. I looked down at the spot on my shoulder and up at him.

"No, it's fine, Zeus." Mocha stopped our interaction. "Men that have to showcase their dicks, are only trying to convince themselves of something. Mean ass."

I snuffled at her comment. Shawty was barking up the wrong tree. But I could respect the fact that she ain't cower at my demeanor.

They all spoke among themselves as I scrolled through my phone and waited for my food. Every Christmas Eve, Apollo cooked drunken French toast, eggs, grits, bacon, and hash browns.

Braiza's name popped up on my screen, so I got up to leave the room.

"What's up?" I answered.

"So, you really didn't care that I left?" she asked with an attitude.

"Nah. Your grown ass made a choice, and my grown ass chose to respect that. If you wanted to talk to me about something, then you should've stayed and communicated," I replied.

"Communicated," she scoffed, following it up with an unenthused laugh. "OK, Nyx. You're one to complain about what you don't get from somebody! Especially when it comes to communicating. I'm too old to be going through this shit with you. Either grow the fuck up, or I'm done."

"Braiza if you don't like—" My rebuttal was interrupted by the sound of Apollo's front door opening so hard, it hit the wall behind it. "Aye, hold on."

I stepped through the rest of the sitting room, ready to meet whoever the fuck it was at my place of business. The fucking morgue. I came from one entrance and Apollo and Zeus came down the hall from the kitchen. The three of us were halted by a camera flash and my mother screaming, "Merry Christmas!"

"Ma, what the hell are you doing here?" Apollo asked with his face twisted up. Zeus and I, on the other hand, hugged her while trying to regain our full eyesight back from the shock of the flash.

"I came to see my sons for Christmas. Is that a problem?" she snapped, craning her neck to see what the movement was behind Apollo.

"Not at all." Zeus cheerfully took off her coat and hung it up. "Apollo is cooking, come on."

Apollo groaned as Zeus pulled Ma toward the kitchen. I laughed and patted him on the back as we turned to the kitchen. Zeus knew damn well he was about to set these women up, and it was going to be my kind of show. If anyone had ever wondered where I got my mean streak from, they found out the moment they met Venus.

"Ma, this is Hazel, and thisss..." Zeus slid behind Mocha's chair. "Is your future daughter-in-law, Mocha."

"Daughter-in-law?" Venus scoffed. "Looks like the hoe is already someone's wife with that wedding band on." She stuffed a piece of bacon in her mouth and rolled her eyes.

I laughed so hard; they were all shocked. But if I didn't put her smart mouth ass in her place, I knew Venus would.

"Nah, don't try to hide it now." I laughed, noticing Mocha trying to hide her left hand. She gave me the finger and turned to say something to Hazel. Then Hazel spoke up.

"I know this isn't an ideal way to meet, but I think it's possible to respectfully start on the right foot. It's nice to meet you." Hazel extended her arm, and Venus looked at it like it was a germ.

"You're way too prissy for Apollo's ass. You won't last a week." She finished her bacon and grabbed a waffle, tearing it down the middle before taking a bite. I could tell she was high as hell. Venus had always been a stoner. I knew we wouldn't be able to stay in the same room long, but for now, it was good to have my mama home.

SIX
BRAIZA

Tossing my phone on the top of my bag, I finished wrapping up my hands. Then I pulled the hair tie from my wrist and finger-combed my hair into a ponytail. My blue and black spandex leggings and sports bra gave me the space I needed to comfortably stretch. For the next forty-five minutes, I punched and kicked at the bag with all I had. There was so much pent-up frustration inside of me that needed to be released, and with the way Nyx had just hung up on me, this bag was getting the grunt of it all. Kickboxing had been my thing since I was a little girl. Although I could have easily made a career of it, education and adolescence were my things. However, the gym was my happy place at least three times a week.

At thirty-nine, it was a task to look this good. I'd always been thin, but as I got older, I had to put in a little extra work to stay on point. The youngins at the gym always side-eyed me until I took off my jacket and put all their asses to shame.

At thirty-nine, I also wondered why I allowed myself to settle for less. I met Nyx at a science fair at the school. His brother hosted it, and he was helping set up when I walked in to check on things. Once the fair started and people filed in, I was standing in a corner just observing things when he approached me. Nyx was tall, and professionally dressed, with a walk that begged women to approach but a demeanor that one wouldn't dare to approach. His locs were neat and his scent penetrated my nostrils when he was three feet away. Creed. I'd never forget it. I could even smell it when I wasn't in his presence.

Nyx came at me a little direct, but honestly, at my age, I liked someone who knew what he wanted. He asked for my number, and I never saw him again that evening. I wondered why, but after getting to know him, I knew he didn't like crowds.

Our dates, as he would call them, consisted of early morning movies because the theaters were less packed, sex at his place, and when the weather was nice, we'd go to this cliff in Georgetown and eat. It was beautiful scenery, but it was like I was always talking to myself, or we'd listen to an audiobook together. Discussing those audiobooks was the most talking I would get out of Nyx. But those moments let me see the light in him. We'd taken a hard dive into true crime, and mid-book we'd stop to predict what the outcome would be. Nyx would dissect details within cases and be spot on every time.

Our love for sex, food, books, and corny dad jokes bonded us. Unfortunately, that was where the romance stopped. Nyx rarely talked on the phone, and a fun date was completely out of the question. Hell, he surprised me when he gave me a key after four months. One would normally take that gesture as a serious step. However, he just didn't want me bothering him to see where he was or if he was up when we planned for me to come over. So, for me, it was just another gesture to satisfy his fucked-up attitude.

Sweat ran down my body as I grabbed a towel and my water bottle. As I hydrated, I felt a pair of eyes on me. I looked to my left to see my friend and counterpart, Randi.

"Why are you staring at me like that?" I asked, drying the visible parts of my body. Randi stood there with his hands crossed. Randi was fine as hell too. If we didn't play on the same team, and he wasn't the closest thing I had to family, I would have shot my shot a long time ago.

"Because you damn near burned a hole in that bag in less than an hour. And the way you just side-eyed me before you realized it was me, let me know you're in a mood. I know it has something to do with that little boy toy of yours." Randi flickered his fingers as if Nyx wasn't shit.

"I am not in a mood," I debated.

"Ma'am, I would have hated for an actual person to be behind those jabs."

"Whatever. It has nothing to do with Nyx, and he is not a boy toy." I put my water bottle and towel in my gym bag and began to bundle back up to leave. Randi knew me, and it was clear he wasn't buying shit I was selling. He was one hundred percent correct, though. My frustration had everything to do with Nyx. "And stop calling him a boy."

"We both know I used it as a figure of speech, but disregarding that tells me you're the one feeling that way about him, not me," Randi responded.

"I don't," I sighed. "I mean, at times you can't even tell that he's almost ten years younger than I am. But then there are times when I can see it as bright as day."

"He may not be it for you, friend." Randi shrugged.

"I keep telling myself that, but from there, the questions just keep coming," I explained. "Like, why does the thought of letting him go hurt so bad? Why do I have this constant urge to knock down all of his barriers, no matter how mean his ass is?"

"Braiza, it's hard to answer that because all I hear from you is the negatives," Randi replied.

"I mean, he's smart and has his funny moments. Shit, he has a job and even a real bed that's not on the floor or inflatable." We busted out laughing at the end part.

"It's funny, but I know how serious you are. These youngins don't give a damn now. Shit be sitting right on the floor. I've even seen a mattress sitting on some crates. I got the hell outta there! I saw the crate challenge and he wasn't about to set me the fuck up!"

"Randi, for real?" I laughed.

"Girl, I'm not playing. That boy blew my phone up for a week until I sent his ass some links for a full bedroom set and blocked him." We were wheezing. I thanked the heavens for a friend like Randi. He would have me bent over in laughter all while giving me the real. And that was exactly what he gave me as we left the gym.

"Seriously, though. You can see the good in someone all you want. What matters is the good they put out when it comes to you."

That was something I really needed to hear. I'd been trying when it came to Nyx, but I could only do so much. "Stop being so accessible to him and see how he acts. Girl, the new year may be the time for something new."

"Thanks, Randi." I hugged him, and we felt a presence behind us.

"What's up, Braiza?" Leon, one of the guys who worked at the gym, gave me a head nod before heading into the gym. Randi and I observed him through the glass window.

"And that is what I mean by something new." Randi pointed toward Leon.

"Really?" I turned my lip up at Randi. "I mean, he's fine but, he doesn't seem a little off to you?"

"The only thing a little off is that mean-ass boy toy of yours. Merry Christmas, friend." Randi waved me off and went to his car. I hit my trunk to drop my gym bag before getting inside. Maybe Randi was right.

The shit I'd been through with men left no space for dating potential. I needed to be dating with intention and I deserved someone who wanted the same.

I observed Leon from my driver's seat as he moved around the gym and thought it just might be time for some changes.

SEVEN
HAZEL

"OK, I think it's time to go," I said. I stuffed a few more forks of food in my mouth and slid off the chair that was up against the island. Apollo's mother had come in stronger than last week's snowstorm and I wasn't here for it. I barely knew this man, and I wasn't about to tolerate being disrespected. We'd been sitting here for almost an hour and I knew that Mocha was five seconds off her ass.

"Yes, I think that's best," Venus said, throwing her hippie scarf tighter around her neck.

I let out a sarcastic laugh. Venus was barking up the wrong set of trees and before my sister and I disrespected our elders, it was time to go. Swiftly, I grabbed my jacket and stomped toward the front door with Mocha in tow.

We were halfway across the street when we heard the door open and close behind us. Looking back over my shoulder, I witnessed Apollo zipping up his coat with one hand and a plate wrapped in foil in the other. Even as he balled his face up against the bitterness of the cold weather, he was a beautiful man.

"Nina has called me three times. I'll call you later," Mocha announced, pulling me out of my lustful thoughts. I turned to see her walking to her car with her phone in her hand.

"OK, sissy. I love you." I winked at her, and she winked back. Since we were younger, that had always been the way Mocha and I showed our love when departing.

"Love you more!" she shouted. Apollo waited until she drove off before apologizing about his mother.

"Sorry about that. I know she can be a bit much at times. It's freezing out here though, can we talk inside?" Apollo gestured toward the house and began walking before I could even answer him. I shook my head at how he'd made a statement seem like a question. However, I followed.

Unlocking my door, I kicked off my boots at the entrance and put a little extra in my steps. I was only going across the street, so I'd put on some leggings with my *UGG* boots, and I knew my hips and ass were giving what I needed them to.

I sat on my couch sideways, folding one leg underneath me and propping my arm on the back, and waited for Apollo to join me.

"That's not how I envisioned our first date." He tossed his coat over the couch and took a seat. I grabbed the plate out of his hand and dug in. His simple attire had me eyeing him the entire time he cooked, but with him sitting this close to me had my ass feeling like I was relaxing in an infinity pool and my panties and leggings were the thin floating device between me and the deep end.

"That was not a date," I replied, studying his eyes and those thick eyebrows. There was something so dark and mysterious about this man that I'd found attractive since he shoveled my snow. But stepping back onto the dating scene scared me. Apollo was a force that was pulling me out of that fear and it was weird. He watched me from his window daily, which was creepy as hell, and any other time he was simply being a gentleman and helping me out. Those moments, along with the mixed energy of his brothers; along with how everything seemed to shift in three different directions when their mother walked in, had me lost as to what to expect this man to be. With all of that, I was open to still figuring it out.

"OK, well, I guess I'll see you on New Year's night at 7:00. Dress comfortably." Apollo got up, threw his jacket on, and was walking back across the street within fifteen seconds, leaving me sitting there dumbfounded. I guess my ass had a date in a week.

I sat up in bed and stretched. Apollo's breakfast settled on my stomach and had me dead to the world for a few hours. I picked up my phone and saw that it was already three in the afternoon. I was due to meet Mocha and her family at our parents' place at six, which gave me enough time to make a stop.

I brushed my teeth and went over a couple of curls that my nap had out of place and slipped on my clothes. My fingers lightly brushed against one of the permanent scars on my stomach as I was pulling my sweater down.

Habit made me go to my full-length mirror and observe the scars on my body while my fingers brushed over it lightly. Battle scars and exit wounds were what I referred to them as now. So many reminders of what I'd gone through. *No, Haze, it's what you survived.*

Quickly, I pulled down my sweater, stormed away from the mirror, and left the house. As I pulled out of my driveway, I looked toward Apollo's bay window and a part of me hoped to see him standing there, gazing at me with his cup of coffee in his hand. But, the space by his window was empty, and his car was no longer in his driveway. I wouldn't have blamed him for getting away from his rude mother.

A long beep sounded after I pressed the numbers to my friend Jordyn's condo entry gate, praying she was home already. The sound stopped and the gate lifted for me to enter. I stepped off the elevator on the top floor and Jordyn was waiting for me with a puzzled look on her face.

Jordyn Drescher was a decorated detective, and little did she know, I had become familiar with her work schedule. She stood there dressed in a black fitted suit with a black turtleneck underneath. Her badge and weapon were still in place, so I knew she had just gotten in.

"It's Christmas Eve, Hazel. I thought you would be headed to your parent's place," Jordyn said as she stepped to the side to let me in.

"I'm heading there next. I just thought I would stop by to see a friendly face. You know this time of year is always hard for me." I flashed a forced smile.

"It'll take some time for things to get easier, and being with family should help. Do you want a glass of wine?" she asked and led the way to her open kitchen. I wondered why she needed so much space when it was only her, but shit, I wouldn't mind staying in a penthouse condo with large, floor-to-ceiling windows all around, providing a beautiful view of the nation's capital.

"Yes, that would be great."

Jordyn poured us two glasses of white wine and took a sip before setting it down and blurting out the words I needed to hear.

"Give me a few minutes to get out of these clothes. These shoes have been killing my feet for the last three hours. That's what I get for trying to be cute. But I'm weighing the chief of police down. Just give me a little more time and watch this ring finger get heavier!" Jordyn flashed her left hand and walked away, doing a little shimmy. We laughed until she was out of sight, and I heard her bedroom door close.

Setting my glass down, I peeked down the hall to ensure her door was all the way closed. I grabbed her keys from the bowl by the door and then made my way to the first room on the left of the long hallway. Jordyn's home office had files and paperwork everywhere, but I knew exactly where to find what I was looking for. I sat in her swivel chair and quickly unlocked the drawer to my right. The flash drive that held all of Jordyn's cases was exactly where she'd left it for the past year.

I plugged it into the desktop and typed in the password I'd

watched her type when this specific case was still open. The files folder opened, and I scrolled down to *Quincy Norwood*.

I relaxed when I noticed that there was no change in the cause of death. Just as it was every other week when I snuck into Jordyn's office just to calm my anxiety. Putting everything back the way it was, I took my place at the counter and continued sipping the wine until Jordyn walked back into the kitchen in her nightclothes.

"No plans tonight?" I asked.

"Girl, no. My parents fly in in the morning, so I'll take tonight to relax since they will be on my case tomorrow about how I work too much and how I need to start a family." The look on her face held her own stress, and now that I'd gotten the answers I needed, I suddenly and selfishly felt bad for intruding on her evening.

My phone chimed in my coat pocket, and it was my mother asking me to see if I could find her favorite eggnog.

"I have to go. My mother just asked me to go to the store. It's Christmas Eve and I know the stores are wiped out. I'll go to a few stores for her, though," I explained to Jordyn.

"OK. Try to enjoy your holiday, Hazel." She came around the corner and hugged me tightly. Although this friendship started with a motive, Jordyn had become the closest thing next to Mocha and Majiq.

I flopped in my driver's seat and took a moment to gather my thoughts. There was always this moment of regret after leaving Jordyn's; however, paranoia wouldn't let me stop snooping.

After three different stores, I finally found the eggnog I was looking for. There was still an hour left before I needed to be at dinner, so I stopped at the liquor store to kill some time. Just as I expected, the line was long, and the entire thing took at least thirty minutes.

I pulled into the driveway and noticed that Mocha and Pierre had already arrived. Thank goodness because, much like Jordyn, I had to endure the talks about my future from my family as well. Just with different consequences.

"Auntyyy!" Nina, Mocha's stepdaughter, ran up to me and squeezed me. As I stated before, I wasn't sure where Mocha and Pierre were in their marriage, but I did know that she had overcome a lot of shit when it came to him. Including him having an affair at the beginning of the marriage with a white woman and getting her pregnant. When Mocha announced that she was staying with Pierre, we welcomed the innocent child with open arms. Nina was now six and you couldn't tell us she didn't belong to this family.

"Hi there, beautiful!" I squeezed her tight. I walked around and greeted everyone. My mother took her eggnog out of my hands and shooed me out of her kitchen while she finished dinner. Chai Cox was a southern woman who moved to the DMV after meeting my father in college. She was in her mid-fifties and rocked her slightly gray curls with pride. She was warm in skin tone just like Mocha and I and had that homegrown southern ass and hips for days. I left the kitchen and allowed her to spike her eggnog in peace.

My father, Leo, and Pierre were playing dominoes on the living room coffee table, and Mocha and Nina were engaged in a Christmas movie. When Mocha first introduced Pierre to the family, my father was adamant about getting him acquainted with the black culture. Playing spades and dominoes were both a part of that. I curled up beside my sister and watched as well until Mama called for dinner.

"How are things at the office, girls?" my father asked Mocha and me.

"Things are good." I looked at Mocha and smiled. "Mocha has been showing interest in becoming a marketing agent."

"I don't know why," Pierre mumbled while cutting his turkey.

"And why is that?" My mother set her fork down and propped her elbow on the table, waiting for Pierre to answer her.

"Well, Mocha and I agreed she would be a stay-at-home mom. She complained about not having a life and I allowed her to work for Hazel, but she spoke nothing of her starting a new career. Especially since we should look to have more children soon." He chewed his food and didn't bother to look up at any of us.

His choice of words had us all confused as to who the fuck he was talking to. But, we knew we did not have to say anything. Mocha was on his ass already.

"No, Pierre, *you* suggested I be a stay-at-home mom. I never agreed to that. I stayed home to help with Nina while she was young because the trash you knocked up couldn't. Talking about you allowed me to do something," she snapped. I was glad my mother let Nina sit in the living room and finish the movie while we ate.

"Mocha!" Pierre said sternly.

"Hold on, now," my father chimed in. "She only got one daddy at this table. Don't talk to her like you're chastising her." Mocha stormed away from the table and stomped up the stairs. Pierre stormed behind. "Make sure y'all are just talking! I'll send somebody after yo' ass too!" Daddy yelled after them, then faced me. "When did things get like this?"

"I don't know, Daddy," I answered honestly. "I'm just as shocked as you are." I lied. I knew something had to be wrong when she took Zeus's invitation to breakfast and said she was coming for me.

"Marriages go through things." My mother sighed. "Unless he's hurting her, I think we've learned to mind our business when it comes to them."

She was right. Although we liked Pierre, for the most part, things had never been a smooth ride. However, after Nina, it was best to let Mocha tell us how to move behind her. From what I'd seen that morning, she loved the attention of Zeus, and after what I'd just witnessed, I hoped she chose herself for once.

"Speaking of marriage, when are you going to begin dating again?" my mother asked.

"Ma." I sighed.

"Quincy has been gone for a year now. I think it's time you start enjoying yourself again," she replied.

"I'm open to the idea," I replied. It was entirely too soon to mention anything about Apollo. Still, I couldn't help envisioning him sitting around this table, laughing with my father. I fought the urge to blush at the thought of him. I looked up at both of my parents and they were giving one another the side eye. I shook my head and went back to eating. For the first time in a long time, Quincy's name was able to be mentioned and I didn't go into a full-blown panic attack. I wasn't sure if it was because I'd just left Jordyn's with what I needed, or if it was because it was followed by my lustful thoughts about Apollo. Wherever the momentary peace came from, I was here for it.

"With the way your eyes just lit up, I'll take that as a sign that I don't have to push any longer." My mother was now directing her smirk my way.

"You have never had to push, Ma. I needed to move on my way." I'd become a broken record with this conversation.

Mocha stormed downstairs and started getting Nina ready. "Come on, Bird." She called Nina by the nickname she'd given her.

"I wanna stay with Nani and Papa!" Nina whined. Mocha looked up at my parents and they agreed she could stay since she had presents there, anyway.

"You guys are leaving already?" I questioned.

"Yeah. Suddenly, Pierre has somewhere to be," Mocha mumbled.

"I told you I had a prior engagement before we came over here, Mocha," he growled.

"It's Christmas Eve, Pierre! Whatever it was, could have waited." Mocha came over and kissed us all on the cheek.

"You don't *have* to go, Cha," I told her.

"I know." She winked at me. "I want to. But, I'll call you in the morning." She winked again, and that always meant she was up to something. I let her live and would just get the scoop in the morning.

EIGHT
MOCHA

The ride home was silent. Well, at least I didn't hear shit. Pierre was rambling but I'd tuned him out completely. Bird stayed back with my parents, so there was no need to give him my energy. I was out of the car and upstairs before the garage door closed fully.

Pierre went to his closet and pulled out a tux and disappeared into the bathroom. Normally, I would be concerned with his whereabouts, but tonight I didn't have a fuck to give. Fed up was an understatement of where I was in this marriage. I didn't have any more in me to give this man.

The shower turned on and I grabbed my phone and put an address into the *Waze* app. Timing my drive, I calculated how much time I had to get ready. All I needed was for Pierre to hurry up and get the hell out. Trying to maximize my time, I went and showered in the guest bathroom, returning in my robe and bonnet as if I was going to bed. I moisturized my body with my favorite Shea butter while Pierre got dressed behind me.

"I'll be a little late," he said before walking out. I had no interest in engaging with him. Once I heard him pull out of the garage, I went to my closet and pulled out the sexiest thing I could find. Since

Pierre's family held a gang of events annually, I had a fire-ass collection of gowns. I debated with myself about what I was about to do. But fuck it. There was nothing left between Pierre and me.

My curves filled the simple black gown perfectly. The slit stopping just above the mid-thigh mark pushed the sex appeal right over the top where I needed it to be. I grabbed a pair of red pumps and paired them with gold accessories, being sure to keep my eagle necklace on. I paused, looking down at the accessory that hadn't left my finger since my wedding day. Slowly, I pulled it off and placed it inside of my jewelry box.

I had twenty minutes to spare and needed to do something simple with my face and touch up my curls. I filled in my eyebrows and did a natural look with ruby red lipstick. I threw on a fur coat and was on my way to do something I knew damn well I wasn't supposed to.

"Ticket, please," a woman at the turnstile asked. I reached into my bag to retrieve the ticket Zeus left with me. "You're in suite 107. Show the doorman your ticket and you can go right in. The show has started, so please try to be as quiet as possible."

I smiled and strutted in the direction of 107. My nerves were a mess. That morning, I had no intention of joining them for breakfast at Apollo's. However, Zeus Tait was a force that had invaded my every thought since the day I heard him sing. I kept telling myself I was a married woman. Truth was, I was a married woman who didn't know what she wanted in life up until a few hours ago and, within the uncertainty, Zeus was the only thing that felt right.

So, when Hazel begged me not to let her go to breakfast alone, I couldn't resist. In that short time, I drew to Zeus just like I was afraid I would. Nina was the excuse I needed as I left Apollo's. I tried hard to convince myself that I had obligations and that I couldn't go to this play. Yet, here I was, standing in the back of the dark suite, staring at Zeus Tait as he enjoyed the show. He leaned forward with his elbows resting on his knees in one of those arm-less event chairs.

"I thought I was going to have to come after you." His voice traveled like electricity through my body, causing my words to get stuck in my throat.

I cleared my throat to respond. "I, um, I wasn't sure if I was going to come."

I stood in place and Zeus kept his back to me. I'm glad you did. Now, come take a seat. I'm not ready to bite just yet."

Lord, I thought to myself as my clit began to pulsate. I hadn't been in this man's presence for five minutes and I was ready to risk it all.

I sat beside him, and he finally turned to me. His eyes were full of fire as he looked at me.

"Hi, beautiful. You look nice," he said.

"Thank you." I smiled. "So do you."

Since Zeus was a teacher, I'd seen him dressed casually the day he brought me flowers. But tonight, he was on another level. Black slacks, a white dress shirt, and a burgundy blazer hugged his frame. Even sitting down with nothing but the light from the stage hitting us, he looked good. His braids were fresh, and the trim of his goatee was just as crisp.

Zeus licked his lips at me and let out a cocky chuckle before running his hand up my slit and turning back to watch the play.

For an hour, I tried to act like his hand resting so close to my pussy wasn't a distraction. I fucked my husband regularly, yet; it had been a while since I'd gotten dicked down properly and my baby girl was purring to be touched.

Suddenly, Zeus got down on the floor in front of me and rested his back against the wall of our balcony, and stretched his legs out, pulling my chair closer to him.

"What are you doing?" I whispered.

"Calming my new best friend down. If she calls out for me any louder, she just might interrupt the show," he said, face-to-face with my pussy. I frantically looked around. "Relax. I paid good money for privacy. Until the theater lights come on, no one can see you."

Zeus ran his hands up my thighs, pushing my dress up over my hips. I slid to the edge of my seat and relaxed as he instructed. The warmth of his breath at my opening made me bite my bottom lip. My clit felt like it was going to detach from my body and jump in his mouth on its own.

He planted kisses on one side of my thigh, slightly brushing his tongue against my clit on his way to repeat his teasing on the other side.

"Zeus," I whispered in a begging tone. His tongue parted my lips, and he moaned as his tongue felt like a surfboard against my juices.

"That mistake of yours can't have your shit dripping like this." Zeus delivered another run of his tongue up my slit and softly took my clit in his mouth. I gripped the side of the chair and threw my head back. "And when I actually give you this dick, the dotted line gon sign itself."

Zeus's words vibrated against my clit and the sensation along with the pressure of his tongue had my orgasm already building. I grabbed the back of his head and gently grinded against his face. The way he slowly made out with my pearl, delivering flicks of pressure in between kisses, had me about to draw blood from my bottom lip, trying not to scream out in pleasure.

I knew that marrying Pierre was a mistake. But the way Zeus has me in the stars right now was even more proof. My thighs began to tremble, and I felt Zeus smile while still buried nose deep.

"Mm, cum for me." I came so fucking hard; I almost fell out of the chair. Zeus leaned up on his knees and kissed me, letting me taste myself. That shit was sexy as fuck.

The light came on as soon as I pulled my dress down. Zeus stood, towering over me. Just as I thought, he looked even better in the light.

"After you." He gestured for me to exit the suite.

I reached up and wiped his beard with my thumb. "You wasted some of your food," I smirked.

"You should've rubbed it in; it's good as a moisturizer too," he replied.

I stepped closer to Zeus, sliding my arms underneath his and wrapping them around his waist. "Thank you, I needed this distraction."

"Oh, all I am is a distraction?" His thick eyebrows furrowed.

"I didn't mean it like that, it's just a lot going on." I sighed, hoping he still didn't take my wording wrong.

"It's cool. But I'm nobody's distraction, Shawty. When I take you away from what you want to be distracted from, ain't no going back. There's a difference. Let's go." He gently pulled out of my embrace and locked his finger through mine, leading the way into the hall of the theater. I secretly couldn't stop stealing glances at his side profile and it was good to genuinely smile.

"Mocha?" My smile dropped immediately at the sound of Pierre's voice. Before I could move, Zeus stepped in front of me.

"Zeus, it's OK," I whispered. Once again, my voice was stuck in my throat. "This is my, um, my husband."

"Oh, the mistake in the flesh." Zeus's ass extended his hand. My heart sank to the pit of my stomach, hearing this man call Pierre a mistake to his face. Let alone attempt to greet him. Pierre looked down at Zeus's hand and left it dangling in the air, then looked behind Zeus at me.

"Mocha, I didn't know you enjoyed the theater," he said. Zeus made his presence known and undeniable once again, taking another step forward before speaking.

"Yea, well, she tastes good. I mean, she has good taste." Zeus placed his hand on his chest like he'd unintentionally made a mistake. At this point, my heart had tumbled down the hall, out the glass door, and was playing in traffic.

Pierre was about to square off with Zeus when the only shoulder I could see over Zeus's tall frame was touched by a perfectly manicured hand. I stepped around Zeus, and I was ready to set the building ablaze.

"Hey, babe. Sorry, the line at the restroom was long. I'm ready." Penelope, Pierre's baby's mother, stood beside him, dressed like money.

"Babe?" I screeched. "So y'all been out playing house and shit while my parents watch your child?"

"She wasn't supposed to be with your parents," Pierre sighed.

"Oh, so I..." I pointed to myself for emphasis. "I was supposed to be at home babysitting while y'all gallivant around town?"

"Precisely." Penelope looked me up and down. Knowing me like a book, Pierre pulled her down the hall before I could hit her in the throat. He and Zeus locked eyes until Pierre finally turned away.

"You're not going home tonight," Zeus stated, grabbing my hand again.

"Yes, I am. I can handle myself." I dug inside my purse for my key fob and stomped toward my car. "Thank you for tonight. I'll call you."

I took a few minutes to calm my nerves before pulling off. Though my hands were still a bit shaky, my thoughts were becoming clearer.

Pierre presented Penelope as a deadbeat, and to see them out the way they were had me on another level. The ride home was made through blurred vision, but I made it. I kicked my shoes off at the door and went right up to my closet to change.

The holidays were supposed to be cheerful. But every year, I was at one of his family's events or arguing about how Nina's time should be split between us and her perceived deadbeat ass mother. I put in the work for years when it came to everything Nina. But it turned out that I'd been taking care of another bitch's baby, for her to be sleeping with my husband.

I slipped on some jeans and a long-sleeved black shirt. I heard the garage door lift and my adrenaline rushed again. I grabbed my all-black Air Max sneakers and then my little friend that rested in the corner of my closet. I named my bat Casey and she'd been by my side through a few of these moments with Pierre.

I did an exciting jog down the steps and waited by the garage door that led to the kitchen. Pierre twisted the knob, and I cocked Casey back. His head made its way through the door frame, and I swung with all my might. Unfortunately, he ducked, causing me to put a hole in the door. I struggled to release the bat from the wood, and Pierre took that opportunity to limbo underneath the bat and backpedal into the kitchen.

One forceful pull released Casey.

"Mocha, put that fucking bat down!" Pierre shouted.

"Fuck you! Penelope, of all people? You son of a bitch!" I swung again and he moved back.

"You're standing here enraged, like you weren't out on a date yourself!" he barked.

I pointed the bat toward him, lunging toward him with every word I spoke. "That's after you broke the camel's back in front of my parents, you smug bastard. I agreed to be a stay-at-home mother to my own children. Not one you conceived with your whore! To blatantly tell me I have no room for a career when I made plenty of room for your betrayal was a whole other level of audacity."

"Then you allowed your daughter to stay at my parents' house while you paraded that no-good bitch around? You're lucky my parents love her and vice versa. She's good there tonight, but as of now, this shit is over."

I turned and swung at the large wedding photo on the wall. The sound of glass shattering and hitting the tiled floor filled the air before I moved around the house, shattering every memory of what was supposed to be the happiest day of my life.

When I calmed down, the sound of someone banging on the front door and laying on the doorbell was heard.

"That must be your bitch." I let out a crazed laugh and threw Casey over my shoulder. Swinging the door open, I was ready for round two.

As bad as I wanted it to be Penelope, seeing Zeus standing there satisfied me more. His shoulders rose and fell with anger as he looked past me at Pierre.

"Did he touch you?" he asked, never taking his eyes off Pierre.

"No," I answered.

Zeus stepped into the foyer. "Put a coat on and go wait in my car."

I didn't debate with him. I grabbed one of my coats out of the front closet and left what used to be my home.

Pierre's voice halted me. "Mocha, I will never give you a divorce!"

"You will. One way or another," Zeus threatened, before joining me on the porch. He didn't say a word as he led me to his truck and opened the door.

"Where to?" he asked.

"Hazel's," I replied and sank into the seat. I could have gone to my parents, but as much as I loved Nina, I couldn't look at her—not tonight. My anger wouldn't be fair to her, and she didn't deserve that.

"CHA, wake up. Ma and Daddy are on FaceTime. Nina wants you to watch her open her presents. Oop!" Hazel brought me out of my slumber. I hadn't been asleep a good three hours after I was able to turn off my thoughts. When I looked up through still crusty eyes, Hazel's hand was over her mouth and the sudden movement behind me told me why.

"Y'all loud as hell in the morning." Zeus stretched from under the covers and rubbed his eyes.

"Hazel, who is that?" My mother's voice came through the speaker.

"Nobody, Ma. It's just the TV." Hazel covered for me, but still gave me a sneaky grin.

"Oh, now I'm nobody?" I pushed Zeus, letting him know to shut up.

"Ma, I'm getting dressed. Tell Nina to hold on for five minutes and we'll call back." I reached up and pressed the red button on Hazel's screen. "Are you always like this?"

"Yep." Zeus stretched, flipped the covers back, and started to get dressed. Hazel went on and left the room. "You got a kid?"

"Sort of. I'll explain later." I got dressed as well. Waking up to Zeus would have been nice if my circumstances were different. I didn't want what could be the start of something, to begin with him consoling me after the hurt of another man.

"Cool, I'll hit you later." Zeus leaned down and kissed my forehead as I slid into my pajama pants. I heard him speak to Hazel about something before I watched him cross the street to his brother's house.

"Cocoa?" Hazel offered when I entered the kitchen. I nodded, pressing the FaceTime icon beside my mother's name. Nina's face popped up and the sparkle in her eyes reversed my solemn mood. She had her father's eyes but hers didn't hold the malice he did.

She was so happy with what my parents had for her. We stayed on the phone until I heard Pierre's voice in the background. "OK, Bird, I'll see you later."

It was the first time she'd spent Christmas morning without the both of us present. But it was about to be the first of many.

NINE
APOLLO

"Ma, can you sit the fuck down?" I coughed. Venus was dancing around my damn living room, burning some kind of herb that was fucking my throat up.

"Watch your mouth, Apollo Tait!" she snapped. "It's bad enough neither of you got me anything for Christmas; now you wanna complain about me wanting to remove the negative energy in here."

"Ain't nobody even know you were coming!" I rebutted.

"And even if we wanted to send you something, you don't stay still long enough for it to reach you," Zeus countered. Nyx kept his head buried in his phone as always.

She'd been on our case all morning about how we chose to spend our holiday. I worked Thanksgiving, so I was able to talk my supervisor into giving me this holiday off. We hadn't given presents on Christmas in years. The three of us just ate breakfast, smoked a little, and sat around, watching football all day. This was what my brothers and I put into play since neither of our parents were around and Venus came in here, randomly disrupting shit.

"This is not how I raised you three to spend the holidays. I mean, for goodness' sake, Apollo, you don't even have a tree." Her arms lifted and flopped to her sides in disappointment.

"With all due respect, we're grown now." I shrugged. I heard her still complaining, but my mind went to Hazel. We'd shot texts back and forth all morning, and half of that was me trying to get her to understand it was just who Venus was.

The Tait household wasn't exactly tight-knit growing up. In my opinion, my parents struggled to juggle three different personalities. Especially as we got older, they conformed to who we were in some ways, and in others, they didn't.

"How's work?" She plopped onto the sofa with her arms crossed. "And I mean your actual career, not that shit your father has you doing."

"The shit my father has me doing is my real career." I shot her a sinister, yet genuine smile. She shifted in her seat uncomfortably and got up, mumbling how my pops had turned me into the devil. "Fuck this, I'll be back."

I grabbed my jacket and found myself across the way on Hazel's doorstep. She opened the door in some green pajamas, her curls flowing loosely. Before she could say anything, I scooped her in my arms and nuzzled my face into her neck. Her natural scent was soft and intoxicating.

"What are you doing here?" she asked, still standing with the door open.

"You can close that shit; I'm not going anywhere. I'm liable to toss my mother into the fireplace if I go back over there." I chuckled but was halfway serious. I couldn't be who Venus wanted me to be, and it didn't do shit but anger me when she tried to change me.

"Come in. We're making gingerbread houses." I watched as she walked away. Her ass jiggled in the cotton fabric, and I refrained from grabbing it. Mocha sat at the table and gave me a short wave.

"My brother knows you over here?" I fucked with her. Zeus and I were much alike when it came to what we wanted. We didn't stop until we got it. He went full speed ahead in pursuing Mocha. I wanted to do the same, but I had to be cautious with Hazel.

"He should." Hazel laughed. "Being as though he woke up in my house this morning."

"That doesn't surprise me," I replied honestly. I pulled out my phone and texted Zeus. It wasn't long before the doorbell rang, and Hazel was escorting Zeus to the kitchen.

The four of us worked on two separate gingerbread houses and talked with one another.

"Green, huh?" I asked. Hazel looked up at me in confusion. "Your favorite color. When I saw you at work, you had on green. Your pajamas are green, and if you put one more green gummy on this damn gingerbread house, I'ma scream."

"Oh," she snickered. "Yes, I love green."

"I'll keep that in mind. My favorite color is red, if you were wondering," I threw it out there, chuckling to myself at the fact that I loved red only because of the satisfaction I got watching it pour freshly from a body.

"I'll keep that in mind as well." She smiled. I continued to look her over, admiring the work of time. The first time I laid eyes on Hazel, she looked so fragile. "Why are you staring?"

"You look so radiant," I confessed. Hazel blushed and looked into my eyes like she was trying to figure something out. Our gaze was broken by the sound of her front door opening. Leave it up to Nyx to bust through the door without ringing the doorbell.

"Excuse you?" Mocha yelled, and Hazel looked at him like he'd lost his mind.

"Don't yell at me, cream!" Nyx grumbled. "Yell at these niggas for leaving me over there with Venus's ass. Y'all dead fucking wrong. I done took a million pictures and she's over there burning that shit again."

His mean ass sat at the table and folded his arms, giving everyone a menacing stare with his arms folded across his chest like a child. All that shit made us do was burst out laughing. When Nyx got heated enough, he was going to do one of two things: tell you about yourself or kill your ass. This was probably the most he'd said in one sitting in a while and that shit was funny.

"Fuck y'all!" he barked.

"Nah, fuck you!" Mocha laughed. "And get my name right before I tell yo' mama I need to see your birth certificate to believe she named you after a goddess on purpose."

"I told you I can roll my dick around in these gummies to show yo' ass! Man, why the fuck did I come over here? Shit ain't no better." He shook his head and pulled out his phone.

Hazel looked around at the three of us and looked like she'd come up with a bright idea. "Why don't you guys sing for us again?"

"Aww, hell nah." Nyx got up and stormed out the same way he came in.

"Why is his ass so mean?" Mocha complained.

"He's always been that way. You'll get used to it," I assured.

"What makes you think we'll be around to get used to it?" Hazel asked, craning her neck back.

"The fact you're spending the holiday with two strangers at your kitchen table and ain't kicked our asses out yet does," I replied.

"I already told your sister she's mine. And I meant that shit. Ma blowing my shit up, man. I'ma head back over there," Zeus said, looking at his phone. He and Mocha walked to the door, leaving Hazel and me alone. Hazel smirked as she witnessed Mocha blush at something Zeus said.

The room was now eerily quiet, and I studied Hazel even more. I assumed my gaze made Hazel uncomfortable because she avoided my eyes and moved a few curls to the back of her ear before starting to clean up. Instinct made me start to help her. Something about making her life easier felt good.

"You don't have to do that, I have it." She waved me off and tossed extra gingerbread pieces into the trash. I followed suit, causing her to run into me when she turned back around. I reached around her, tossing the candy and icing container in the trash. Hazel looked up at me and I pushed her against the closest wall.

"Apollo, I, um," she whispered.

"*I wanna put you in seven positions for seventy minutes, you get it, babe,*" I sang Tory Lanez and Chris Brown's "The Take", while nose to nose. My left arm gently swept up under the back of her pajama top and caressed her skin before gently pulling her closer to me. "*You got a lot on your mind, and I want to ease it and slip it in.*"

"I guess the Tait men are two for two today, huh?" Mocha's voice made us both jump, and Hazel used the opportunity to pull away from me. "Y'all can't say shit about us anymore. But um, Apollo, your mother is tryna burn your house down!"

My eyebrows furrowed and I rushed out of the house. My front door was open, and Nyx was on the lawn, laughing so hard, he had tears. Light clouds of smoke escaped through the doorway, and I darted in.

"What the fuck is going on?" I asked, running into the kitchen.

"I wanted to start dinner, but something went wrong." My mother shrugged nonchalantly.

Zeus looked at her, befuddled with his mouth wide open. "Something went wrong? This shit is unbelievable. First of all, you know Dad was the cook in the house. Second..." He faced me. "Your mother just tried to dump a cup of water in a grease fire! Thank God, it was small. I caught her just in time. I told her ass I was across the damn street and to wait!"

"So yo' ass knew she was 'bout to burn my shit down before you left Hazel's and ain't say shit?" What the hell type of shit was that? "Y'all get the hell outta my shit. I'm putting your ass in a hotel, Venus!"

I shook my head and went to my basement, my place of solitude. Relaxing in my recliner, I let my thoughts and annoyance settle.

"I'VE LIVED HERE ALL my life and have never been here." Hazel daunted over the *Enchant* event they had every year at our baseball stadium. There were Christmas light fixtures and attractions, a maze, ice skating, and even a market that offered spiked winter drinks.

"Time to expand your experiences," I replied. Although we spoke on and off throughout the day for the last week, this was the first time that I'd been in her presence since Christmas Day.

"Here! Take my picture." Hazel shoved her phone in my hand and jogged into the walkway made of white lights. I pushed a few buttons on her *iPhone* to get the best lighting against the Christmas lights and got the angle.

"Look up slightly and smile," I instructed. The photo came out just how I wanted. I snuck and sent it to myself before handing her back her phone.

"Come on with the angle!" she squealed, pleased.

"I mean, my mother is a photographer, and as crazy as she is, she's talented, nonetheless. She made sure to include us in her extra-curricular activities when we weren't spending time with our father." I complimented Venus. She hated how we clung to our dad, so the times when he went on jobs were her times to live her dream through the three of us.

"He cooks and knows his way around a camera. Why become a paramedic?" I chuckled at Hazel's switch to third person. She looked at me with interest, and we continued along the lighted path. There was a pause between the lingering question and my answer because I needed to be sure to word it correctly.

"You should know by now that I enjoy helping people. Blood never really bothered me either." I saw the mixed reaction Hazel had to my answer and I didn't really expect anything different. "How did you get into volunteering?" I inquired about how I knew she spent most of her free time.

Her head lowered and I was about to get pissed until she adjusted her fucking crown herself. I was proud to see Hazel gather herself and stick her chest out.

"I know how it feels to need help, and how ashamed one can feel to ask for it. I wanted to create a space where those in need feel safe enough to come and get help. No matter the circumstance," she boasted with pride. She'd grown and it looked good on her. A nigga could only appreciate that.

"Well, if it isn't my nephew, the paramedic." My Uncle Ace blocked my path with some lady on his arm. The way he drew out the word paramedic, let me know he still held on to the animosity of my father trusting me with the family business. But I didn't give a fuck about the chip on his shoulder. In the middle of this stadium wasn't the time nor the place for his bullshit.

"Uncle Ace," I huffed. His eyes traveled to Hazel and recognition flashed in them. I stepped forward, countering my stance and blocking his view of Hazel.

"Nephew, nephew, nephew." He smirked. "How's my brother?"

"Still running shit," I affirmed. "Fuck yo' slithering ass been up to?"

Ace's eyes narrowed at my description of him. "Apollo, you've always thought your balls were bigger than mine."

"Correction. I know they are."

"We'll see about that. C'mon, Hunnie." His ol' Alonzo wannabe ass grabbed his date's hand and stepped off.

"Why did that feel so tense?" Hazel questioned. Looking back at her, she seemed rattled. I knew the answer to her question, but now wasn't the time to answer it.

"Just some family shit."

"No, I feel like I've seen him before." Hazel searched within for answers. "Jordyn," she whispered to herself.

"What?" I asked.

"Nothing, I think we may just have a mutual friend is all. I'm sure it's nothing." Hazel shook it off, but I took heed to every word she said. I wasn't going to press it for now, though.

"Let's just continue our night. You wanna do the maze?" I led her toward the maze and allowed her to take the lead. Hazel was a breath of fresh air. Even as my urge to kill was present, she made the night easier to get through without seeing the life drain from my uncle's face being my relief.

Her smile was bright, her laugh was hearty and contagious. By the time we made it out of the maze, our stomachs were tight from laughing at how long it took us to get out.

"You don't get to lead the way anymore!" I told her.

"This was supposed to be a team effort! I'm not taking all the blame."

"Shiiitt, I went everywhere you told me to and ended up tripling back each time," I debated.

"It was not that bad! It was only forty minutes."

"That's a long ass time." I laughed, grabbing her by the waist from the side, and turning her to face me. "I like the sound of us being a team though."

"It does sound nice, huh?" Hazel blushed.

"Mmhm." I leaned down and pressed my lips against her lingering smile, delivering a peck. She cupped my neck and pulled me back down to her, returning my gesture. Pulling back with that smile flashing again, Hazel thought she was going to leave me with that. She had me fucked up. I covered her lips with mine and pushed my tongue into her mouth.

She welcomed it and gripped the sides of my coat while seductively feasting on my tongue and bottom lip. I wanted to dick her down right in the middle of this cold ass building, but I had self-control and I knew it was time to pull back.

"Aight, let's go get something to drink," I warned her.

The rest of the night, we checked out the market.

"I like these." Hazel picked up a pair of vintage earrings in the shape of an infinity symbol. I pushed her hair back over her shoulder to confirm my suspicions. There was a small infinity tattoo behind her ear.

"They're yours if you can tell me what this symbol means to you," I told her. She swallowed hard and fiddled with the earring.

"When it comes to love, the symbol means everlasting," Hazel began, looking up at me. "I've been through some things and I needed a reminder that the everlasting love I needed to focus on was for myself. So I got it tattooed."

I removed the earrings from her hand and held them up to her now exposed ear. "They're going to look good on you on our next date."

"Oh, I won date number two?" she joked.

"Yup. My goal is to show you another everlasting love." I spoke intently while adoring every feature on her face. Hazel cleared her throat and looked away.

"Are we trying ice skating?" she asked.

"Hell nah." I'd decided against ice skating when she mentioned she wanted to come here. We called it a night after a few drinks. I don't know why she chose to drive herself but I walked her to her car and didn't exactly have to follow her home since we live by one another. However, Hazel took a detour and since I chose not to follow, I spent the rest of the night wondering where the hell she was. I was so restless; I couldn't even sit in the house.

TEN

NYX

I was just about done with the night's work when my aggravating ass brother popped up. Apollo sat on one of the metal tables that weren't being utilized at the moment, running his mouth about Hazel.

"Where do you think she went?" he asked.

"Nigga, I don't know. How about you ask her?" I went over the last bit of details and submitted everything in the system while he continued to ramble. I tuned him out but he had my full attention when I heard Uncle Ace's name. "Wait. What about Ace?"

"I ran into his sketchy ass over at the stadium. He low-key threatened me," he explained.

"Y'all niggas have always been in a pissing match."

"Pissing match my dick! That nigga always wanted to be Pops, and now wanna be me. Gon' fuck around and be the first Tait in the dirt," he barked.

"Speaking of Dad, did he ever tell you why he wanted all of us to come visit instead of delivering a job like any other time?" I wasn't about to sit there and listen to Apollo go on about Ace or Hazel. Yeah, Ace wanted to run the business, but it was handed to Apollo. That was it, that was all. I didn't see what Apollo was even worried about it for.

"Nah. He just said to make sure y'all are there. Don't be in there acting like a dickhead, man." Apollo always thought he was somebody's daddy. Talking about how Ace wanted to be Alonzo, but this nigga acted just like his ass sometimes.

"I'ma be me like I always do. Alonzo don't fuck with me like that and vice versa. I do this shit for y'all, so ain't shit gon' change once we walk through them gates," I told his ass.

Karmen peeked her head into the room and waved, letting me know she was there and I started grabbing my shit.

"Nigga, we need to be there early, so don't take yo' ass home and stare out that window, stalking that girl, either."

"Fuck you." He jumped off the table and walked out.

Thinking about the visit with my pops the same week we had to deal with Venus's ass was just too much. Therefore, I wasn't taking my ass home. I wanted to be alone, yet still wanted company. Shit never made sense to anyone, but I got it, so that was all that mattered.

Braiza had been pissed at me since I hung up on her Christmas Eve when Venus came storming through Apollo's door. I'd never missed a woman a day in my life, but I had to admit I actually missed her. I knew she was growing tired of my shit, but to be with a nigga like me, you just had to go with the flow.

I put my key in her door and attempted to turn it. When that motherfucker didn't turn, I paused and looked around like that would help me figure this shit out. Then, my ass kept trying to twist it like it was going to change something. Braiza had me fucked up.

There was a toolbox in my truck and I kindly took my time to pick her lock. Once I pushed the door open, Braiza stood there with her arms folded over the silk teddy that stopped just below her pussy. She looked good as hell, but I was too pissed to even fuck some sense into her.

"Nyx, I changed the locks for a reason!" she barked.

"And we're going to talk about that shit later. I'm going to bed." I walked past her, straight to her bedroom. Kicking my shoes off on the side of the bed, I laid my clothes on her dresser.

"Nyx, I don't want you here." She pouted.

"Too bad. Lay yo' ass down, I'm tired." I was now in my tank top, boxers, and socks, sliding underneath her comforter.

She could be mad all she wanted. I had a lot on my mind. Although I wasn't for all that emotional shit, I needed to be near her. I felt her angrily flop onto the bed and fight her pillow to get comfortable. Shit ain't make me no never mind. She better take her ass to bed or stay up thinking about a good reason as to why she changed them damn locks. As for me, I was going to sleep.

THE SOUND of the gates opening sounded like nails on a chalkboard. I hated coming to the prison, and in all eight years that Alonzo had been inside, I'd only been there twice. I knew I wasn't a nigga to be in jail because I didn't fuck with people. So, having a motherfucker in my face, telling me how to move every day, wasn't going to do shit but have me catching extra charges every day.

I'd have shit my way like Alonzo simply because he ain't raised no bitch, but these walls weren't shit I wanted to be confined to.

After we got searched, Zeus, Apollo and I were let into a small room where Alonzo was sitting at a table, waiting for us.

"Fuck is this? *The First 48?*" Zeus's stupid ass joked.

"Nah, it's an attorney visitation room. They can't listen in on these rooms, so this is the room I requested." Alonzo stood and hugged Apollo and reached across the table to dap Zeus and me up like we weren't his seeds. See, that was the fuckery I was talking about.

"Man, why are we here?" I wondered. I didn't want to spend any extra time here than needed.

"Because I told y'all to come!" Alonzo hissed.

"Nyx, I asked you to chill." Apollo looked down the table at me.

"And I told you I ain't fuck with this nigga!" I reminded him. "Now, what is this job?"

Alonzo glared at me for a minute, like it was supposed to do something. Then he began explaining.

"This shit is big, and I needed to make sure everyone was here so nothing got misconstrued. Nyx, your disrespectful ass is going to have to step away from the office for this one."

I ignored him calling me disrespectful and shifted in my seat to listen. I ain't been in the field in a minute and was curious to know what the hell he had planned.

"There's a corporation and someone needs the entire board picked off. It will take some strategizing because this shit must be done right. It can't look like they were targeted, so of course their deaths need to look like an accident. My suggestion is to find a way to catch them all together. I'll leave it up to y'all, but y'all know not to have that shit come back on y'all."

"We are not new to this shit," Zeus said.

"Neither was I, lil nigga, and you see where I'm sitting," Alonzo replied in a monotone voice.

"That ain't because you slipped up. But that's a conversation for another time," Apollo said. "Anyway, is that all for the job? Will I receive the details the normal way?"

"Yea, but I do wanna say something. I talked to your uncle this morning. I hear you're sleeping where you shit." He stared at Apollo. Zeus and I sat there confused.

"I got it under control, Pops." Apollo defended himself against whatever Ace had said.

"Y'all can have y'all lil pow wow. Let me know when you get the details, Apollo. I'm out." I went back through all the security gates and shit and leaned against my car, sparking a blunt.

"Nigga, put that shit out in front of the jail." Zeus laughed, coming out behind me.

"Fuck them. Are they still talking?"

"Yea. I'll see what that shit is about later. I need to get to work. I told my boss I'll be there for the second half of the day." Zeus dapped me up and we both got in our vehicles. Him going to work reminded me I had a bone to pick with Braiza's ass. I took a few more pulls off my blunt before pulling off so Zeus didn't get suspicious about where I was going.

These lil badass kids running through the hallways reminded me of how my brothers and I used to terrorize these exact hallways. It shocked me when Zeus decided to teach here because we sure made a name for ourselves before going to high school.

It was clear that they were in the middle of changing classes and I pushed through the crowd and damn near ran past Zeus's classroom to get to the principal's office.

"I'm here to see Ms. Daniels," I told the administrator at the front desk. I assumed he was about to tell me she wasn't in her office because Ms. Daniels walked into the office as she opened her mouth to speak.

"Why are you here?" Braiza sighed, shifting her eyes back onto the clipboard she held.

"We need to talk," I answered. She gestured for me to follow her to her office. I sat down and kicked my feet up on her desk. She shoved them off and folded her arms across her chest. "Damn, you look good. Why don't you wear those glasses for me?"

"You have the nerve to come in here like this. And the shit you pulled last night? Only to get up and leave without saying shit?" she barked through gritted teeth.

"I wanted to be near you." I shrugged. "Why did you change the locks?"

"Because I'm tired of your mean ass! This shit is one-sided and it isn't fulfilling for a woman like me!"

"My dick ain't fulfilling? I'm hurt." I placed my hand on my chest.

"Nyx Tait, I swear if you don't get the hell out of my office." She pulled her glasses off and pinched the bridge of her nose.

"I'm gone." I got up and made it to the door before turning around. "Don't take your frustration out on these kids, either."

"Get out!"

I chuckled and left. I heard her loud and clear. I normally stand on who I am when someone asks me to be something other than myself. This time, I deflected instead of telling her to kiss my ass and that shit had me feeling a little weird. I can't lie and say I didn't miss her ass when she ghosted me for a week. However, I was who the fuck I was. At least that was what I was telling myself. Braiza had a nigga feeling a little off and I ain't like that shit. Not one fucking bit.

ELEVEN
BRAIZA

My office door closed and I tossed the pen I was holding down on my desk. Nyx Tait worked on my very last nerve with his audacity, but as weird as it was for him to break into my house, it was the very first time that he'd applied that kind of pressure. But then he followed it up with the shit he'd just pulled and there was the audacity again. How the fuck do you treat me like shit, let me be upset for damn near two weeks, and ask me why I cut off easy access?

Then a tune in the form of a knock on my door let me know it was Randi. Only his ass knocked on my door using a beat.

"What?" I grumbled. Randi opened the door and leaned against my doorframe, eating a chocolate chip cookie. "Don't start."

"I'm just saying. Ya ass been having a day and finally seeing that fine specimen of a man waltz up out of here tells me why." He bit the cookie and smirked.

"I have not been having a day. And now he's a man, huh?"

"Now that I've finally laid eyes on his ass, yes, he's all man. I see what is making you mad now. He walks like he's hanging like a horse."

"Randi!" I shouted.

"I'm just saying." He tossed the rest of the cookie in his mouth. "And yes, you are having a day. You've had two cups of coffee, suspended three students, and even added a few choice words in these emails you sent out." Randi sure knew how to tell me about myself, and most days, it was appreciated. Today, it just aggravated me even more.

"Don't you have some work to do?" I asked.

"I'll do some work when you figure out your love life." He stuck his tongue out at the same time as me, reaching for the block of sticky notes on my desk and launching them at him. I was going to be mad that I had to pick them up later, but as long as he cleared my doorway.

I retrieved my phone from my top drawer and texted Nyx.

Me: Are you out of the parking lot yet?

Nyx: Nah, what's up?

Me: Stay there.

I grabbed my coat and the keys to my office and headed to the front of the school. I was glad to see that my halls were empty. All except for one kid.

"Xavier, if I walk back through here and see you again, I'm suspending you for a week," I told my damn problem student as I caught him wandering down the hall, twirling the hall pass around his finger.

"Don't do that, Ms. Daniels. My mama gon' be pissed that she can't see Mr. Tait when she picks me up," he responded.

"Watch your mouth and get to class," I sighed. Xavier was a smart young man but the fact that his mother was a walking thirst trap didn't help his behavior. Xavier was saying something as I was walking away, but I wasn't trying to hear it. There was only one solution to the problem, and it was to take his little butt to class or he'd have an even bigger problem.

Once I spotted Nyx's car across the parking lot, I went to join him. Thankfully, he had the heat pumping. This winter was kicking our asses. He leaned back and waited for me to speak first.

"What are you doing?" I asked him.

His face twisted up. "Sitting here waiting on you to tell me what I waited on you for."

"No, Nyx. What are you doing with me and to me?"

"Ain't nobody got time for the riddles and shit." I could hear him begin to get upset. "Ask what you need to, Braiza."

"I did, Nyx." I returned his attitude. "It's been six months and I'm still lost on what your intentions with me are. I'm even more unsure about why I still feel myself falling for you, even with your lack of effort."

"Say what you mean, Brai."

This man. I let out an exhaustive sigh.

"Save the dramatics. I'm telling you to lay out what you want from a nigga. I can't guarantee that you'll receive them all at once, but at least it'll be on the table."

"I need *you*, Nyx. I need more communication, more affection, and more exclusivity. Hell, I need you to grow up!" I expressed.

"I'm a grown ass man, Braiza. Don't play with me." His voice got dark like it does when he's about to shut down. I was surprised that this conversation even lasted this long. "You know all that other shit not me. You can't say that you need me and give a list of shit that ain't even my character."

"And you can't expect someone to deal with that shit." I reached for the door handle, only for Nyx to grab my arm and damn near pull me over the center console into his space. He released my arm, and his hand gripped the side of my neck.

"Where you going, Braiza?" he asked. My pussy tingled, because for once this nigga didn't tell me I could get the fuck on. His lips were so close to mine that my heartbeat sped up, hoping I would finally feel his full lips on mine. I was dying to know how his tongue tasted, and I thought this was finally it. "Keep talking all that shit about why you falling for a nigga and you may just get what you're asking for."

I felt his hand slide underneath my skirt and easily tear a hole in my tights. Slowly, he rubbed up and down my pussy.

"The way yo' pussy dripping feels like you gon' drown soon instead of falling."

"Nyxxx," I moaned.

Nyx's mouth was so close to mine, that I began to tremble. Especially with his finger having its way with my clit. Our eye lock was intense, and my breathing was heavy as I was on the verge of an orgasm.

"I hate explaining myself, Braiza. But, I heard you, and I got you. OK?"

I couldn't even speak. I just nodded and broke our eye contact to let my head fall against the headrest. My orgasm was strong, but not one of those clench your legs and embed your nails in something types. It was the euphoric, legs trembling kind.

"You good, now?" Nyx whispered. Again, I nodded. "Now take your ass back to work and stop acting like you're leaving a nigga."

Kicking off my heels, I removed what was left of my tights and slipped my shoes back on. I knew that this conversation would end in disappointment if I went in for a kiss, so I took the fact that Nyx heard and acknowledged me and went back inside.

"Bitch, you're missing something!" Randi snickered as I tried to hurry into the front office and past his desk. I flipped him off and closed my office door, immediately going to clean myself. I didn't know what I was going to do with Nyx Tait.

TWELVE
ZEUS

"Mr. Tait, I have to use the bathroom," one of my students blurted out and danced in her seat.

"Raise your hand next time. Get the hall pass and go." I pointed over to the wall where the hall passes hung and continued my lesson.

Today, we were going over the elements of the periodic table, and while teaching, I was also putting chemicals together that could blow some shit up. Ever since we'd left the prison, I'd been pondering how I could fulfill my part of the job.

"Are we doing an experiment this week?" Xavier, of all people, asked.

"We are, but the only thing we will do and talk about is that experiment only. Since your daredevil ass wanna go home and do the most," I spat. The rest of the class groaned in annoyance at Xavier's stunt they all had to suffer from.

I was the cool teacher, and a few times, I allowed my fascination to spill over into my lessons, but not anymore. I was liable to go in on Ms. Daniels's old ass the next time she called herself pulling me into her office.

Plus, I actually enjoyed my job and had to take responsibility for my part in what happened before the break. Young minds are curious, and I should've known *somebody* was going to eventually try some shit.

"All right. Read over this chapter and answer the unit questions at the end." I gave out today's assignment and started to get comfortable at my desk when a figure walked past the small window in my classroom door. I could've sworn it was Nyx. I went to the door, but by the time I looked down the hallway, they had bent the corner. I was mad that my classroom was on the opposite side of the building than the parking lot because I knew my brother when I saw him. What I didn't understand was why he would be here.

The day went by slowly and the kids tested every damn nerve in my body. Relief came over me once I heard the last bell ring. Being a teacher was satisfying, but it was not for the weak.

———

"THAT WAS FAST." I looked around Mocha's new place. She'd texted me all excited, telling me to come to see her new place. It was a nice two-bedroom with an open floor plan. Plush gray carpet was throughout the apartment except for the kitchen and bathroom.

"Money talks," she beamed. "When I say I'm done with something, I'm done. And Pierre is a thing of the past." Mocha pulled glasses from their boxes and set them on her kitchen counter.

"This says otherwise." I lifted her left hand, observing the ring that still adorned her finger.

"Well, I am still married, Zeus." She sighed.

"That doesn't mean that you have to wear the reminder of it every day," I attested.

"Are you going to help me, or are we going to go over something that I know we're both tired of going over?" I sensed the attitude in her voice and didn't give a damn. I let her live, though and grabbed a box. But this conversation wasn't over. I opened so many boxes from *Amazon,* and everything she'd purchased had some kind of bird on it.

"Don't know why you ain't just move in with me," I half-joked.

"Because my life of living under a man's thumb is over. I've been saving my money since I started working at the firm with Hazel and I'm finally able to stand on my own. My independence is my main priority right now."

"You wouldn't be under my thumb. But I can respect that."

"Plus, it's too soon to jump into something that serious again," she claimed.

"I don't know what the fuck you talking about. We go together!" I countered.

"Zeus."

"Zeus my ass. You heard what the fuck I said. We can move at your pace for now, but you're mine. I told you we all have a chance to make up for our mistakes; I'm your one and only chance. Play with me if you want." I stared at her, waiting for a rebuttal. One that didn't come. Her ass was over there blushing like a schoolgirl. "That's what I thought."

We put up the rest of the necessities and went to the grocery store since Mocha had been screaming about wanting some damn tacos.

"Just like a woman. We did not come in here for that." I watched as she threw snacks into the cart.

"Hush. I want some chocolate." She pushed me softly.

"Tacos and chocolate? Make sure you get some spray. You 'bout to fuck that bathroom up." This time, she playfully punched me in the arm. Mocha gathered the ingredients for the tacos and picked up some kind of yellow salsa. "What the hell is this?"

"Mango pineapple salsa."

"Shit sounds sweet as hell." I tossed the plastic container back into the cart.

"It is. But it balances out the flavors of the taco. You'll like it." I watched her as she moved around the store. Mocha's spirit seemed so free from the first time I met her. I'd always observed and loved her outgoing and outspoken personality, but now she seemed a lot more open to completely being herself and it looked good on her.

"Stop staring at me like a creep." Mocha looked over her shoulder and smiled.

"Just admiration, baby." She blushed harder and my dick jumped.

Down, boy! I told my manhood. These slacks weren't thin, but neither was my dick. These people were going to see all eight inches, fucking with Mocha.

I paid for the groceries, and after Mocha admitted to wanting my company for the night, I stopped by my place and grabbed some clothes.

"This is not how I envisioned your place looking," Mocha said, picking up picture frames.

"How did you envision it?"

"With one of those futon couches and mismatched furniture." She laughed.

"I'll pretend not to be offended. I'll be back. Unless you wanna see what my bed looks like and test it out. It ain't on the floor."

"Save it for later. Go get your things." Mocha shook her head and so did I. I just knew that was going to work.

I grabbed some things from my closet and caught Mocha pulling at my basement door when I returned.

"That sign says caution," I said, causing her to jump.

"Oh, I was just curious. What's down there?"

"A lab, where I mix shit to either burn shit down or blow it up." I shrugged.

"Yea right." She giggled.

"Aye, believe me, or don't. Are you ready?" I held the front door open, and Mocha looked at me like I was crazy before crossing back over the threshold.

Back at her place, we showered and ate. She was right, that salsa was bomb as hell. I had the itis but we both had some work to do. Now, we were laying in her bed with notebooks and papers everywhere. I was grading today's papers and writing out my lesson plan for the next day while Mocha went over a few marketing strategies she was excited to show Hazel.

I heard her close her laptop and slide closer to me. Mocha laid her head on my arm and slid her hand underneath my shirt, rubbing my abs.

"I'm not done yet. Don't bring yo' ass over here starting shit," I warned her. I hadn't put this dick up in her yet, but I could hear her pussy calling out for this motherfucker.

"I'm not. I'll let you finish."

"You gotta stop touching me like that, though, mama," I warned her again. I picked up my next paper and began to read over the questions and answers. Shawty must've thought I was playing because she slightly sank her nails into me and ran her hand up and down my side.

I tossed the papers on the floor and flipped her ass over.

"Zeus," she called out, laughing like I was playing with her ass.

"Nah, you wanted this dick, so I'ma put your ass into a coma so I can finish my work." I pulled the little ass shorts she was wearing over her ass and pulled her by her waist, arching her back the way I wanted it. I smacked her ass and the little jiggle it gave me along with the glisten I saw seeping from her pussy lips had my dick at full attention.

I plunged into her so hard that I know I hit rock bottom in that bitch. The sound and feel of her wetness, mixed with her moaning my name with her face planted into the sheets, had me occasionally pulling all the way out so I wouldn't bust too early.

"Damn you gripping my shit, shawty," I let out as I grabbed onto her hips, slowly dipping back inside of her. She started to throw her shit back and it had a nigga grinding his teeth. "Throw that shit, baby."

Her ass bounced against my abs, and I alternated smacking each cheek with every thrust. The way she was creaming on my dick let me know she liked that rough shit. Shawty's pussy was getting wetter and wetter.

"I'm cummin', Zeus!" She had the sexiest voice while I was inside of her. I felt her walls tightening and pulled out. Mocha was about to complain until my tongue plunged inside of her from the back while she came. I was in a sniper position while I held her thighs and flickered my tongue deep inside until her ass was squirting. "Oh Gooooddd! Zeus!"

Getting up, I looked down at my work with a smirk full of pride. Her shorts were soaked, and Mocha looked like I'd just fucked the soul out of her. I did, but she hung in there like a champ. Prints from her ass had my glasses blurry, so I tossed them to the side. Closing my eyes, I slid back into her waterfall. Mocha started throwing her ass back again.

"Your turn." She looked back over her shoulder. She was right; the sight before me had my nut building. I fucked her hard and Baby Girl took all this dick like a pro. I pulled out and came all over her ass.

Walking to the linen closet, I grabbed two of her new towels and wet them both.

"Boy, I'm getting in the shower. I got both of our cum running down my ass and thighs, and a lot of it, might I add. A towel ain't gon' do it." Mocha weakly scooted off the bed, still on her stomach, and fully removed her clothing.

Round two went crazy in the shower and put us both out for the count. Those grades had to wait.

THIRTEEN
HAZEL

"What are you about to do?" Apollo asked on the other end of the phone. "And why won't you come to the camera?"

I had my AirPod in, moving around my office, getting ready to go. My phone was on the charging stand on my desk. "I'm getting my things together, Apollo. I told you I was meeting Mocha and a friend for happy hour at Rio's. I'll FaceTime you once I get in the car."

Instead of answering, Apollo hung up the phone. I shook my head at his stubbornness. He wanted to see me tonight, but I had other plans. I would gladly dip on the girls later, but I needed a few drinks first. I'd never been the type to not have a life outside of a man, and I wasn't about to start now. That was also a problem in my previous relationship, and I'll be damned if I was going for that shit again. *Quincy.* My past invaded my thoughts.

After my date with Apollo the other night, I found myself at the cemetery, staring at Quincy's tombstone for an hour. A part of me questioned myself about why I was there, but the other side knew I went there to gloat. I finally felt like I could breathe with Apollo, and for once, it felt like I deserved it.

Quincy was abusive. Three years together and the abuse began verbally. Then mentally, and eventually, physically. Things started as a fairytale and the man that I fell in love with slowly faded away. Of course, I tried to leave but the mental abuse was real. Not being good enough for anyone else was spoken into me daily and I'd started to believe it.

Aside from Apollo's weird ass uncle, I was made to feel like I deserved the world that night. It was like I was gaining my power back outside of maintaining my independence, and the one person who I felt needed to know was in the ground. So, I pulled up on him, not even knowing what to say. So, I just sat there. Time went on and my conscience started fucking with me. An hour later, I was sitting outside of Jordyn's condo building, talking myself down from going to this woman's door at midnight. I was unsure of how to just allow myself to be happy, and the results of what had been an amazing night showed just that.

Apollo was now making me have flashbacks and he wasn't even my man, but he sure as hell acted like it. I enjoyed spending time with him and talking to him, and I missed the fuck out of him when we were apart; however, things like this were why I was determined to take things slow.

"How'd you like my ideas?" Mocha popped her head into my office.

"I loved them." I smiled at my sister. The excitement about her new journey was beautiful on her.

"I'm so nervous to send them to Mr. Jenkins." She fully entered my office, biting her nails.

"There is nothing to worry about. Your ideas are innovative, and you've provided the right amount of research to back your theory of reaching a broader audience. He's going to be throwing accounts your way left and right." I lowered Mocha's hand from her mouth and winked at her. She winked back and her shoulders relaxed. "Now, are you ready to get some drinks?"

"Hell yeah. I've been stressing about these presentations all day. Let's get fucked up! I'm riding with you."

We made it to the lounge, where Jordyn was waiting for us.

"Why you ain't tell me she was a cop?" Mocha asked.

"How do you know that?" I asked.

"She's sticking out like a sore thumb."

"That's not true. All of us are dressed for work." I looked around the room at what some may consider a blue-collar crowd.

"Yea, but that gun bulge on both her hip and ankle is a dead giveaway."

"Girl, come on. She's cool." We approached the bar where Jordyn was on her phone, per usual. "Off the phone! We're supposed to be releasing all things work related," I teased, and I went in for a hug. "Jordyn, this is my sister, Mocha."

"Nice to finally meet you." Mocha leaned in for a side hug. I'd mentioned Jordyn a few times, but never brought her around.

"You too. I hate to cut things short, but I can only have an hour. There's been a new development in one of my old cases."

My heartbeat sped up. "An old case? W-what old case?" I felt sweat beads begin to form on my forehead.

"And old robbery that we never really solved. I can't really get into it," she responded.

I tried to catch my breath and gather myself. I needed a shot, and fast. "Three shots of Patrón, please," I told the bartender when she came to our end of the bar.

"Here's to a long day!" I toasted.

"You can say that again," Jordyn sighed. We clinked the small glasses together, tapped the bottom of them on the bar, then took the shots to the head. I closed my eyes as the warm feeling of the alcohol calmed my nerves by the second.

"Damn, sis, was the day really that stressful?" Mocha asked. I opened my eyes and looked at her with a smile.

"Mentally, yes. I'm good though. Y'all eating? The wings here are good!" I spoke loudly over the music. The place was quickly getting packed, and I was glad we'd gotten there early to grab bar seats.

Fucking Robitussin! Blasted through the speakers and the three of us sang Chris Brown's "Under the Influence" at the top of our lungs. I even got up and started dancing. Mocha pulled out her phone and began filming me, so I turned around, so my back was facing the camera and did the funny viral TikTok dance that was trending to this song.

They both laughed and we waved the bartender over for another shot.

"I really need to get—" It sounded like Jordyn was about to make her exit, but she looked behind me and looked like she'd seen a ghost. My heart pounded before I even turned around. When I did, it dropped to the ground. Apollo stood there, looking like a menace to society with his eyebrows furrowed. A fine one, but a menace, none-theless.

"What are you doing here?" It was so toxic the way my pussy was tingling, even though I was pissed.

"You said you would call me when you got in the car, and since I've been calling you for the past half hour, I thought I would make sure you made it safely," he said calmly.

"I thought your brother was crazy. That shit must run in the family." Mocha looked him up and down.

"You can say that again," Jordyn shockingly interjected. "How've you been, Mr. Tait?"

Jordyn's face of horror was now stoic as she stood and squared off with Apollo. I looked back and forth between the two in what seemed to be a familiar standoff.

"Could be better, Detective." He shot her a smirk that made even me uncomfortable. Jordyn stepped back and reached into her bag, pulling out two twenties.

"I'll call you later, Hazel. It's time for me to go." She briefly hugged me, and I watched her disappear into the crowd.

"What the hell was that?" I questioned.

"Just a little first responders' tension." I shrugged.

"Mm. Well, can you leave? You already give off stalker vibes, and this didn't help." My irritation was at an all-time high.

"Not a stalker, baby. I'm just protective of what's mine." His toxic ass kissed my forehead and was gone as quickly as he came.

Mocha found that shit funny, but I was lost.

"That shit is not funny," I stressed.

"All three of their asses touched in the head." She continued to laugh.

I ordered my next round and ignored her ass. She and Zeus loved that toxic shit, but it was a no for me. My body reacted to this man against my will, and I had an amazing time on our date, but this was too much. Plus, too many weird ass moments happened when I was around him.

"IS THAT ALL?" The *U-Haul* worker asked after sliding the last box of clothes into the truck.

"Yes, thank you. I'm ready now. You guys can just follow me." I locked up my house and made my way to the center. Every year, right before the seasons changed, we did a clothes drive. I'd bring everything home gradually to be washed and separated.

Now, I was regretting not taking everything back to the shelter as I washed them because I ended up having to rent a truck to take everything back. Things were in my favor today because if Apollo wasn't at work, he would have surely jumped in to save the day. All that would have done was pull me right back into his orbit and I didn't need that. At least that was what I was telling myself, but I'd be lying if I said I didn't miss him.

I unloaded the boxes when we arrived at the center, and the other volunteers jumped right in to help. It was times like this that my heart was overjoyed. So many people showed up. Those who were there to help, and those in need. We provided spring clothing for everyone from infants to seniors.

"This is amazing work you're doing here." Jordyn's voice made me lift my head from the bag I was packing for an awaiting family.

"Thank you. The Christmas turnout was bigger than this one, which is expected, but this was more donations than we expected for this time of year. I'm happy with the turnout. What are you doing here?"

Jordyn walked around the table. "I wanted to talk about the other night."

"OK?" She had my full attention. Apollo played their interaction off as some work thing, but the look in Jordyn's eye let me know it was more.

"Not here. Is there someplace we can talk?"

I asked another volunteer to finish helping the family and led Jordyn to the storage space in the back. "OK, what's going on?"

"The man that showed up, what's your connection to him?"

"I think the real question is, what's *your* connection?" I countered. My personal business would be shared only when I was ready. Jordyn had blindly warned me about someone and questioned me rather than tell me what the hell was going on.

"I was the lead detective on a case that lasted years. A little over a year ago, it concluded and resulted in the incarceration of Apollo's father," she explained.

"OK? What does that have to do with Apollo?"

"His father is doing time for attempted murder. However, the entire Tait family was under investigation. Any evidence of them being dirty always seemed to slip through our fingers until we were able to catch Alonzo Tait in the act."

"Again, why does that warrant a warning about Apollo?" I was still confused. I knew people were held accountable for their parent's actions all the time, and I'd never agreed.

"Shortly after sentencing, I began receiving threats. I can't prove it but I know for sure they came from Apollo."

"You seem to be throwing around a lot of accusations with no proof," I debated. Something was surely off with Apollo, but murder couldn't be it. *Could it?*

"You don't have to believe me. Just please be careful, friend. I care about you, and I want to see you happy again. Just don't ignore red flags or dismiss me for telling you this. I got your back and I only want to see you win, Haze." Jordyn grabbed my hand and squeezed it. I knew she was genuine, and I appreciated having a friend like that. Shit just wasn't adding up.

Her phone chimed, and just like that, she was racing back to her patrol car. I stayed in the back for a while, replaying Jordyn's words. *Nah, Apollo saved lives, not took them. She must be mistaken.* This shit just wasn't adding up.

FOURTEEN
MOCHA

"You're pregnant, Cha?" Hazel stood over me in the bathroom stall and I threw up my breakfast.

"Honestly, Haze, I don't know." I rinsed my mouth out at the sink. "I'm going to see if my doctor can fit me in today."

"Doctor my ass. I'll be back." Hazel stormed out of the bathroom. I washed my hands and went back to my desk. I'd spent the weekend getting settled into my place and Monday had come around again. The last thing I needed right now was for the stick I knew my sister was retrieving to prove what I kind of knew.

The timing was horrible. Hazel was right when she stated that Mr. Jenkins was going to throw accounts my way once he saw my trial presentations. Everything that I wanted career-wise was finally starting to happen, and now this. The worst part of it all was that I knew it belonged to Pierre. We'd had unprotected sex the morning I was supposed to go to his event. Ironically, the same day I met Zeus.

Zeus. He wouldn't want anything to do with me if I was carrying another man's baby. Zeus had stood on everything he said about wanting to be in my life, so hard that the fact that the *other man* was my fucking husband was irrelevant.

Zeus: I miss you

His text came through like he knew I was thinking about him. Blushing at his words had become so natural. My cheeks got hot every time I saw his name pop up on my screen.

Me: I miss you too.

"Tell Zeus you're going to text him later." Hazel grabbed my hand and pushed me into the bathroom again. I let out a groan, dreading the results. Fifteen minutes later, I was staring at the digital screen reading, **Pregnant.**

I leaned against the stall and bumped my head against it a few times.

"Ooouuuu! You're pregnant! I'm telling Mama!" Hazel shuffled around a little before I heard her nails tapping at the screen.

I darted out of that stall so fast and snatched the phone. "Can you not be so childish?"

"But, Cha!" She was smiling hard as hell, not even knowing this was not about to play out how she thought.

"But nothing! I'm about to file for a divorce; I don't want to raise a child in a broken home," I explained.

"You have a lot of support. Fuck Pierre. You know Ma and Daddy will be full-time grandparents. Look at how they are with Nina. Auntie duty will be the closest to me becoming a mom anytime soon, so I'm here 100 percent."

"It's not the same, Haze. Plus, Zeus is not going to want to be around me having another man's baby," I grumbled. The thought of losing Zeus before we really began hurt and I didn't know why.

"So, this is about Zeus?" Hazel looked at me with her head cocked to the side. All I could do was stare at the tile floor. "Look, I suggest you go talk to Pierre first and then decide. Just let me know what happens. I have a conference call in a couple of minutes, so I have to get back to my office."

"OK. I'm taking my lunch break."

Hazel winked at me before walking out of the bathroom. I winked back and followed her out.

Pierre should have been my first visit, but I found myself sitting outside of the middle school. Zeus and I tried this Thai restaurant over the weekend, and I loved it. On the way over, I placed the same order for both of us and went to pick it up. What I wanted to be a nice lunch date had the potential to go to hell if I brought up the news. I decided against speaking about it for now. I knew I couldn't have been more than about four weeks, and I wasn't sure what I was going to do, anyhow. So, telling Zeus would be pointless.

The front office explained that the bell dismissing the kids for lunch should be soon and directed me to Zeus's classroom. I stood at the door as he explained something to a student who had approached his desk with a textbook and paper. For those short minutes, I watched how patient he was and how the student walked away, nodding in understanding.

Usually, I was graced with the Zeus Tait that was outspoken, assertive, and got what he wanted. To see him in his element was exciting and turn-on. I tried to hide the huge smile on my face when he spotted me, but it was too late. He smiled back and refocused on his class.

"Anything that's not done, finish it for homework!" he yelled seconds before the bell rang.

"To what do I owe this pleasure?" He approached me and pecked my lips.

"Mr. Tait, you can't do that in school!" a male student yelled from the hallway.

"Mind your business! Worry about not being late for my damn class tomorrow!" Zeus yelled back. I giggled at the exchange. My Zeus was still in there, but it was still clear that he took this job seriously and I admired that.

"How long do you have before your next class?" I asked, setting the bag of food down on the table.

"About an hour," he said. Zeus walked to the back of the class and grabbed another desk chair and rolled it to the side of his desk so I could join him. He took the containers out and separated our food. "How's your morning been?"

"Stressful," I sighed.

"Why?"

"Um, just work," I lied. "I have a few new accounts and I'm struggling to get started on."

Those accounts were a walk in the park. I could have them all done in the next two days, but that was my story and I was sticking to it.

"We can have a study session later tonight if you can focus." He smirked.

"And why wouldn't I be able to?" I mimicked his teasing tone.

"Cuz this dick ain't no one-stop shop, baby!"

"Something is seriously wrong with your ass." I laughed. "You're right, though! But business first!"

"I got you," he agreed. I shoved a forkful of food in his mouth.

"You seem to have a good relationship with the students." I expressed my observation.

"Yea. My goal is to teach them that learning new things can be fun while giving them the room to express themselves as children. My parents already had it set in their minds of who they wanted us to be growing up instead of allowing us to grow into ourselves, and *not* try to mold us." For the first time, I witnessed Zeus kind of shy away from a topic and not boldly look into my eyes when speaking. I knew how personal passion could be uncomfortable, so I understood.

"Was this food on your mind like it was mine?" I asked, looking at how he was crushing his food.

"Hell yea!" he answered. "I was taking your ass back here when I got a chance. I'm glad you surprised me though."

"I thought it would be nice to do something for you for a change." I smiled proudly. My mission was accomplished. My phone vibrated in my purse, and I immediately answered it when I saw it was Bird's school. They said that Nina had been sick, and Pierre wasn't answering. "I have to go."

I took one more bite of food, leaned in for a kiss, and tossed my purse over my shoulder. I didn't get far down the hall when a woman's voice echoed through it.

"Oh, you already ate," she said with disappointment. My entire body did a 180-degree turn, and sure enough, a woman was entering his room.

"You're in a school, Mocha, keep walking." I had to push myself not to go back. I was sure these women threw themselves at his fine ass all the time. *And your ass is still married and pregnant.* That thought alone made me want to throw up.

"HEY, GORGEOUS. WHAT'S WRONG?" I squatted in front of the chair Nina was sitting in in the main office.

"My stomach hurts," she mumbled with her lip poking out. I didn't want to be insensitive, but my mama would tell our ass to go to the bathroom and go back to class.

"What did you eat?"

"Cereal." She avoided my gaze.

"You know you can't have milk, Nina. Why would you do that?" I sighed and stood to sign her out. I dreaded taking her home. I hadn't been to my old home since the day I left and never planned to return. However, amid me telling her parents to actually be parents since they wanted to fuck, it slipped my mind that I was Nina's legal guardian. "Come on. Let's get you home."

"Wait, Mrs. Sapora!" Nina's teacher, Mrs. Powell, called after me.

"Yes?"

"I've been calling Mr. Sapora since yesterday. There was a meeting scheduled to discuss Nina's progress and no one showed."

"Why didn't you call me?" I questioned. I was right beside Pierre on Nina's contact list, so I was confused.

"Nina's mom came to pick her up last week and said that either she or Mr. Sapora would be the ones to attend the meeting. We contacted you today because she was sick."

The anger that boiled inside of me at Penelope's audacity was ready to erupt. But, I knew there was a time and place for everything.

"Mrs. Powell, respectfully, I'm still her legal guardian over her mother. I am also the only one versed in her learning disability. Please call me first unless anything changes legally," I said as politely as I could. "I'm available now for the meeting if you are."

Mrs. Powell nodded and led me to her classroom. Nina was diagnosed with dyslexia two years ago. It had been a journey learning how she learned and seeing how she progressed.

The meeting was amazing. Nina was progressing so well and was catching up to the grade-level curriculum for her age.

As we were in afternoon traffic, Nina became all bubbly again. I looked at her suspiciously through the rear-view mirror as she sang every song that played. Being around my family and me, Nina fell in love with the culture, and I loved that for her. Normally, we would sing together, but I just rushed through traffic to get to her when she could've stayed behind in school.

"Feeling better?" I inquired.

"Yup." She continued to dance and sing. All I could do was shake my head. She'd just played me. I got even more pissed when I pulled up to the gate to see Pierre's truck parked in the driveway. I knew they told me they tried to call his ass.

"Come on, Bird." I opened the door for Nina, and we walked through the front door, hand in hand. Nina sprinted up the steps in front of me and I slowly ascended behind her. I wanted to get her settled before searching the house for Pierre. I had a few bones to pick with his ass.

I made it to the top of the stairs and Pierre came out of our bedroom doors.

"What are y'all doing here? Why isn't she in school?" he questioned.

"Well, if you weren't too busy in here doing what looks like nothing, you would know!" I looked Pierre up and down in disgust. He was clearly naked underneath his robe and the sudden movement through the crack of our bedroom door clarified what he was doing.

"Keep all the sarcasm, Mocha. What's going on and what made you come home after abandoning us?"

"Abandoning you? Pierre, go to hell. My best guess is that your baby mama is the one in my fucking bed right now. I would let y'all handle your child, but it's clear you can't. Next time, tell that trifling bitch to stay in the lane she put herself in when she signed her rights over. As a matter of fact, Bird, come with me." I turned to grab Nina's hand. There was no way in hell I was leaving her in here. Pierre's tight grip on my arm stopped me right at the top step.

"You're not leaving me again." Here we were with his fucking audacity again.

"Watch me!" I snatched my arm away from him, and Pierre's hand was around my throat as fast as I could blink. My eyes widened because this man had never put his hands on me. They say life had a way of revealing who people were, and among other things, this was truly showing me the monster I had been married to. "Let me go!" I gasped, clawing at his fingers.

"Why? So you can go running to that Tait guy?" He applied more pressure to my neck as he said Zeus's name. "Yea, I did my research. You're going to leave all of this to live on a teacher's salary?"

"Daddy, let her go!" Nina's voice trailed down the hallway. Pierre forcefully let me go, and I felt my left foot slip on the top step before everything began moving in slow motion. My ankle gave out first, causing my legs to buckle next. I went headfirst down the staircase, hitting my head on a few steps, then tumbling down further. Pain shot through my side, back, and abdomen from the impact of the fall until I was curled up at the bottom.

A few seconds went by, and my vision remained hazy. I saw Nina's small body trot down the stairs, followed by the muffled sound of Pierre yelling at her. A sharp pain shot through my abdomen and suddenly, I remembered I was indeed pregnant. Using the wall for support, I lifted myself and stumbled to my car. The warm feeling of blood soaking my jeans instantly brought tears to my eyes. Earlier, I had no idea about how to go forward, knowing I was pregnant with Pierre's baby. But to have it ripped from me by that selfish piece of shit hurt like hell.

I wasn't sure how I made it, but I pulled up to the front of Stanton Memorial and walked inside the emergency room. Nurses rushed my way at the sight of blood and helped me to the back. The last thing I remembered before being sedated was Apollo's voice.

I stared blankly at the white ceiling and bright lights while they performed a D&C. I was doped up, and time seemed to roll by. I stayed in my own head for hours until I heard Zeus bust through my room door.

"What happened? And why does my brother have to call me to tell me that yo' ass stumbled into the emergency room?" Zeus's tone was low yet stern enough for me to know that he was both worried and upset.

"Everything happened so fast," I mumbled and turned my head to the side. Zeus's hand gripped my chin, lifting it. I witnessed his eyes get dark.

"Whose handprint?" This time, his tone sent chills down my spine, even in this cold ass hospital. I hesitated to tell him, fearing his reaction. "Mocha, whose fucking handprint?"

"Pierre's," I whispered. Zeus went to storm out of the room. "Where are you going?"

"I'ma burn his fucking house down with him in it."

"Zeus, please don't do anything crazy with Nina there." I reminded him that Pierre wasn't alone. He nodded and stormed out. That was the last time I saw him that night.

FIFTEEN
APOLLO

The ambulance bounced around on the fucked-up streets of the city as we rode to our next call. There was a call about a chemical burn nearby and Gavin was drifting corners to get there. We came to a four-way intersection and slowed to wait for traffic to halt so that we could safely make a right turn when I spotted my brother's car coming from that direction. What the hell was Zeus doing out and about when he was supposed to be at work? And he wondered why his boss always digging in his ass.

It had been a couple of days since Mocha was admitted into the hospital and no one had heard from him since. He couldn't answer the phone, but his ass was bobbing his head to the music like he didn't have a care in the world. We had a meeting set up tonight so I would ask him about it then.

Pulling up to the address, Eddie pulled up to the curb and we filed out. There was a mixed man and white woman on the lawn arguing. The man had what looked like a t-shirt wrapped around his arm.

"I told you to just divorce that bitch!" the woman yelled.

"I am not leaving, Mocha! Drop it!" he grilled back, heaving in pain. I didn't mean to laugh in this guy's face, but hearing Mocha's name concluded why Zeus was coming from this direction. I greeted the couple and reached for the man's arm. Slowly unwrapping the shirt, I applauded Zeus's work with a slow head nod.

The man's skin on his forearm and hand was still crackling, and the meat and bones underneath were visible. "You're going to have to be transported," I informed him. "Your skin needs to be thoroughly flushed, and you're going to need a skin graft."

Mocha's husband agreed, and we loaded him into the back of the ambulance. I chuckled here and there on the ride back to the hospital. This had to be the hand he choked Mocha with.

Gavin's feet hit the pavement first. Pierre began to lift himself to get out, but I grabbed his burned arm and forcefully sat him back down. He groaned, causing me to I peered over his shoulder and raise a hand to assure Gavin he was fine.

I moved in closer so that only he could hear me. "I have eyes and ears all over this hospital. If I get word the police were informed about who burned you, the rest of your body will be dipped into something far more deadly by the end of the day. Got it?"

Pierre nodded with wide eyes.

"Good. Gavin here will take you inside." My voice returned to its normal volume. We only had a few more hours on shift, and although I found Zeus's antics amusing, he also needed to give me a heads-up on shit like this. He was lucky we were the unit in the area.

"What was that about?" Gavin jumped back into the truck.

"Nothing, just letting him know to be extra careful when dealing with chemicals," I lied. "My little brother has been fucking around with that shit since we were kids. Luckily, all his ass had come out with were a few small burns on his hands here and there."

"Yea, that shit ain't no joke," he agreed.

LATER THAT NIGHT, we all met up at the bowling alley. They complained about dinner being our only bonding time, but their asses always ended up back at my spot, raiding my refrigerator for leftovers.

I wasn't sure if he would show up or not, but Zeus walked up on Nyx and me just as I was explaining the shit he'd done today. "I sure did burn his bitch ass up!" He sat down and changed into his bowling shoes.

"Oh, I saw your handiwork. I was just telling Nyx that Mocha got your ass tripping," I retorted.

"How so, brother?" Zeus looked at me like he ain't give one fuck.

"Like not letting us know what the fuck you were doing!" I barked. "What if I wasn't the one who responded to the damn call and threatened the muthafucka not to talk to the police? Yo' ass would've been sitting right next to Alonzo."

"Fuck that. He put his hands on my future wife," Zeus grumbled, tying his shoes.

"Nigga, she still fucking married!" Nyx laughed. I swear he was an asshole. He was right though.

"Y'all both know I ain't tryna hear none of that. Talk about something else." Zeus looked between the two of us with his hands clasped between his gapped legs. It reminded me of the stubborn ass teenage Zeus who drove me crazy.

"Anyway. I have the details for this job." I sat down with the two of them. Thankfully, the bowling alley was loud. "The office the board uses to meet seems to be connected to two other buildings. There's a meeting scheduled in less than a week, and since Alonzo wants the entire board wiped out, this is our opportunity. The best way to go about it is making it seem like an accident with mass casualties."

"You know I don't do innocent people, so what's the plan for the other buildings?" Zeus asked as Nyx just sat back and listened.

"There will be a gas leak," I started, putting gas leak in air quotes. "Nyx will be responsible for reporting it and making sure those buildings are evacuated. The explosive you make needs to take down all three buildings. I'll make sure the rest of the buildings are clear and the individuals in that boardroom are locked inside.

"We all report to work like a normal day, and we'll coordinate on how to slip away and make this shit happen quickly and easily."

"And where the hell do you expect me to keep a big ass explosive until lunchtime, Apollo?" I was sick of Zeus and his sarcasm.

"Figure that shit out, man. Let's bowl." He had all the questions and no damn suggestions.

———

I DRUMMED my finger against the countertop as I waited. The sound of a key entering the keyhole made me sit up and turn on the barstool to face the door. I stood as the lock turned and Detective Jordyn Drescher walked into her condo.

Jordyn was the detective on my father's case who had him sitting in jail. Instead of focusing on Alonzo, she got a little carried away and began looking into all things involving the Tait name. I mean, she had a hard-on for our asses, too. Imagine her disappointment when she came up empty, just as she would have if she hadn't caught Alonzo in the act. To see her with Hazel was a red fucking flag, and if her answers didn't add up tonight, I was going to be a raging bull, charging headfirst.

She moved around, taking her coat off and placing her keys in a bowl by the door. Only holding her purse, she walked further in and didn't even notice me until I stood. Dropping her purse in place, the detective immediately went to her waist.

"Don't even think about it." I waved my gun around in the air. I wasn't even a gun-carrying nigga, but I wasn't stupid. I was visiting a cop who wouldn't hesitate to shoot my ass.

"Why are you here?" She stepped toward me. I admired her fearlessness, but that tough shit ain't mean a damn thing to me.

"I think the better question is, why are you popping up again?" I replied.

"Hazel and I are friends. I had no idea she was seeing you." The annoyance was clear, and yet again, I didn't give a fuck.

"So you befriend someone I'm dating, who is also the girlfriend of a homicide victim whose case you were assigned to? That's no coincidence."

"Hazel and I stayed in contact after her boyfriend's death a year ago. Which is a lot longer than you've been in her life. So, don't flatter yourself, Mr. Tait." Jordyn looked me up and down in disgust.

"That better be all it is," I warned her. "Have a good night, Detective. It's a nice place you have here."

"Wait!" Jordyn shouted. "What does my being assigned to Quincy's case have to do with you? And you mentioned a homicide. That case was ruled a death by overdose. Unless you're implying something else." Her eyebrow raised in suspicion.

"My apologies. I must've gotten my words mixed up. I know we're both upstanding first responders, but my legal terminology isn't that great. Goodnight." I gave her a half-ass smirk and exited her condo.

"DIDN'T I tell you to stay out of my kitchen!" I barked at Venus when I finally made it home from Jordyn's. Traffic was a shit show, and it took me over an hour.

"Boy, I'm only making a sandwich!" She waved me off. I know I said I was checking her ass into a hotel, and I did. Who the fuck gets multiple smoking complaints and charges until they don't want your money anymore and tell you you have to leave? Venus, that's who. She showed up on my doorstep again, rambling about how she couldn't light her incense, burn her sage, or smoke her weed.

"I don't care. You almost burned my shit down. Ain't no telling what you would end up doing with that knife in your hand. Next time, make sure it's a PB&J so you can use a butter knife."

"You know, I never thought I would tell one of my kids this, but go to hell, Apollo. You've been talking shit since I arrived and I'm tired of it." She tossed the knife down on the counter for dramatics.

"You can be tired. You've been on the road since Pops got locked up and ain't said shit to nobody but Zeus. So don't come in here acting like you give a damn. Why aren't you over at Zeus's anyway?"

"How, uh, how is your father doing, anyway?" she said just above a whisper, rubbing her neck.

"And there it is. You're here because I'm the only one in touch with Pops." I set the water bottle down on the counter and folded my arms. Venus took a deep breath and batted away the wetness in her eyes.

"I miss my husband, Apollo. He hasn't called, and—"

"It's because you stopped answering! How do you abandon him and us for a year and pop up, thinking shit all good? We dealt with that shit for the holidays, but your time here is running out!" I snatched the bottle of water and retreated to the basement.

I hadn't spoken to Hazel in a few days. She'd been ignoring my phone calls, and whenever she got home in the evening, she'd pull her car into the garage, and I wouldn't get the chance to actually see her. Something told me Jordyn's warning was the reason for her distance, so I chose to give her some time. It was that, along with trying to figure out the ins and outs of this job coming up. But, just like my mother, Hazel's time was up.

I FaceTimed Hazel to see what she was doing, but she ignored it. That only prompted me to call back-to-back until she answered.

"Yes, Apollo." She sighed. She was leaning over into the mirror, putting on lipstick.

"Where you going?" I asked, pulling the phone closer to my face.

"Mocha and I are going out for dinner." She placed the top of her lipstick back onto the little tube and I hit the red button. Two steps at a time, I jogged to the main level of my house and grabbed my car keys. I wasn't worried about a coat because I wasn't going far.

Starting my engine, I backed out of my driveway and straight across the street into Hazel's. Hopping out, I rang the doorbell and slid my hands into my pocket as I waited for her to answer.

Hazel snatched the door open. "You can't keep popping up over here like this. I have somewhere to be." The defeated sigh she let out, let me know that she'd noticed my car.

"I can do as I please. And as you can see, you ain't going nowhere. Excuse me." I brushed past her.

"Apollo!" Hazel yelled after me. I sauntered down the short hallway to her kitchen. She wanted dinner, and she was going to get it. She just wasn't about to leave the house for it. Especially not dressed in the tight-ass jumpsuit she had on. The off-the-shoulder sweater she had on over it wasn't hiding shit. I saw that shit over the phone and immediately knew she wasn't about to make it to that restaurant.

The door slammed and heels clicked my way as I washed my hands and maneuvered through her kitchen.

"What are you doing? I'm hungry and Mocha is waiting. See, she's calling now. Can you just move your car?" Hazel stomped her foot and let the phone continue to ring. Her hangry voice was cute. I looked up from separating the ingredients on her counter and smirked. Her phone vibrated again, so I stopped what I was doing and snatched it out of her hand. I slipped it into my pocket and pulled out a couple of pans.

"Have a seat." I nodded toward the table.

"I'd rather stand," she protested.

"Suit yourself." I shrugged. Hazel watched me intently while I whipped up the batter for my infamous strawberry cinnamon crepes. Before I began, I made some homemade whipped cream. All the while, her phone was going crazy in my pocket. Suddenly, it stopped, and mine vibrated on the counter. I grabbed it, answering Zeus's call.

"Oh, you can have your phone, but I can't?"

I ignored her, waiting for my brother's face to appear on the camera.

"Aye, you talked to Hazel? Mocha blowing my shit up to get you to go over to check on her. Said they were supposed to meet up, but Hazel ain't answering her phone!" Zeus yelled, still not on the screen. I could tell he was down in his lab.

"Yea, she's straight. She is right here. Tell Mocha they're going to have to reschedule." I peeked up again to see Hazel roll her eyes so hard, I was surprised them bitches came back around. I ended the call and chuckled before sparking a conversation. "Why have you been ducking me?"

"I'm not saying shit until you feed me," she barked. I scraped a piece of butter in the pan to melt, lifted the spoon from the whipped cream, and put it to her lips. Her pretty ass lips open and closed around the spoon. Hazel's reaction to what I knew tasted amazing was sexy as fuck. Her eyes remained closed as she exhaled and licked the remainder from the corner of her lips. "Damn, that's good."

"I know," I said confidently, moving back to the stove. "Now, is Jordyn your reason for ducking me?"

"And why would Jordyn have me ducking you?" Hazel's head cocked to the side and her hands clasped together. It was one of those moments where a woman knew something was up but couldn't quite tell you what it was, so they sarcastically and impatiently waited for an answer when it came up.

"I heard the warning she gave you before leaving the bar."

"OK?" Hazel waved her hand in a circular motion, impatiently telling me to continue.

"Jordyn was the lead detective on the case that my father is incarcerated for. She got him with some bullshit evidence, and after that, it was like she had a hard-on for every nigga rocking the Tait name," I explained.

"But all of you have upstanding careers. Why would she take an interest in you?"

"As I said, it was some bullshit-ass eyewitness. My pop wasn't perfect, but he made sure the three of us locked down a career. After a year of trying to find something to pin on us, Jordyn came up short and has had a chip on her shoulder ever since. I'm just making sure she wasn't using you to get to me."

"Oh, I don't know what to say, Apollo." She wore an apologetic look while twiddling her fingers and shifting back and forth in her heels.

"You ain't gotta say shit, beautiful. Just go kick those heels off and find us a movie. I'll meet you out there when the food is ready."

I took my time perfecting a pile of crepes and layered them on a dish with the whipped cream and the strawberry cinnamon filling between each one, using sliced strawberries as a garnish.

In the living room, I noticed she'd changed into shorts and a tank that displayed her pierced nipples.

I approached the side of the couch and Hazel immediately reached up to grab the plate.

"Chill, Fat Ma." I laughed and swatted her hand away. I lifted her legs and slid underneath them. Cutting a corner piece, I put the fork to her lips. She took the crepe into her mouth slowly.

"Where's your plate?" she asked, licking and wiping whipped cream from the corner of her lips again.

"Are you telling me you'll eat this big ass stack of crepes by yourself?"

"Hell yeah. I love food!" She snatched the plate and cut another corner, stuffing it into her mouth. This time, I didn't wait for her to lick off the remains; I leaned in and did it myself. Hazel quivered at the lick that I followed with a soft kiss.

I moved down to her neck and chest and showed them the same love. The heat coming from her shorts felt like an active volcano just waiting to erupt. I took the plate from her and set it on the coffee table. Lifting her left leg, I put it behind me so I could position myself between her thighs.

I moved closer to lift over her and press my harness against the warmth in between her legs.

"Apollo," she sighed. My lips were no longer on her. We were face to face, brushing our noses and sharing air space that was full of lust.

"What's up, Fat Girl?" I whispered.

Hazel swallowed hard and closed her eyes to gather herself. "If we move forward, I need to take it slow. Aggression and uncertainty don't work for me," she let out.

I grinded my hips one time. I could feel how wet it was through her shorts. "Your pussy is saying otherwise. But I'll wait. And when I do give you this dick, be ready to gobble this muhfucka up with some of that whipped cream you can't get enough of. We can watch a movie tonight, though."

Sitting back up, I placed her legs back in the original position across my lap. I picked the plate up and we continued eating. That was the start of a sexually frustrating night.

SIXTEEN

ZEUS

"Fuck!" I pulled my hand back and shook off the pain. I was in my basement, which had been transformed into my personal science lab. Apollo had put me up to the challenge of figuring out what explosive was safe to move to the job location, was strong enough to take out three buildings, and leave no evidence behind.

The best way to go was a gas explosive made of carbon and nitrogen. Once the chemicals were mixed, they created yellowish crystals. While testing the compound and measuring things to figure out how much was needed for this size job, I found out that this particular compound was just right. Small amounts were very powerful and detonated by heat. A casing of the buildings was needed soon to measure everything accurately. But for now, I was done.

I went upstairs to my first aid kit to tend to my new burn. Once my hand was wrapped up, I sat down to open my laptop to grade some essays and ended up on the phone with Mocha. We'd quickly developed a habit of working together after work hours. I would grade papers and do lesson plans while she worked on projects that have been assigned to her.

Mocha hadn't physically been back to work since being released from the hospital, but she was determined to keep up with her workload. She also requested her space for a while, and I would always respect that. However, my birthday was in a few days, and she'd better be there. Mocha hadn't brought it up, but I knew all about the miscarriage. I told the nurse at the hospital I was her husband, giving her the green light to run down Mocha's condition.

It fucked with me that she was pregnant by the bitch ass nigga she called a husband, but it pissed me off even more that he would have the audacity to put his fucking hands on her. That was why I burned the same hand he choked her with and didn't think twice about it. I bet he'd think twice before fucking with her again.

"Yo' ass over there sleep?" I said loud enough into the speaker to scare her if she was.

"No," she mumbled, sounding like she was laying with the side of her face pressed against something.

"Take yo' lying ass to bed. Call me in the morning." There were noises of her fumbling around before the call ended.

Never in a million years would I have ever thought I would be ready to go to war over somebody else's wife. Mocha was special, though. Her beauty and feistiness originally drew me in, but her drive and growing independence captured me more and more. I was clear on the fact that I wasn't going anywhere, and I loved how she let me know what she needed to grow. She respected my hold on my self-proclaimed position in her life and I respected her boundaries. However, I'd blow a motherfucker to pieces behind her.

Apollo was right; I moved wrong, doing what I did to Pierre. But the mere thought of him touching what I'd decided no longer belonged to him sent me over the top. The only thing I thought about was making sure Nina wasn't in the house when I approached Pierre.

It took me another hour to get through the rest of the papers and I called it a night. Ms. Daniels had me on duty at a pep rally tomorrow at the school and I was dreading it. The kids be hyper as fuck after lunch, and as much as I love my profession, I love it even more when students listened.

. . .

JUST AS I ASSUMED, the pep rally was chaotic. I get that pep rallies were designed to get students excited about an event, but damn. It took us at least an hour to get everyone filed into the gymnasium and seated.

"Mr. Tait! China took my phone!" A student named Paris ran up to me and pointed back into the bleachers.

"Give it back!" I yelled, then diverted my attention back to Paris. "And you put it up! You're not supposed to have it out, anyway."

I heard them exchange words as Paris climbed the bleachers and snatched her phone away from China.

"Separate!" I yelled. I didn't need to be breaking up a fight in the middle of all this chaos.

Once everyone settled, the cheerleaders ran on the floor. I took a seat on the bottom bleacher at the end just as my phone went off. My brothers were hitting up our group chat.

Apollo: Somebody better come get y'all mama.

I held my stomach in laughter at the GIF of someone pinching their nose in annoyance. I knew Venus and Apollo were going at it in there. Those two were like oil and water.

Me: It can't be that bad, I replied, fucking with him. Nyx sent a laughing emoji, which I knew also pissed Apollo off.

Apollo: Shiddd! Nigga we are about to push your party up. She claims she's waiting until after your birthday to hit the road again.

Nyx: Why she ain't staying at Zeus's?

I loved my mama, and we had a better relationship than she did with my brothers, but she'd drive my ass crazy too if she stayed with me.

Apollo: That's a whole other conversation. She thinks I can get Pops to talk to her.

. . .

NYX RESPONDED with the GIF of LeBron James exiting his press conference. Nyx was being Nyx, especially when it came to our father. He only indulged when it came to money, which was the reason he went to the visit with us.

"Mr. Tait, you can't watch these children and be on your phone." Ms. Daniels came and sat beside me. She was fine as hell, but just as annoying. "Who were you speaking to that is more important than your job?"

This broad loved to annoy me. But I had an honest answer for her ass. "My brothers."

My family would always be more important than anything.

"Well, not on my clock, you won't. Stay off your phone." She stood and damn near stomped away. I didn't know why the fuck everything I did seemed to get under her skin to the point where she had to be dramatic about the shit but the time frame for me figuring that shit out before spazzing was quickly closing.

"YOU PULLING UP TONIGHT?" I asked Tina as she oiled my freshly braided hair. My casino-themed birthday bash was tonight, and I needed all who mattered to be in attendance. I know they said friends ain't supposed to touch each other's private parts, but Tina was my dawg years before we got physical.

"Of course. I wouldn't miss it." She smiled.

"You can bring ol' boy if you want." I shrugged.

"Yea right. I don't have time for his shit. It's your birthday and I won't be the one responsible for the drama." Tina took the cape from around me.

"Suit yourself. And you better stick to the dress code!" I gave her a pound and headed home to get dressed. It was a Saturday afternoon, at the end of January, and the streets were lit, freezing and all. I smiled at the kids across the street on the blacktop, playing basketball with puffy coats on, and the old heads talking shit on the corner.

I offered to move Tina's shop out of the hood, but she wouldn't budge. She said she was at home here and I could respect that. At times like these, I understood why. Although Alonzo moved up when we were young, the intimate lifestyle he introduced us to kept us connected to the hood. There wasn't any way I could stay there though.

I got home and went down to the basement until it was time for me to get dressed. I was getting closer to fulfilling my end of this job, and I must say that my little experiment was thrilling. The scars on my hands showed I wasn't a stranger to experiments, but never to this capacity. My dick got hard just thinking about how beautiful it was going to be.

I'd begun testing the crystals as much as possible with the space and protective equipment I had in my basement. I asked Apollo to send over the square footage and blueprints of the buildings, and from there, I began estimating how powerful I needed this thing to be. The only downfall was transporting it. The crystals were sensitive, and I learned that once combined, the only way to keep the compound from crystallizing was to keep it on ice. Meaning, I would have to put this thing together in the basement of these buildings and get my ass out of there undetected.

Apollo had all the bright ideas, and Alonzo trusted his ass to make sure things went smoothly, so he needed to figure this shit out. I wasn't blowing myself up fucking with his ass. I fucked around down there for a couple of hours and then went to take a nap before getting dressed. I needed all of my energy because a young nigga was about to turn the fuck up tonight and hopefully carve my name in Mocha's pussy afterward.

THE TAILORED Mahogany's Fashion custom red and black tuxedo I wore had me feeling like the sexiest nigga in the world. "The sexiest Tait in the room," I mumbled with a cocky chuckle.

"Nigga, what?" Apollo adjusted his suit jacket and looked me up and down like I'd said something off the wall.

Again, I chuckled. "I said what I said."

"Why all the tension?" Mocha strutted her fine ass through the middle of the three of us. I kicked my lips at how she filled out the back lace gown. I think that shit was called a mermaid-style dress or something like that. Whatever it was, she was wearing that motherfucker.

"The gworls are fighting," Nyx dry ass said in the funniest sassy tone he could muster. The three of us were too shocked to even give it the laugh it deserved, all because it came from his ass.

But we all knew Mocha wasn't going to let him live. "Oh no, Mr. Goddess! Don't do that no more!"

"See, just when I thought I could have been nice to yo' ass, you fuck it up! Did you bring your abusive, cheating ass plus one?" Nyx looked behind Mocha, stretching his neck around dramatically.

"Too far, bruh." I stepped in. I grabbed my woman's hand, and we entered my party together. Something that was meant to be done with my brothers by my side as well, yet they lingered behind me, carrying bad energy.

The crowd was thick as hell and that shit was unexpected. My two worlds had combined into one space to celebrate the kid, and so far, it looked like it blended well. I walked through and dapped up niggas from around the way, people my brothers and I pulled jobs with and for, along with a few colleagues and friends from college. I hoped this would turn out to be a great night.

There were blackjack tables, Russian roulette, craps, spades and poker tables, slot machines, and more. I knew this party cost a bag, but with the way the tables were set up, we were about to get that shit right back. The DJ stayed on point the entire night, but when he hit a reggae mix, the building went crazy.

I mean, left their chips at the table to hit the dance floor. Y'all know how niggas always claim they got some type of Caribbean in them around these parts. They sure as hell were showing it tonight. All kinds of winding was going on, and my baby shocked the hell out of me when she grabbed my hand and hit the wind herself. Mocha dipped and popped her hips, and I knew she could feel my dick through that dress.

"I need you to do all this on my dick tonight," I said in her ear. Immediately, she got uncomfortable. My face frowned for a second before I remembered she'd just had a miscarriage and a D&C. She still hadn't spoken on it, but since I knew, I decided to divert her attention elsewhere. "Let's go fuck up the craps table."

"I don't know what I'm looking at." Mocha stood confused as the craps game commenced.

I pulled her in front of me and more than my dick reacted to the way her body felt on mine. Damn, I missed her. My heart rate sped up and I had to take a few deep breaths to speak clearly. Life introduced us at a weird ass time but fuck it. If I had it my way, Mocha and I were going to roll through the punches together. I said fuck her husband the first day I met Mocha, and that shit was times ten now.

I called for the dice and let them know that Mocha would be the shooter. "Aight, you start by making a bet," I spoke intently in her ear.

I explained more and more each time she rolled the dice what each number meant. Twenty minutes later, shawty had cleaned their ass up.

"Don't let me call yo' ass and you up in MGM fucking around," I joked as a smooth hand rubbed my shoulder from behind. I turned to see who it was and Tina clung to the side of me, now rubbing her hand across my chest.

"I told you; I'd be here." Tina smiled. She backed up, did a 360 spin, and placed her hand back on my chest. "And I stuck to the dress code."

I looked between the two awkwardly and I could feel Mocha tense up beside me. She reached across me and swiped both of Tina's hands off me. Then, dared to extend her hand. "I'm Mocha."

"Well, Mocha, next time you lay your hands on me, these heels are coming clean off." Tina looked at her hand in disgust.

"You find yourself all over my man again, we damn sure can square up." Hearing Mocha finally be a little possessive turned me on. But I had to tell my lil nigga to calm down when he jumped for joy because I was in the middle of two people who wouldn't hesitate to swing.

"Girl, my brother ain't pale!" Nyx grumbled, coming to lean over the side of the craps table beside Tina. "Talking 'bout yo' man. What's up, sis?"

He fist-bumped Tina. They'd always been cool.

"Hey," Tina replied.

My brother could be a pain in my ass sometimes. "Nyx, can you mind your damn business?" I hissed, then turned to face Mocha. "It ain't even like that. Tina and I are like best friends."

"Best friends my ass. Why are you explaining this to her like she got room to talk? Just 'cause she ain't wearing her ring doesn't change shit. Plus, Mama likes Tina better, anyway." Nyx smirked at Mocha, making her storm out.

I was going to beat his ass, and just as I was about to let him know, Mrs. Daniels walked the fuck up and wrapped her arm around this nigga, smiling and shit.

"Hey, baby." She grinned.

"Oh, hell nah!" I yelled, throwing my hands up. This was turning out to be a fucked-up birthday.

SEVENTEEN

NYX

"Nigga, you fucking my old ass boss?" Zeus yelled.

"Ain't shit old about me, Zeus!" Braiza yelled back before I could respond.

"Zeus?" My brother's eyes got big as he dramatically leaned forward at the waist. "Nah, it's Mr. Tait to you!"

"Nigga, chill yo' ass out and enjoy your party. Better yet, you might wanna be a good lil side piece and check on ya girl," I calmly replied and sipped my drink. "Where I stick my dick is none of your concern."

"It is when she's on my ass all the time. It's most likely because she's mad at your simple ass. It makes sense now. And watch your damn mouth before I burn the bitches off." Zeus pointed to my lips and jogged in the direction Mocha did just a few minutes earlier.

"So, you didn't tell him? Why would you let me walk in here to get ambushed, Nyx?" Braiza asked, disappointed.

"Braiza, please don't come in here with that shit. I'm in a good mood, don't piss me off. You said you wanted more exclusivity; this was me trying," I groaned.

"This is what you call a good mood, you crazy—"

"Watch your mouth." I stopped her before she made me embarrass her. "You wanted more from me, and if inviting you out wasn't enough, I don't know what you want from me."

Braiza let out a sarcastic laugh. "This is unbelievable. Excuse me." Her ass bounced in the long sleeve satin dress as she stomped to the bathroom.

"She must be a new one," Tina said from behind me. I laughed because I knew for sure they were sick of us collectively for the night.

"About five months in," I answered.

"And she still doesn't know who Nyx is, huh?"

"Nah, she knows. But for the first time, somebody is telling me I need to do better, and I want to. This shit is hard, though. Not giving a fuck works better for me," I said honestly.

"It can work for you but don't mess up something good and end up alone, expecting that shit to work for someone else. I'ma get out of here before Zeus comes back. You done got me into some shit." Tina leaned in for a hug.

"Me? I was just your backup for his married bae."

"I ain't need no backup. I told you, Zeus and I ain't fucking with each other like that. And if she would have approached shit differently, I would've respected their shit. Married or not." Tina crossed her arms and no matter what she said, I knew she was fucked up about the whole thing. Shit, so was Apollo and I. Zeus ain't never been gone on a bitch like this and the one time he was, she was married with a smart-ass mouth.

"You're better than me."

"Yea, well, I'll see you later." Tina fist-bumped me and left. I opened my phone and checked out some sports stats while I waited for Braiza. Her heels clicking against the marble floors made me peek up.

"I'm ready to go," she announced with her attitude still on one hundred.

"I can take you back to yo' place if you gon have this attitude all night."

"Oh, my attitude ain't going nowhere. I just did my hair and makeup and put on this damn dress for no reason. Nyx, I am not in the mood for your bullshit. I can call for another ride home if needed but I think giving me a ride is the least you can do."

Leading the way to my car, I mentally put together a playlist to ignore her ass. Braiza had this thing about talking to a nigga like I was one of her students and after having a few drinks tonight, this would end with me putting her ass out on the side of the highway.

I opened the door for her before getting in myself and immediately opened my *Apple Music.* It took me a minute but autocorrect saved me some time selecting the album. It was a twenty-five-minute drive, so the *Quavo and Takeoff* album was perfect. Braiza wasn't aware of how dope my voice was, therefore; my one-man concert was a no-go on this drive.

Braiza was tapping away at her phone as I bobbed my head to the music. Things were good until I almost went headfirst into an oncoming car, turning onto a side street. I swerved and cussed their asses out.

"Nyx, calm the fuck down! Are you not paying attention? You went down a one way!" Braiza yelled.

It took me a second to process what it said on the sign at the beginning of the street before I realized she was right.

"My bad, I zoned out," I lied. This was the longest I'd been in the car with Braiza and a quick reminder of why.

"Well, whatever had you distracted, can you put it to the back of your mind and get me home safely?"

Her tone set me off. "Yea, let me get you the fuck out of my car."

I turned the music up some more to block her out. Braiza had nothing to do with what had just fucked me up mentally, but I couldn't take for someone to witness my shortcoming. Even if they didn't know they had.

I backed into her driveway and shifted the car into park. I was pushing the engine button when Braiza looked at me.

"Where do you think you're going?" she asked. Habit and

comfort prompted me to follow her inside. Shockingly, those two overrode the fact that I was just upset and feeling exposed.

"I'm staying here."

"No, the hell you're not. You wanted me out of your car and now I'm getting out. Alone!" Braiza stepped out of the car. Through the window, she could be seen digging around in her purse for her keys. I killed the engine and stepped out myself.

"Come on, man. It's cold and my key is already out!" I yelled around the car.

"What damn key?"

"The key I had made. Fuck you thought? You were going to have a key to my shit, and I wasn't gon have yours? Plus, I told you you had me fucked up when you changed your damn locks."

Braiza went back to frantically digging in her purse. The sound of jangling keys got louder when she finally pulled them out. A few seconds passed before she was throwing my keys at me over the top of the car.

"There! There are your damn keys. Nyx, just go."

I wiped the side of my face in frustration. "I didn't ask for that shit back, Braiza. Can you stop being so dramatic and come the fuck in the house?"

"I'm going inside my house, but I'm doing it alone." She strutted past me without making eye contact and I grabbed her arm.

"Do we have a problem?" a voice came from behind us.

"Who the fuck is this?" I pointed over my shoulder with a strong thumb. Braiza looked like she'd just seen her dead granny standing in her driveway.

"Leon, how do you know where I live?" Fear was etched all over her face and that shit had me heated. There had to have been a furnace sitting there with us on this cold winter night because when he spoke again, the only coldness present was in my eyes.

"I followed you after our date to make sure you were safe and—"

My hand was around his throat in a matter of seconds. It had been a while since death was at my fingertips before the body was cold. Leon's ass was not only a creep, but I guess he also called himself protecting what the fuck was mine. Now, life was leaving his eyes behind those thick ass glasses over some pussy he hadn't even tasted. He better not have tasted it.

"Nyx, stop! You're killing him!" Braiza came and grabbed my arm while I tightened my grip. I looked away from Leon's falling body and up at her. She stepped back, fear still lingering. Once his body went limp. I held onto him and hit the trunk button on my key fob.

Tossing him in, I checked his pockets for car keys. "Drive his car and follow me."

Braiza stood there crying and shit and it only pissed me off more.

"Braiza," I said in a low tone and moved closer to her. "Don't stand here and cry now. You shouldn't have been going on a date in the first place. Drive the damn car!"

I shoved the keys into her chest and closed the trunk. It took a minute, but she got into Leon's car and followed me to the mortuary. There, I stripped him of his clothing and tagged his ass under a John Doe to be cremated.

"You do this with such ease," Braiza whispered tremulously.

"Protecting those I love will always be effortless." I didn't even think twice about my response, but it paused the both of us. My shoulders dropped when I saw the flicker in her eye. Shawty was slowly breaking me down. In the past months, Braiza had more than proved that she wanted me. Hell, she'd proven that she also wanted the best *for* me. "If that nigga followed you home, his capabilities stretched far past that."

Braiza walked closer to me. It fucked me up that she visibly struggled between the fact that I scared her and that I'd just dropped the L word.

"I love you, too, Nyx." She reached up and caressed my beard, still trembling. Then she leaned in and kissed me. I didn't care about her witnessing me kill someone, or that I'd just told her I loved her, that was still too intimate.

I turned my head, and defeat washed over her like any other emotion was never present.

"Take me home," she sighed. I nodded and she exited before me. I had to get rid of Leon's car, but it was best that I did it without her. It was like I took a step forward, but those two steps backward were almost always inevitable.

EIGHTEEN
BRAIZA

I rubbed my hands up and down my legs. My mental and emotions were all out of whack. The man I'm foolishly in love with just confessed his love, all while getting rid of a body and still denying me affection. I needed to be alone tonight, and I was thankful that Nyx left without a fight.

The entire weekend, I lounged around my home watching comedies and my phone on DND. I had so much to sort out and didn't want to be bothered while doing it.

Monday morning came fast, and I'd come to terms that I was an accomplice to murder.

Nyx was right, what Leon pulled was creepy. It made me wonder how long he may have been watching me. We went on one boring date and I drove my car to the restaurant, so I was unsure of how he knew where I lived.

I showered and straightened my hair for work. I went through my suits and went with a blush skirt suit. The skirt was pencil style while the blazer was quarter length and kind of ruched around the elbow area. A cream blouse, silver accessories, and nude flats finished the look. I hit the hallway exiting my room and the smell of *Folgers* hit my nose. I grumbled under my breath, knowing I was about to face Nyx. Other than Randi, he was the only person who entered my house without asking.

"Good morning, Nyx," I said dryly.

"What's up?" he replied, pulling the coffeepot off the machine and pouring some into one of my canisters. I stood back and observed him make my coffee the way I liked. I didn't want to smile, but I couldn't contain it. He'd been paying attention.

"My brother made breakfast, so I brought you a plate." He put the top on the canister and turned around with a wrapped-up plate and the canister. He sat them both down on the island in front of me. The sound of the canister hitting the marble with him being so close to me since I watched him choke the life out of someone, made me jump.

Nyx looked at me with shock and disappointment. I didn't want him to think I thought of him differently. Well, I did. I just wasn't sure how to explain it all at the moment, so I just avoided eye contact.

"Have a good day and take your phone off DND."

That was all I heard before hearing the front door slam. Gripping the edge of the island, I did a quick breathing exercise so I could continue my morning. I needed to be in the right headspace today. Last week's pep rally was to prepare for statewide testing that would commence all week. These kids deserve the best of the staff daily, so I tried to go in with a clear head, however; Nyx made it somewhat impossible at times.

———

"I LIKE THAT." I sat and watched Randi try on some new work clothes. "I envy your closet at this point."

It was a Thursday evening and Randi suggested a trip to the mall after work and I was all in. The distraction was needed. Randi knew he could dress his ass off and went shopping at the change of every season.

"You need to be trying on something. I know you have a date for Valentine's Day," he said, looking at himself in the mirror from different angles.

"I don't. And I won't even set myself up to think that there's a surprise waiting to happen with Nyx." I sipped the Coke I had in my hand. I truly thought he was ready to step up when he invited me to Zeus's birthday party. I was ready to pop out a child for him when I thought I'd finally broken his shell.

But to be embarrassed like that, crushed me. Then to witness a darker side of him afterward was another thing. Still, my body reacted to the mere thought of him. Not just sexually, either.

I suddenly got hot and felt sweat beads form on my forehead and the tip of my nose.

"Did you ever go out with Leon?" Randi asked, then dramatically turned around on the balls of his feet. "Biiitttcchhh, I forgot to tell you. Hold on, I just thought about something. Why haven't you been to the gym this week?"

"I've just been tired, that's all," I lied.

"Oh well, girl, they said Leon hasn't shown up to the gym all week. No call or anything. The owner even did a welfare check, and his place was empty."

I was weak under pressure and the way I began to sweat and breathe heavily made Randi look at me with curiosity.

"What do you know?" I took the next few minutes to explain everything, and I was now on the brink of tears.

"Girl, if you don't get it together." Randi waved me off and went back to looking at the pile of clothes he pulled to try on.

"Huh?" I was lost at his reaction.

"That man got rid of someone capable of and obviously planning to do something to you. If you don't hop on that young dick and thank him, I will!"

"Randi!" I shrieked. He shrugged and went back into the dressing room. I wiped my sweaty hands in my pants and then dried my eyes. I kept telling myself Nyx did the right thing, but I wished I could take the visual away.

NINETEEN
MOCHA

I rolled over, holding my stomach in laughter. *TikTok* had become my guilty pleasure since dealing with back-to-back disappointments. After my miscarriage, I kept my distance from everyone because even though I lost the baby the same day I found out I was pregnant, I was still a wreck mentally. I still felt like I'd lost a part of myself at the hands of the father. Zeus had been all that I'd allowed him to be during that time, but I wasn't ready to tell him yet. I mean, was it even relevant to him now?

The day of his party, it took me hours to put on a smile and show up for him, only to find out that someone else was doing the same thing. The same woman who showed up in his classroom was the same woman hanging all on him at his party. I'd just left a marriage full of infidelity and I'll be damn if I would walk into something like that again. I was that woman for years and despite how dating Zeus while still married looked, I wasn't trying to be that woman again.

I swiped past a dancing video that had me moving around in my bed, so I decided to have a little fun and record my first *TikTok*. I threw on a cute outfit and practiced the dance to "Touch It" by

DVSN. Once I got it, I looked around my room for a place to set my phone up.

"Shit, I need a tripod," I hissed. The light inside my room just wasn't there, so I went into my living room and did a bootleg set up on my bookshelf. The chandelier gave me the lighting I needed to hit record.

After at least five attempts, I finally got it right. It took me almost an hour to post it and I did one of those screams into my pillow and was scared to look at my phone every time it lit up.

I was too nervous, so I went to shower so that I could meet with this attorney. I've been closed off from the world for a week after Zeus's birthday party and all I wanted was to be completely detached from men. That started with getting a divorce.

I didn't feel like doing too much, so I went with a long-sleeved, all-black catsuit and an army fatigue bomber jacket, and some black and red *Jordan 1s*.

I exited the front of my building and sped up my pace to my car.

"Mocha, can you just talk to me?" Zeus stepped out of his truck that was parked in the row behind mine. My complex was gated, and I was so unsure of how he got his crazy ass inside.

I got inside of my car just in time, he was at my window as soon as I closed the door. Acting as if he wasn't standing there, I placed my purse in the driver's seat and brought the engine to life. The simple motherfucker knocked on my window like a sad puppy and mouthed for me to roll it down.

I hit the button to roll down the window. I looked at him out of the corner of my eye, giving off nothing but annoyed vibes. "Why the fuck I gotta do all this for you to hear me out?"

"Zeus, watch your toes." I looked him in his eyes as I rolled my damn window back up. He'd been warned, so if any body part was in the way when I pulled off, it was on him. Unfortunately, he moved out of my way, and I was able to leave without running his ass over. I approached the gate and saw that the damn access pad was fucking melted. "This nigga done lost his mind."

"MRS. SAPORA, DID YOU SIGN A PRENUP?" the divorce attorney, Angela Jarez, asked me.

"No," I answered.

"Great. That means that you can go after half of everything."

"I don't want it," I informed her. Angela looked away from her computer with a puzzled look. "I would like to keep my car, and I want to know my options for staying in my step-daughter's life. I was assigned her legal guardian years ago, but I don't know how binding that is if Pierre and I get a divorce."

"Do you want to take some time to think about this? We could literally take him for everything," she pressed.

"No. I was never with him for his money, and I don't want it now. Can you start the paperwork please?" A lump was in my throat. The tears were a mix of emotions, and Zeus had put the last drop in the cup to make it overflow. But, I refused to break. It was tough, though.

One, I didn't get married to get divorced. Two, although things didn't turn out the way I envisioned, I was proud of myself for finally breaking away from Pierre, and last, I'd just lost the one person who gave me hope of my future shining brighter than I ever imagined. Yea, I was a ball of emotions, but I was choosing the latter to focus on.

"I have a friend in family court. She can help with the custody battle. And yes, from what you've told me, this is going to be a battle. Are you sure this is the route you want to go? We have him on infidelity and abuse." She pushed me to rethink my decision.

"I'm sure, Angela. Can you call me when everything is drawn up and we can work on getting him served?" I stood and threw my purse over my shoulder.

"I'll be in touch."

I didn't let out a full exhale until I made it out front. I knew Pierre was going to put up a fight, I just hoped that at some point he'd get tired and just sign the papers.

Since I took the day off, I decided to go pop in on my parents.

There's nothing like the unconditional support they've always given me, and I surely needed it at this moment.

"Hey, Daddy." I walked in the front door, and he smiled in the rocking chair as he held the phone to his ear.

"Zo, give me a callback. My youngest beauty just walked in." Daddy hung up the phone and stood to embrace me. "What brings you by?"

"I took the day off to speak with a divorce attorney," I confessed.

"So, you're going through with this, huh?"

"Yea, Daddy. It's time. I just hope he doesn't contest it too much." I sighed.

"Let me know if he does. I'll make it easier for ya." He looked over his glasses at me like he was trying to make sure I heard him.

"How so?"

"I have my ways. Just let your old man know when you're ready for him to step in." He pushed the frames back up his nose and looked back down at his phone.

"OK," I let out. "Where's Ma?"

"She went to get her hair done, and last I talked to her, she was walking in the grocery store. She's making me some of those neck bones your grandmother used to make."

"Oh, I'm staying for dinner." I got comfortable in my seat. "Let me tell Haze. You know her greedy behind will be over here in a hot second when it comes to Mama's neck bones."

"You know she cooks for twelve, although it's only us, so there'll be plenty. Have you spoken to Nina?"

"Yes, she sneaks and calls me every day so that I can help her with her homework." I opted not to tell my parents about my miscarriage and how it happened, so they only worried about the basics of my divorce.

"I hate how she's being affected by all of this. We're going to miss her around here." He shook his head.

"My attorney is referring me to a family law attorney to help with Nina. I hate that she's in the middle and it's obvious that her parents don't give a rat's ass about her. She is going to need someone, and I feel like we've been a part of her life for too long to abandon her," I explained.

"Again, let me know if you need me. I'll be back. I have to go to the restroom."

I called Hazel a few times and she didn't answer. Unlike me, she went to work today. She was probably in a meeting, so I sent her a voice recording.

"Girl, call me back so you can come get yo' daddy. He's in here acting like he's Al Pacino while we wait for Mama to get home. She's cooking neck bones, too!"

I opened my *TikTok* app and was shocked to see the reactions to the video. I had over 500 new followers and the comment section was crazy. I scrolled and hearted all the comments until I came across one that had people responding to it.

@TeachemZeus Ain't nobody touching shit. *angry face emoji*

His simple ass wasn't even following me but harassing me in my comments. He wanted to be petty, but I lived for some petty shit.

@MochaAdiem You're worried about the wrong bitch. Where's Tina?

In less than sixty seconds, Zeus was calling my phone. I ignored his ass just as I'd been doing for the last week and continued checking my notifications. The bar at the bottom also showed the number of messages waiting to be read. Opening them, my mouth dropped when I read different designer brands, asking me to be a brand ambassador.

Dollar signs popped up in my eyes as they did in cartoons and my mind began to wander. I could monetize *TikTok* by doing promotions. I could even bring the idea of social media to the firm as a way to gain more clients and to also push marketing to another level. I grinned to myself and sat there and began preparing a presentation to present first thing in the morning.

TWENTY

HAZEL

"No, no, no! What did I do?" I paced back and forth in the living room with the empty bottle in my hand. No matter how many times I told myself I did the right thing, it just didn't feel right. "You had to. Right? He was going to kill you."

I was going back and forth with myself over something that couldn't be undone now. My hands began to tremble, grabbing my rib cage where a fresh bruise resided. What the fuck are you crying for? He hurt you.

Bang! Bang! Bang! My head shot toward my front door.

"Hazel, open up! It's Jordyn!" I panicked at the sound of the detective on the other side of the door. Bang! Bang! Bang! The knock got louder and so did my heartbeat. I looked at the door and then back down to the lifeless body on the floor of my apartment.

Bang! This time, the door flew off the hinges and Jordyn and her counterparts rushed inside with guns drawn.

I jumped out of my sleep, and my boss was staring at me from my office door.

"Are you OK?" Mr. Jenkins looked genuinely puzzled.

"Yes, what can I help you with?" I tried to gather myself and fix my hair which I was sure was out of place.

"We've been waiting on you. The meeting started fifteen minutes ago."

"Oh, I'm sorry. I laid down during my lunch and fell asleep. I'll be there in five." I stood from the couch and began looking through the files on my desk.

"Five minutes, Hazel or this account will go to someone else." He walked back to the conference room, and I was finally able to breathe. My hands rested on the edge of the desk while I did a slow breathing exercise to calm my anxiety. These dreams came randomly and were repetitive. The shit was like a nightmare that taunted me on some shit that didn't even take place. I didn't kill Quincy. *At least I didn't think so.*

"Not right now, Hazel," I coached myself and breathed in and out for a few more seconds. "OK," I sighed and continued looking through the files.

This meeting was an introduction to a new sneaker. I've come up with marketing strategies for many shoe brands, but there weren't so many ways to continue doing this. Thank goodness I kept a compact mirror in my drawer. Pulling it out, I made sure I was presentable and popped a mint in my mouth before heading to the conference room.

"Hi, I'm Hazel Cox. I apologize for my tardiness. We can begin with you telling me about your product and what audience you're looking to reach with your advertisement." I greeted the young lady, who introduced herself as Daija.

"Well, I'm new to the industry and want to present something comfortable, stylish, and affordable for my generation. I've noticed that a lot of what people consider to be in style is uncomfortable or costs way too much. My goal was to create something that met all needs," Daija explained.

I jotted down her expectations. "I'm sure we can help with that. Did you put together anything to show us the sneakers?"

"Yes, Mr. Jenkins has the flash drive." Daija and I both turned to him and waited as he pushed a few buttons on his laptop. Pictures popped up on the projector hanging in the back of the room. The shoes reminded me of a mix between *Converse* and *Balenciagas*. It wasn't something that I would wear but it was definitely what today's generation considered in style.

Daija made me proud to see someone her age come in with a presentation so professional. It wasn't just pictures of the sneakers, she actually had professional photos taken with models.

"Would your models mind being a part of the campaign?" I asked.

"Not at all. They're close friends of mine, and would do anything to help," Daija beamed.

"Perfect. The agency also had a modeling sector. We can get contracts in place. They can if they want to, but it's not mandatory to completely sign with ADM, but they will have to sign some paperwork if they're going to be a part of the campaign."

"Great. When can everything start?"

"Give me a few days to put together a few ideas and we can meet back here at the end of the week." I gathered everything I needed and stood to shake Daisha's hand.

"Don't be late for the next meeting," Mr. Jenkins reprimanded. "I told that young woman that I had my best assigned to this and it was unprofessional for you to keep her waiting."

"It won't happen again." We parted ways and flopped into my chair in my office and got to work. I wanted to jump right into doing research for Daija's account, but I had a few due the next morning that took priority.

My phone buzzed, and Mocha gave me the laugh that I needed.

Cha: Girl, call me back so you can come get yo' daddy. He's in here acting like Al Pacino while we wait for Mama to get home. She's cooking neck bones, too!

Her voice sounded like she was completely over my dad, but I knew her ass was staying for those neck bones. I didn't blame her; I was making my way over there as soon as I clocked out. Apollo could cook his ass off, but he ain't have shit on my mama.

On the ride to my parent's place, I thought of Jordyn. It's been a few weeks since she gave me that warning about Apollo, since then, she's been MIA. I've even attempted to call to get her side of the story Apollo gave, but nothing. Not an answer or call back. Hell, I even stopped by around the time I knew she got home on a normal day. I didn't want to be too overwhelming, but I needed to try again. Especially after the dream I had earlier.

The phone rang and went to voicemail.

"Hey, Jordyn! I was just checking on you. I know work can get busy. Shoot me a text to let me know you're OK." I hit the red button on the screen of my dash to end the call. If I didn't hear from her tonight, I would stop by again soon.

"Thank God you're here! Get yo' daddy!" Cha laughed and winked at me.

"Dad, what are you in here doing?" I asked, leaning down to kiss his cheek.

"Just letting my baby know I got her back is all." He shrugged with the remote in his hand. "Sit down and watch Family Feud with us."

Cha shook her head and gave me a look that let me know he was downplaying it. A commercial was on so I asked Mocha why she wasn't at work today.

"I had an appointment with an attorney. Save your questions for later because I'm not about to get him going again." She nodded toward my dad.

"Whatever," he said, still staring at the TV.

"Anything interesting happen in the office today?" Cha asked. I told her about Daija and her sneakers. "Let me see."

I handed her my phone once I pulled up the digital copy that Mr. Jenkins sent me of Daija's presentation. A smile crept onto Cha's face.

"What is it?" I asked, side-eyeing her. She immediately grabbed her phone, pulled up *TikTok,* then shoved the phone in my face. "OK? You did a *TikTok*."

"Look at the numbers!" she pointed out.

"Whoa!" She'd posted a dance video that morning and she already had almost 3,000 likes and half of that in comments.

"Exactly. I have messages from all kinds of designers asking me to be a brand ambassador, so I thought I would pitch the social media idea to Mr. Jenkins, and this works perfectly to do it. Especially if Daija is looking to reach the younger generations."

"I told you you were going to be great at this!" I cheesed proudly at my little sister.

"Well, I learned from the best."

"Yes, you did," I confirmed, cocky with every right.

A horn beeped outside, and my dad immediately got up. He knew it was my mother outside with the groceries. In a house full of women, he never let us touch those bags if he could help it. It was moments like this where we realized how good we had it growing up. Then, it saddened me the way we both still ended up in shitty relationships.

"Wash your hands and join me in the kitchen," Mama said, entering the house. Chai Cox even went to the grocery store looking good.

Cha and I followed instructions and helped prepare dinner. Mama went to work on her neck bones while Mocha and I sat at the table peeling the greens.

"Mocha, what's this I hear about you about to be in some fight last weekend?" Our eyes locked, widening in shock like we were still teenagers.

"How did you hear about it?"

"You know the shop I go to on the south side? Well, a guy stormed in, and he and the owner were arguing about it while I got my hair done. Who is this guy you've been seeing?"

"The guy I *was* seeing. His name is Zeus Tait, and—"

"Tait?" my mother and father said in unison. We didn't even know he had entered the kitchen.

"Yea," Mocha answered slowly. She looked just as scared to hear their follow-up comments as I was.

Dad cleared his throat and changed his facial expression. "So you've started dating already. You are done."

Something wasn't right and Cha and I knew it. "Yea, but I'm not seeing him anymore. Hazel, however, is seeing his brother Apollo."

"Chai, call me when dinner is ready." Daddy damn near turned blue in the face and excused himself.

"What's wrong with him?" I asked.

"Nothing, he's always hated the smell of fresh greens. So, Hazel, what's been going on at the shelter?"

"We have a clothes drive that's coming up. It's driving me insane keeping everything organized by sizes and getting everything cleaned, but I'm managing."

"That's good. Send me a reminder through text so I can put it in my calendar to help." She smiled over her shoulder, but her hands were visibly shaking as she cleaned the neck bones. Dinner was awkward as hell, and Cha and I couldn't wait to bolt out of there.

"What was that about?" I wondered aloud.

"I don't know. But I told you Daddy been tripping all night. I'ma head home and grab a glass of wine. I'll see you in the morning."

"OK."

"MOCHA AND HAZEL, I know all about social media. I have a Facebook account and so does the company. We also have an Instagram," Mr. Jenkins stated like we were wasting his time.

"Yea but not like this." Mocha showed him her page. "And this is only in twenty-four hours. The company page hasn't made a post in two years."

"OK, so what are you suggesting?" he inquired.

"Let me rebrand the online presence and let me do it using Daija's shoe line. Reels are going crazy online, and the interaction is insane. We need a *TikTok* page as well." Mocha showed Mr. Jenkins different brand pages and how followers love it.

"Set everything up and have something to show Ms. Collins when she arrives."

I high-fived my sister when Mr. Jenkins left the conference room. Mocha was stepping into her purpose, and I loved it for her.

Knock! knock! My new assistant, Paisley, knocked on the door. "Ms. Cox, someone is here for you. They insisted on waiting in your office."

I rolled my eyes because I knew the only person who would push to have their way carried the last name, Tait.

"Have fun. I'm going to get some lunch," Mocha grumbled. I gave her a pursed smile and we both went to our offices. I was sad that she was on the other side of the office now.

Apollo stood in his work uniform with a glass vase full of carnations in one hand and some food in a Styrofoam container in the other.

"To what do I owe this pleasure?" I smiled and greeted him by slipping my hands around his waist and resting my chin on his chest to look up at him. He was so handsome, but I couldn't help but wonder why his name boggled my parents.

"Just because you're beautiful and you deserve to be treated like a queen." He was smooth talking too. He leaned down and pecked my lips, and suddenly we heard glass crashing and Mocha yelling.

"Please don't tell me that Zeus is here," I sighed and lowered my arms.

"He insisted, thinking that he could get her to talk to him."

"Get that fool out of here before my sister loses her job!" I yelled and pointed down the hall.

"Enjoy your lunch." He kissed my forehead and jogged down to Mocha's office. I waited until I saw them get in the elevator to go check on Mocha. She was bent down carefully, picking up big chunks of glass and placing them into a pile. Water was everywhere and a dozen tulips spread sporadically through the small office.

"Hey Cha, you OK?" I asked from the door. Without a word, she stood and slammed her door in my face. "Well, OK then."

She was past the point of being pissed if she wouldn't even talk to me. I was going to fuck Apollo up.

TWENTY-ONE
APOLLO

This office was nice. They had set the DA up nicely. They could've given him a better desk though. I heard it squeak when I kicked my feet up. I checked my watch and saw that it was almost three o'clock, almost time. I watched traffic build up out of the large window while I tapped the tip of the expensive pen on the desk, waiting, and got excited when I heard the door finally swing open.

"So, are you saying you finally have something on him or don't you?" Hearing that familiar voice was amusing. An evil smile formed, and I turned around, revealing myself.

Jordyn and my Uncle Ace halted suddenly and their eyes damn near popped out of their sockets.

"Oh, don't stop talking on my account." I smiled, dropping the pen back into the holder on the desk.

"Where is DA Danson?" Jordyn hissed. I didn't know why she always did this thing where she would change her shocked expression to hatred and act all tough.

"Oh, he took a late lunch," I replied. They looked at one another, making me laugh even harder this time. "Don't worry, he's alive."

"Why are you here?" Jordyn questioned. My bitch ass uncle

hadn't spoken since I turned this chair around. At times it's so hard to believe that he's a Tait.

"Originally, I was meeting someone here to file an appeal on my father's conviction."

"On what grounds?" Now Ace decided to speak up, and I knew it was out of fear.

"Shut the fuck up." My tone made it evident that I was bored with him already. Nigga even made me roll my eyes back to Jordyn.

"Seems like your little eyewitness lied on the stand."

"You don't even know who the witness is," Jordyn debated.

"Really? We're playing that game?" I pointed to the motherfucker who was cowering behind her this whole time. "See, this is why I like to kill muhfuckas," I mumbled under my breath.

"What was that?" Jordyn asked again.

"Nothing, bitch." I waved her off. "Like I was saying. Initially, I came to file an appeal. But, why go through all the waiting when I can get you and that bitch ass DA to handle it. Before you ask and piss me off further, I'll continue to explain.

"Now that I know who your eyewitness is, I can prove that he wasn't even in the state when my father was arrested. See, this was a setup from the beginning. Doctored reports are stating he was on the scene when you arrived, I can prove that shit to be false."

"What do you want?" Jordyn's voice was shaky.

"That's where you come in." I looked at Ace. "You are going to recant your story and the DA will throw out all the charges."

"I'll go to jail for perjury!"

"Ehh, I'll make sure that doesn't happen as well. You'll have a week, or my lawyer and I will have it to where he'll make a mockery out of you and your career in open court. Enjoy your day." I let my feet hit the floor and stood to make my exit. A thud came from the only closet in the room and made the two of them jump.

"What was that?" Jordyn asked.

"Oh, that must be Danson. I guess he's finished with lunch." I laughed and walked out of the courthouse.

I was about a block away from the sight of the politician job my father gave us, so I decided to sweep the place. Work interfered with me casing the building weeks ago, so it pushed the job off. Now, we were two days away from the time of their next meeting, and I still hadn't given Zeus a final answer on how he could successfully transfer and detonate his explosive.

"Hi, how can I help you today?" The receptionist in the front lobby greeted me. If I wasn't hellbent on being with Hazel, I would've tried to bag her.

"Someone put in a ticket for a leak in your basement. The job isn't for a couple of days but I need to check to see what parts we will need before we show up," I lied.

"What company are you with?"

"Warren and Sons."

"Do you have an ID?"

"Yea, but I left it back in the truck. I was doing a job down at the courthouse and parked down there since parking is bad around this time. I tossed everything in the truck and my wallet was in my bag. It'll take me a half hour to go and come back, but I guess I'll be back." I let out a frustrated sigh.

"Oh no, that won't be necessary. Please, just be in and out if possible. Follow me." Her thick ass strutted to a stairwell and unlocked the door. "It opens from the inside, so when you're finished, just come on back up."

"'Preciate you, lil mama."

She blushed and hurried back to her desk. The basement was laid out just as it was in the blueprints. Now that I knew the receptionist was sweet, I knew how to get Zeus in. Pulling the paper out of my pocket, I followed a pipe in the ceiling to where the buildings should connect. The blueprint didn't show the pipes connecting but the way they were entering the wall on each side let me know it ran into the next building.

"Bingo." I got what I needed. Zeus was the expert on how to set that shit off, so that was on him. I folded the piece of paper and stuffed it in my pocket. Jogging back up the stairs, I waved at the receptionists "Thanks. We'll be back in a few days."

Business had been taken care of for the day, and now it was time to give in to my final satisfaction for the day. Hazel. I've been craving this woman more than I craved death at times.

The flower arrangement I gave her at her office also contained a spa day set for this afternoon. I'd purposely booked her time slot for after I was off work, just for this reason. Plus, this was the last day of my morning shifts. Quarterly rotations were done, and I was moving to the overnight shift.

An hour later, I was slipping a masseuse a hundred-dollar bill. "She's in room C," he informed me.

Creeping through the door, I allowed the original masseuse to step in and issue an apology. "About time. I've been waiting twenty minutes," Hazel complained. She was face down on the table with a sheet covering her naked body and her curls sprawled all over the top of her head.

"My apologies, ma'am. Let's get started," he told her and slipped out of the door. I closed the door and locked it behind him. This spa had always been sensual to me, and the aesthetics of the room kept that vibe going. The soothing sound of heavy rain played while the digital wall mimicked an equally soothing thunderstorm. The flash of fake lightning mixed with the shadows of raindrops covered Hazel's body.

Pulling the sheet down to her waist, I put a few pumps of oil on my hand and began at her shoulders. Her skin was always so soft, and I yearned to taste her. She moaned through the massage, and I fought hard as hell to not put my lips on her.

Moving down to her bottom half, I massaged up her calves and worked my way to her thigh. There were those fucking moans again. My thumbs moved closer to the inside of her thighs. She jumped a little, but it was too late. Lifting the sheet just a little, I saw Hazel was wet as fuck.

"Who the fuck are you getting this wet for?" I barked, making her jump out of her skin.

"Apollo?" Hazel sat up, holding the sheet close to her body. "What are you doing here?"

"Nah, answer my question. You ain't know it was me, so why the fuck your pussy dripping like that?"

"Oh my God," she groaned and let her face fall into her hand.

"Yea, you gon be calling for him some more in a minute. Lay back down." Hazel tried to turn back over on her stomach. "On your back."

Keeping the sheets close to her, she turned over. I came out of my shirt to get comfortable. I noticed how tightly she clinched the sheets to her body, and I knew why. But being the woman of a Tait didn't come with insecurities.

I spread her legs and mounted the table, letting my legs hang off the sides. I reached under the sheet, careful not to move too quickly.

"Apollo, I—" Hazel attempted to sit up, but I stopped her, holding a strong hand in the middle of her breasts. I pushed gently, laying her back down. I was going to do my best to calm her and make her comfortable. Especially with her body.

I heard her breathing pick up once I pulled the sheet away from her. Her glistening pussy was right in my face, and I was going to get there, but I had another obligation at the moment. Going right to where I knew the first scar was, I kissed it. Hazel's breathing picked up. I let my lips linger on the old wound of a knife slit for a few seconds before letting up. Turning her over to her left side, I held onto her hips and kissed the one that was a full-blown stab wound.

At this point, she was shaking. Laying her back flat, I moved up her body and kissed her ribs on each side. Both of which I knew had been bruised before. I knew just where her last set of scars resided, but I wouldn't dare touch them without asking.

"Do you want me to stop?" I asked.

The tears falling down the side of her face were barely visible due to the shadows of the raindrops. Hazel shook her head no.

Sliding down the table, I cuffed her legs in my arms and glanced down at her pretty waxed pussy. Her wetness seemed like it sparkled every time the blue and white lights hit it from the digital thunderstorm. Instead of going down, I lifted her abdomen to where her pussy was positioned right in my face.

I kissed the scars on the inside of her thighs repeatedly before resting her legs on my shoulder and gripping her waist, pulling her pussy into my mouth.

"Apollo," she cried. I let my tongue glide against her soaked lips, and around her clit before sucking the soul out of her through the swollen button. Her legs shook as she closed them around my neck. It was fine because I was holding her in place. It took about thirty seconds to familiarize myself with what was now our pussy. Rotating my tongue around her clit with slow, sensual sucks had her raining harder than the fake shit on the walls. "Fuuucckk!"

Waiting until she came down from her orgasm, I reached down and freed my dick from entrapment. Then I took her legs off my shoulder. "Sit up."

This time, she didn't reach for the sheet, and my mouth watered her D-cup breast. They had a slight sag to them but were big enough that the combination made them beautiful on her curvy body. I lowered her on my dick slowly, positioning her legs over the top of mine. Her tightness resisted me at first, but the way her shit was still dripping, she even welcomed me in. I moved my hands underneath her ass, as she rocked back and forth.

"Fuck." This position always fucked a nigga up. Hazel held on to the back of my neck, leaning back a little, allowing my dick deeper into her. She rocked her hips in a slow motion while I thrust upward in a circular motion. She gasped and let out a shuttering exhale. I knew then, I'd found her spot.

Hazel felt so fucking good, I knew I wouldn't last in that position. Grabbing her waist, I laid her back down, so I was on top. I placed my hands back underneath her ass, having her lifted off the bed slightly. Staying deep, I hit that spot over, and over and over while she pierced my skin with her teeth. Her pussy tightened and contracted around my dick. Her uterus had to be in her throat with how deep I was in that bitch.

"You cumming again, Fat Girl?" I growled in her ear. I was holding the fuck outta my nut, but Hazel was pulling it out of me each time her shit contracted around me.

"Yess." A low rumble of thunder accompanied her moan. This time I had to cum with her. Letting her ass go, I pulled out and stroked my dick while I came on her stomach. Grabbing a towel, I wiped us both off. Hazel laid there, staring at the ceiling.

Going to the top of the table, I kissed her forehead and leaned down beside her ear. "Let your pussy get wet for another muhfucka again, and their blood is on your hands."

Exiting, I delivered a head nod to the masseuse and went to my truck.

TWENTY-TWO
HAZEL

My body and soul felt amazing. But my mind was racing and if my heartbeat got any faster, I was for sure going into cardiac arrest. No other man had touched me since Quincy and Apollo had imposed on my darkest moments so delicately.

I stared at the ceiling for a half hour after Apollo walked out and all I kept asking myself was *how?* One may think that Apollo was just pleasing me sexually, but he deliberately tended to my most flawed areas. But, how did he know?

The pleasure ceased, and the longer I lay there, the more disturbed I was. My chest tightened as I thought back to the worst day of my life.

A YEAR AGO.

"WHERE ARE THE GROCERIES?" *Quincy asked as I walked in from work. "And who the fuck are you smiling at?"*

My sister and I had been texting back and forth about Mr. Jenkins.

Mocha had started as my assistant a few days prior, and she and Mr. Jenkins just wouldn't stop with the catty back and forth. Cha was going in on that man and I was trying to convince her that aside from him being overly opinionated, he's really a nice person.

"Mocha. And I just went grocery shopping. Why didn't you take something out?" I placed my purse, phone, and keys on the counter so that I could go shower. I wasn't in the mood for him today. If push came to shove, we could just order out.

I took my pants suit off and dropped it in the pile that needed to go to the dry cleaners. After presenting and closing three accounts today, the hot shower was the perfect wind down. I moisturized and slipped on a cute nightgown before making my way back to the front so we could figure out dinner. My eyes went to the back of my head when I noticed my phone in Quincy's hands.

Taking a deep breath, I tried to prepare myself for his words because that's what he did. He was verbally abusive. I've gotten to the point where I just let the words roll off my back and keep it moving. I checked the refrigerator to see if there was anything quick that I could throw together.

"Who is Mr. Jenkins?" Quincy asked in an attitude-laced tone.

"You know that's my boss." I closed the refrigerator and leaned against the counter.

"Why the fuck are you advocating so hard for this nigga?" He tossed the phone down and faced me. He was inches away from my face when he forcefully grabbed my jawbone with one hand and squeezed. My hands instantly went to his, trying to relieve the pressure. "You fucking him?"

I shook my head no. I heard the drawer beside me open and began to cry. The sound of him shuffling through the knife drawer terrified me. I almost pissed on myself when I felt the blade gliding along the inside of my thighs.

"Somebody else been in my pussy, Hazel?" he gritted. I clenched my eyes closed and said a prayer. The knife pierced my skin just enough to draw blood. Again, I shook my head. "You sure?"

He sliced the inside of the other thigh. Blood was running down my legs and onto the floor.

"You stay walking out of here in all that sexy shit." Quincy scraped the knife against my skin until he got to my right side.

"Agghhh!" I yelled. The sound was muffled due to him still having a tight grip on my face. He sliced at my side and then moved to the other. Now the tip of the knife was pointed into my side.

Quincy dug into me slowly, and I just knew that he was about to kill me. "If I find out you're fucking any of those niggas at that job, I'll kill you." He pulled the knife out of me, and blood gushed out. "Go put some pants on so we can go to the hospital."

That night, his manic ass sat at my bedside at Stanton Memorial and curated a lie about how I was attacked. The next day was when I began my revenge. For the next few months, I slowly placed powdered metal poisoning in his food. But only the takeout so that he wouldn't get suspicious. He would get sick every time and think it was food poisoning. I was just waiting for the day he kicked the bucket. Then, he caught me. He beat me so badly; he bruised and even cracked a few ribs.

When I was released from the hospital, he was sprawled out on our apartment floor, dead. The medical examiner said that it was a drug overdose. I knew that even with his sporadic behavior, Quincy had never touched a hard drug. Not while he was with me anyway. However, Jordyn was still suspicious afterward and something told me she wasn't letting it go easily. So, I've befriended Jordyn to make sure that poison never showed up in his reports.

Present Day

Jordyn seemed to have let it go, and after meeting Apollo, my anxiety about the situation calmed a lot. Until now. I could barely breathe lying there fully engulfed in real-time feelings about my past. I rushed out of the room and got dressed.

"Why are you banging on my door like this?" I ran into my sister's arms and let out a wail. My family knew nothing of Quincy and I's business, but I think it was time I let Cha know. I had to get it out.

After explaining Apollo's actions, she took my next statement right out of my mouth. "Oh, you're staying here for a while. I wouldn't say it's creepy, but it's definitely disturbing."

I agreed and we got comfortable and watched movies and drank for the night. It felt good in the moment but the hangovers that hit our asses the next morning had us regretting it.

TWENTY-THREE
ZEUS

"Aht! Aht! Apollo, you're riding with me." I stopped his ass from trying to climb in the car with Nyx.

"Shiddd! I ain't getting in there with no damn explosives," he shot back.

"This shit was you and Pops's idea. You had one job the other day and you failed to fully complete it because you ain't told me how I would have time to get this shit together at the location. So, if I'm blowing up, so the fuck are you!"

That nigga still reached for Nyx's door handle, and because my lil brother played so much, he locked the doors just before Apollo was able to pull.

"Y'all stay on some bullshit," Apollo hissed and practically stomped to my car. "Let's hurry this up, don't y'all both gotta get back to work?"

It's wild as fuck that I was taking lunch and free period to blow up a damn building.

"Drive slow, man!" Apollo shouted and I laughed. The chemicals were sitting on ice, keeping them from crystallizing. I knew we were safe, but why not fuck with Apollo a bit. He and Alonzo always found a way to randomly pull us back on the front lines so yeah, I was about to have fun fucking with him.

I started slow but was fucking the corners up, making him look at me with the fear of God in his eyes.

"I'ma beat yo' ass after this, watch."

"If we live to get through this, we can definitely square up." I hit another corner. The drive wasn't long, and as soon as I parked, Apollo jumped out and went to get in the car with Nyx.

I lifted the middle console and retrieved my disguise bag. We all had contacts to alter our iris patterns and a fake nose that matched our skin tone. The goal was to throw off any kind of facial recognition. I saw Apollo and Nyx do the same in my rearview mirror. I took a can of color hairspray and sprayed my shit blonde before balling it up underneath my hat. I checked myself over and got out to retrieve the cooler from my trunk.

Apollo approached my truck carrying a large carved-out toolbox big enough to sit the cooler in. While we prepared, Nyx headed down a few blocks looking like Fire Marshall Bill, to get his part started.

"Can y'all hear me?" he asked through the earpieces we all wore. We both confirmed transmission and waited about five minutes before we walked the opposite way to get around the corner. Both Apollo and I held onto the toolbox, keeping it as still as possible.

"Welcome back. Oh, you have contacts today. I like them." The receptionist smiled at Apollo. I let him handle it and kept my distance until she led him to a door and unlocked it. I went right to work and told Apollo I needed his help to remove all these tubes from the ice. There were two spots they needed to be placed and I didn't have long to get the fuck out of that basement after they were off ice. Apollo helped with the tubes for the first side and then slipped back upstairs to ensure that the door of the office that we were targeting was secured from the outside.

"Aight, ain't no way they're getting out of here," Apollo said. "I'm headed back your way, Zeus."

"Nyx, you're up," I said.

"Ma'am, there is a gas leak in the building. We're going to have to evacuate. Seconds later, we heard the fire alarm go off. That was Apollo's cue to pull the one in this building as well.

"Three minutes," I warned, watching the crystals form. Everything was in place. I sparked the lighter and held it to a torn piece of paper. I waited until the flame expanded and dropped it onto a pile of newspaper. Once the entire pile was inflamed, it would be large enough to reach the trail of gasoline that will travel to each explosive. The heat will instantly detonate the explosives on both sides.

I sprinted up the steps and Apollo was waiting for me at the side door.

"Nyx, talk to me," I said into the earpiece.

"I'm a block up," he responded.

We walked past the buildings and saw that the congressman's security was attempting to open the building door.

"Too late." I chuckled." We stepped off the curb, heading away from the evacuated crowd just as we heard the explosion. Looking back, all three buildings crumbled simultaneously. "Beautiful."

"Good shit, lil brother." Apollo dapped me up.

"Did you really doubt me?" I placed an offended hand on my chest.

"Not at all," he replied, pushing me and squaring up.

"Nigga, calm yo' over muscular ass down. You were safe the entire ride. I just had to fuck with you for thinking this shit is a cakewalk. Now hurry up, I have class in a half hour."

"YOU HAVEN'T SEEMED like yourself lately, son. Do I need to stay?" Venus asked from my passenger seat. I was dropping her off at the airport. She'd stayed a couple of weeks past my birthday, and she was finally ready to get back to her adventures. Neither of my brothers wanted to be bothered, so I told her to book something in the evening to assure that I was off work. "Is it about that girl?"

"Her name is Mocha, Ma. We hit a lil hiccup but I'm good. Nothing for you to worry about," I replied. Mocha was still pissed, and I got it. Coming from a marriage filled with infidelity, I would be on my way at any sign of another motherfucker too. But, if she gave me a chance to explain, she would understand that shit ain't like that with Tina.

The last time I tried to surprise her, she threw a vase at my head and told my ass I thought she was Boo Boo the Fool. She had me fucked up, though. Valentine's Day was the next day, and luckily none of my brothers were big on the holiday so I'd probably spend it with them.

Shit, Apollo going crazy about Hazel's ass too. Apparently, he dicked her down and she ghosted his ass. How the hell does somebody that lives across the street from you ghost you? I guess it was doable with his new work schedule, but damn.

"She's married, Zeus. You had fun for the moment but that's not who you were meant to be with."

"You picked up and left the person you thought you were meant to be with. Now you wanna give me advice?" I did a double-take between her and the road.

"Your father left me!" she yelled. "If I recall, he was locked up before I left."

"For all of five minutes!"

"You don't even like him, why does it matter to you?"

"It doesn't. Pops held us all back from a lot of things, including you. All I'm saying is don't sit here and judge Mocha when you have your shit too."

I felt her stare at the side of my face like she was trying to figure something out. "You're falling for this girl."

"I am. And she's going to be around. I'ma make sure of that. So, you and Nyx stop with all the unnecessary bullshit. We're here." I put the car in park in front of her terminal and popped the trunk to retrieve her bags.

"I'm sorry, son," Venus leaned against the car while I sat her bags on the curb. "I've always wanted the best for you boys. Even when I saw what your father was trying to mold you into. You fell victim to it, but you also followed your own path. I'd hate to see a woman be the thing that destroys that."

"Have a safe flight, ma. I love you." I leaned down to kiss her cheek after handing the employee her bags to be checked. "You checked in yesterday when I told you to, right?"

"Yes."

"Call me when you can."

Venus wasn't about to get a reaction out of me. It hadn't even been ten minutes since I told her not to play with Mocha and she just couldn't resist. I returned to my driver's seat and scrolled through *TikTok* before pulling off. @MochaAdiem was the first video to pop up on my For You page.

Mocha had her hair pulled up into a tight ponytail, with her natural curls falling to the side. Looks like she was doing a lash tutorial and did one of those things where you point, and something pops up on the screen. Some shit about the way lashes can enhance your beauty.

She was fucking gorgeous, even with those big ass lashes on her face. I noticed everything about her, and I knew she wore them frequently, but they always looked natural. I guess those were just for advertising.

There was a knock on my window, and I could smell the chemicals I wanted to mix already.

"Fuck you want, Mistake?" Mocha's husband was standing at my car window with a bag over his shoulder and some blonde bitch not too far behind.

"I guess you're the reason Mocha served me with divorce papers. You were also there when I told her she wasn't leaving me. That still stands. She won't see me, so I'm telling you and you can tell her, I'm not signing."

"No, that bubblehead bitch behind you is the reason she served yo' ass. You will sign, I can put my life on that. Now get the fuck on because I can spot three different things that I can set your ass on fire with right now. So, unless you want me to fuck your good arm up, don't miss ya flight." I rolled my window up.

This nigga had balls the size of China. It felt good to know that Mocha filed for a divorce. I went back to watching her video and that smile she flashed at the end was contagious. I smiled at the screen like a lil bitch and couldn't stop myself from commenting.

@TeachemZeus Will you be my Valentine? 🚔

I strolled through the rest of her recent videos, and it looked like the advertising had become a thing. I loved how she knew what she wanted and was going to get that shit. I was lost on how the fuck she ended up with a square like Pierre.

@MochaAdiem 🤏

"Damn." I laughed. Her fire was always sexy to me. This shit was cute but the playing hard thing was getting old. Like always, I would respect what she wanted, for now. But she not going no fucking where.

TWENTY-FOUR

NYX

I unlocked Braiza's front door and heard the tv on. The night I told Braiza I was falling for her didn't go how I planned. Shit, I ain't plan on telling her I loved her at all, let alone doing the shit after she'd witnessed me kill somebody.

"This is how you're spending your night?"

She jumped so hard that the bowl of popcorn fell out of her lap. I hated how nervous she seemed around me since that night. She always warmed back up, so it was good to know she wasn't entirely running for the hills. I was trying the best way I knew how to show her this was what I wanted. I started doing shit, like making her coffee in the morning and sending gifts and shit to her house. Tonight, I was stepping it up a notch.

"Didn't I ask you to return my key?"

"Didn't I tell you I wasn't?" I sat down on the sofa, and she shifted her body so that she was further away from me.

"Why are you here, Nyx?" Brai paused her movie with a sigh. She had her straightened hair pulled back into a ponytail, no makeup on, with a pajama set on and some fuzzy slippers.

"I'm here to get you out of the house. I ain't the best at planning dates, but it's a start."

Braiza's eyes lit up but then her shoulders dropped like she didn't really wanna get her hopes up. "We're going on a date? Like a real date, Nyx?"

"Why do you gotta say it like that?"

"Because the last time you got me excited, you set me up to be embarrassed." Braiza picked up the bowl of popcorn and walked to the kitchen. All that was heard was the sound of her feet dragging on the hardwood floor.

"Yes, we're going on a real date. Now go change before I change my mind!" I yelled, knowing I was about to piss her off.

"You can leave if you're going to talk crazy to me. Your rude ass really shows your age sometimes!" There she was. She came around quicker than normal and the dragging of her slippers became more aggressive as she returned to the living room.

"I was joking, man. Can you go change please so we can enjoy this dumb ass holiday?"

She turned on the ball of her slippers and I watched that ass swinging in her pajama pants until she made it to her stairs.

A group FaceTime call came through, and I answered it to see Zeus tilting a bottle to his head. "What's up, bruh? We outside?"

This nigga was clearly fucked up. "Nah. Unlike your lonely ass, I have a date."

"Oh, you and Ms. Trunchbull are really doing this shit, huh?"

"Yep. Who would've thought that out of the three of us, I'd be the one with my love life in order?" I taunted him.

"You ain't about to act like you ain't have a part in my shit being fucked up," Zeus said.

"And you ain't about to act like you ain't spend last Valentine's Day with Tina," I debated.

"Nigga, we spent that night fucking cuz her dude was fucking up. That's all that was," he explained.

"Yea, well I hope your sideline hoe ass can explain that to the Mrs." I chuckled. "We've been on the phone too long nigga, bye."

I could see the steam coming from his ears. He was feeling this broad. But just like they say a married man ain't about to leave his wife for a side piece, I wasn't believing it to be the opposite with a woman until it actually.

"I'm ready. Am I too dressed down?" Braiza appeared, doing a spin. She had on dark jeans, a brown sweater that twisted in the middle, exposing a little cleavage, and some brown *UGG* boots.

"Brai, I got on jeans and a hoodie. You're good."

She locked up and I opened the passenger side door of my car, revealing the roses sitting on the seat.

"Thank you." She blushed and climbed in.

I got in and closed the door. Braiza jumped and tried to look away like I didn't notice it. This car wasn't moving until we discussed this shit.

"You scared of me?" I asked outright.

"I, um, I don't know. I don't feel like you'd hurt me, but I can't get the sight of you killing that man with your bare hands out of my head," she expressed.

"What needs to happen to fix that?"

"I don't know. How often does that happen?" She looked at me inquisitively.

"Not often at all." I wasn't lying. As I said, before this recent job, I hadn't been in the field in years. Them niggas are dead before they even get to me these days.

"But it has happened before, Leon?"

"It has. About eight years ago, and the circumstances were quite the same." Now that was partially true. The circumstances were the same but it ain't have shit to do with me or anyone I loved. "You're right about the fact that I wouldn't hurt you. But I'll always protect you, and if you feel that entails being protected from me too, I'll let you go back inside."

"That's not necessary," Braiza whispered, letting her eyes soften.

"I've seen a lot in my life, and I'm capable of separating self-defense from someone being a monster. We can leave."

Her ass always had to go too far. She reached over and tried to interlace our fingers.

"I drive with this hand." I removed myself from her grip and placed her hand on my knee where I was more comfortable. Shawty was breaking me down, but all that affectionate shit would take some time.

I pulled out of her driveway. This time I paid closer attention so I wouldn't have any mishaps. Misreading that one-way sign had Braiza's antennae up, and I'm sure if something like that happens again, she wasn't going to let it go.

"Why are we at your place?" Her rising attitude was presenting itself as I parked and turned the car off. "You said that we were going on a date."

I ignored her and went around to open her door. "That look on your face ain't sexy at all. Fix it." For Braiza to be damn near a decade older than me, she sure did act like a brat at times. Instead of going through the front entrance, I led her through the gate leading to my backyard. Stealing glances out of my peripheral, I noticed her frown curve upward.

The heated camping tent hit a nigga pocket for a nice piece of change, but it was worth it. It was huge and allowed for a projector, an electric fire pit, and one of those inflatable couches people used for camping. There was fruit and champagne on a table waiting for us, and a thick blanket.

"Well, this is thoughtful." Braiza slid her arms around my waist and looked up at me.

"Nah, don't give me the googly eyes now. You were ready to chop my head off a second ago."

"My apologies. I just didn't know what was going on. So, what are we watching?" She cheesed, removed her coat, and got comfortable on the couch. She unfolded the blanket and grabbed a glass of champagne.

"You'll see." I set things up and pressed play on the projector. Getting comfortable myself, I sat beside her. Leave it up to Braiza to snuggle against me and throw the blanket over me as well. I gritted my teeth at the gesture but held my tongue on asking her to move. I let her do her thing and just kept my arms resting on the back of the couch.

The beat to Barry White's "You're the First, the Last, my Everything" started and she got excited as hell. Braiza mentioned on many occasions her love for the comedian *Chris Tucker* so I knew this movie would be perfect.

I sang the lyrics low as the first scene of the movie played.

"You sing?" She gasped with an amused smile.

"Watch the movie, Brai," I replied.

"My kinda wonderful! That's what you are!" We sang together and mimicked the way he hit the steering wheel to the next line of the music. We fell out laughing and she snuggled back against my side. The night was filled with us reciting the movie word for word. Shit was a vibe, and it felt weird as hell anticipating our next date.

"Thank you." There she was with those damn eyes again. "It wasn't what I expected. But you've made a step. A thoughtful and well put together step and I appreciate it."

"Oh yea, how much?"

Braiza smiled and went down, throwing the blanket over her head. My belt and button were undone with ease before she took me into her warm mouth. It took less than five minutes of her deep-throating and stroking my shit before she swallowed my kids. All I can say was I hoped the neighbors were minding their business because round two could've been seen in HD with the way the dim lights magnified our shadows inside the tent. If not, they got a good show.

TWENTY-FIVE
APOLLO

I used the door knocker to knock on the door of the nice condo. My fingers drummed against the door frame while I impatiently waited for the door to be answered. Knocking one last time, I prepared to kick this bitch off the hinges. Just as I lifted my foot, the door swung open. Ace tried to close it just as fast as he opened it.

"Aht! Aht! Aht! I know Granny taught you not to treat family that way!" I growled, kicking the door anyway. Ace stumbled back but quickly regained his stance. I looked around the living room. This snitch-ass nigga was sitting pretty in a high-rise condo. I continued to scope the place until my eyes landed on luggage in the corner of the room. "Going somewhere?"

"Look, Apollo, Alonzo is being released like you wanted. You said that you would stop them from bringing charges against me. But they're coming after me, so I can't stay here," he heaved.

"Oh, I meant what I said. I'm going to stop that from happening. You see, they can't charge a dead man." I laughed wickedly.

"If I end up dead, Jordyn will come after you with all she has!"

"What she has is nothing! If she did, I would be behind bars. Plus, you committed suicide. You panicked about spending time in jail and decided to end it yourself. At least that's what's going to circulate the media." I slowly walked toward my uncle, never taking my eyes off him. He didn't even realize he was walking right into his death trap.

Ace backed up more and more until he backed into the glass leading to his balcony. He had nowhere to go. I grabbed his neck using my gloved hand, jacking him up by his jacket, and used the other hand to slide the balcony door open.

A quick and precise right hook curved up and hit me dead in my jaw, twisting my head to the side. Slowly, I turned back to look at him. Again, the fear in his eyes made it hard to believe he was a Tait.

"Apollo, don't do this!" He begged for his life while dangling over the railing. His condo was on the thirteenth floor, and I was going to enjoy watching him plummet to his death.

"You expected my father to place you at the head of this business when not only are you a fucking rat, but you can't even die with dignity. How about I go ahead and put us all out of our misery?" I tossed Ace over the balcony and didn't stay to watch his body flail around until it hit the concrete. I heard it on the way out of his condo.

People immediately began to gather around screaming and shit. I was out of dodge and on my way back through the alley the moment I heard him hit the concrete. I zipped up my jacket and waited by the ambulance until Gavin and Eddie received the call. I suggested a dinner around the corner purposely for dinner just so I could be in the vicinity. I stepped out for a phone call and knew not to go missing for more than fifteen minutes. I was thankful for the many alleyways that connected streets through the city.

I was already inside the truck when the two of them rushed out of the diner. I'd heard the call and climbed in the back with Gavin.

"What happened to your jaw?" Gavin asked. He was a nosey motherfucker.

"I heard the call and tried to rush to get in the driver's seat and hit myself with the door."

"See, that's why we let Eddie drive."

We arrived on the scene and put on an Academy Award-winning performance. Dropping to my knees by Ace's body and let out an emotional sigh.

"Sir, do you know this man?" a police officer asked.

"Yea. He's my uncle." I shook my head. "How am I going to break this to my father?"

"HOW DID YOU PULL THIS OFF?" my father asked as he walked through the gates of the prison.

"We've got a lot to discuss." I hugged him and my pops held on to me like he hadn't embraced me in a lifetime. I had never been behind the walls so I'm sure it felt like an eternity to him.

We got on the road back to the city and I broke down to him how it was his brother that put him behind bars.

"He's glad that you got to him before me. He would've died slowly if I had anything to do with it." He pulled at his cigarette and blew the smoke out the crack of the window. I always hated that he smoked them and would have to get my car detailed to get the smell out. "I heard the job was successful. I have the wire scheduled for the three of you in a few days. Where are your brothers, anyway?"

"They both should be at work. I kept your release a secret. If I would've said something, Ma would've stayed in town and I needed a break," I explained.

"Your mother was here?" he asked. I was still able to hear the mixture of excitement and disappointment that he felt when he spoke about her.

"Yea, she surprised us for Christmas."

"And you didn't tell her you were coming to see me that week?" He sounded upset.

"You know we don't even speak like that. And we were discussing business, I wouldn't have told her any other time. I will say that she was glued to my hip, hoping to speak with you. Now that you're out, I'll give you her number."

"Sounds good." He sat back and took another pull of his cigarette. "Where is she now?"

"Her flight was to Greece. But she never stays in one place long. Zeus talks to her the most, so he'll most likely know before anyone," I informed my father. Alonzo answered with a nod.

Once Venus took off around the world, I paid someone to go in and clean their house once a week. I was glad because my pops could go to a place of comfort and not have to totally rebuild. The place would be lonely, but at least it was his.

TWENTY-SIX
MOCHA

"I'm not giving her shit! If she wants to leave, everything that I've bought stays! Let's see how far she gets without me!" Pierre barked, sitting on the other side of the table with his lawyer. It had been three long months of mediation and every time, he comes in here and shows his natural clammy ass.

"Pierre, for once, can you stop the theatrics? All I'm asking for is my car and shared custody of Nina. The car is paid off and there will be no attachment to you. We can agree to a schedule for Nina and deal with one another as little as possible. Can we settle this and sign the fucking papers?" I groaned. This was getting old. Springtime was setting in and my life and career were in a good place. I didn't need Pierre like he hoped I would.

"I'm not signing anything."

"You know what, keep it! If you think holding anything over my head is going to make me stay in this marriage, you're sadly mistaken. Angela, please contact me when you draw up the final papers. Pierre, I'll see you in family court. With the dirt and evidence I have against you, I suggest you don't turn that into an all-out war. Because it will be one you lose."

I picked my purse up and went to the elevator. I scoffed at Penelope sitting in the lobby. Pierre seemed to master the dwindling art of putting on a show, so I knew she heard every word I said. Imagine hearing a man fighting to stay with someone else while you sit like a weak bitch on the sideline. Pierre continues to make this easier and easier for me.

I pressed the elevator button continuously, hoping that it would make it come faster. A tight grip on my arm halted me from entering when the elevator opened.

"How dare you try to take our daughter," Pierre hissed. I looked down at his arm and saw the terrible burning of his skin. Whatever happened, I was quite sure he deserved it.

"You're lucky I'm only going for joint custody. Get your hands off me or I'll be sure you lose that entire hand!"

Fear flashed in his eyes, and he quickly let me go. It was like he recalled something and backed away from me. I pushed the button again and watched the elevator close on Pierre.

My heels clicked against the sound of the asphalt of the parking garage while I fished inside my purse for my keys. The hairs on the back of my neck stood up and I brushed it off as it being a little chilly in the enclosed garage. I stopped in front of my parking spot because between walking with a purpose and my eyes slightly tearing up from anger, finding those keys felt impossible.

I felt the metal at the bottom of the bag and sighed. Stepping around my car, ready to hit the key fob, I noticed my tire was flat.

"You've got to be kidding me." I groaned, starting to go into the car for my insurance information until something caught my attention. My tire wasn't flattened by it being punctured. The bottom of the tire was fucking melted.

Immediately, I closed the app and looked around the parking garage. I couldn't spot him, but I knew his ass was there. Reopening my phone, I went to his number and pressed send.

"Yes, beautiful," he answered calmly. Hearing his voice sent a spark through me that made my eyes fall shut while I clinched the phone tight. Lord knows I missed his presence, but this shit was too much.

"I know you're looking right at me. Come fix my damn tire so that I can go, Zeus," I exhaled and surprisingly, every word flowed out clearly.

"No. That's not how this works." My pussy began to tingle. I tried to tell her not to miss his ass, but she has been cussing me out since the day I stormed out of his party. "I've tried doing this shit the nice way. I tried to explain and even bring you that big ass vase of tulips. Now, we do it my way."

"I don't have the time for this shit, Zeus." I pinched the bridge of my nose. Today had already drained the hell out of me. The mediation between Pierre and me began at one o'clock in the afternoon. It was now four.

The low humming of an engine caused me to lift my head. A gray tinted-out jeep pulled up; the windows rolled down and Zeus was on the other side. From what I could see, he wore a black button-up and black slacks. His hair was getting a little frizzy, but I kind of liked it like that. His gold jewelry was simple, with an earring, a small rope necklace, and his gold frames.

He pushed his glasses up his nose a little before speaking. "You see, the chemical I used on your tire causes it to stick to the concrete, and it takes a special solvent to remove it."

"I can just google what the solvent is."

"You can try. But before you waste your time, remember who you're talking to." I closed my phone. "Exactly. Now, if you get in and allow me to remind you of why you love a nigga, we'll end up in this same spot in a few hours and I'll change your tire."

I climbed into the truck with no hesitation. Zeus leaned against the window, and I propped my elbow on the center console. We locked eyes and the immediate comfort that filled the space was needed with the day I was having. "Who said I loved you?"

"You do. You just don't see it yet." He winked and pulled out of the garage. Three months had passed, and I missed the fuck out of him. But I had to stand on who I was becoming and not let this man play with me. No matter how much I missed him, or how good he dicked me down.

"Where are we going? You have two hours."

"I have however long I want. Sit back." Zeus turned the music up. I listened to him sing low. His voice made me relax. The ride was under an hour since we were already in downtown DC. Rush hour extended the drive, but I got excited once I noticed where we were.

"Wait, why did you park back here?" Noticing that we were parked in the back lot of the National Zoo. "I normally like to start at the front."

"Well, I thought about what you said, and we do have a couple of hours. Maybe less than that until the sun goes down. This is closer to the birdhouse." He winked and killed the engine. My smile had to be a mile wide.

Zeus opened my door and grabbed my hand. I felt like a creep once again as I looked at him while he led the way. I pray that whatever that was with that braider bitch, was in the past. I'd stood my ground for months and I hoped that I made my point.

"How did you know?"

"Every knick-knack in your home is of some kind of bird. Not to mention the necklace you never take off." I lightly grabbed the eagle pendant that hung from a small gold chain. Nina has one just like it.

Zeus opened the door to the birdhouse and the sounds were music to my ears.

"Only time I've seen you light up like this is when you first saw me singing outside of that shelter. You should smile like this more often." I rolled my eyes, but my smile never left my face. He was right, I hadn't felt this happy in a long time.

Zeus interlocked our fingers, and we walked through, looking at and reading about different birds. "Why birds?" he asked.

"Hazel and I were playing in our grandmother's backyard down south and I kept hearing this sound like someone was whistling a song, but it was repetitive. I looked around the perimeter of the yard for hours until I finally spotted the most beautiful little bird hiding in a big bush my granny had.

"It was orange up top, brown at the bottom, with black and white speckles on its back. I listened to it until my mama yelled out of the back door to let us know that dinner was ready. I stuffed the food down my throat and jumped on the desktop my granny had set up. I found out it was called a Musical Wren. They aren't common in the United States, so I felt it was special for me to spot one. That evening was the first time I pushed until I persevered and the only thing that waited for me at the end of that mission was serenity. Birds are my peace."

"Is that the tune that plays on your jewelry box?" I nodded and looked at him lovingly. "Why the look?"

"I'm not used to anyone being this invested now that I think about it," I expressed.

"Sometimes you don't know what you're missing until you have it."

"You're right." I stopped to face him. "But I also know what I had, that I don't want anymore."

"Mocha, you have my word that I ain't fucking with Tina. She's the homie." I opened my mouth to debate the word *homie,* but Zeus stopped me. "I know. I know. Yes, we've gone there, but it has never been serious between us. She didn't feel the need to respect any boundaries at my party because I've never been serious about anyone. But I damn sure let her know I'm with you and we had to keep that shit platonic.

"Don't make me set fire to this zoo with a debate about being with me. I stayed true to that and kept my dick in my pants for the last three months. I'm not doing this shit any longer."

I knew not to debate with him. Especially not in a public place. Instead, we continued our stroll through the birdhouse.

"Summer break is almost here. What do you plan on doing?" I asked him.

"Honestly, I'm going to teach summer school and help with the camp. I have to stay close to my kids somehow." He stopped to read about a red crossbill.

"Your students are special to you, huh?"

"Yeah. You'll be surprised how many kids in a classroom need parental guidance that they're not getting at home. Or in need of a friend, a mentor, or a sounding board. I make it my duty to be all of that while teaching something I love. What about you?"

"Hazel and I have taken off with this whole *TikTok* thing. So, we're utilizing it with her volunteer work this summer," I explained.

"Speaking of *TikTok*, unblock me." I couldn't contain the snorkel that came out. When I blocked him, I played out his reaction in my head. The annoyed look he wore now was a part of that visual. "Keep fucking around. I'ma report your page!"

"Stop being dramatic, I'll unblock you." We'd seen everything at the birdhouse so now it was his turn" "We have a little sunlight left. What's your favorite exhibit?"

"The lions."

"Lions it is." I grabbed his hand, and he leaned in and kissed my forehead. Missed was an understatement when it came to his lips being on me.

Less than an hour later, we were on the way back to my car. Zeus parked his car beside mine and I watched as he opened the trunk and pulled out a bottle of God knows what.

"Get out. You're going to have to roll the car a little forward for me to detach the entire tire," he said.

"How you fuck my shit up and need help fixing the shit?" I looked at him with my head tilted to the side.

"Can you just get out and do what I said? Or we can leave it here. Your choice."

I had an attitude, but I did what he asked. He poured the solution, and I rolled forward once he told me to.

"OK. You can cut the car off." He rose and removed a jack and tire iron from the back of his truck. I hit the trunk button so that he could remove my spare. "So, how was the meeting this afternoon?"

"Same as it has been. He's fighting me tooth and nail and I'm not even asking for shit."

"Mm," he said.

"What does that mean?"

"Nothing." Zeus kept changing the tire, leaving the conversation that he'd just started alone. I was cool with dropping it, but I was also curious to know what was going through his head.

He let the car down off the jack and instead of putting the ruined tire in the spare's original place, Zeus put it in his truck.

"I'll get a new tire put on your rim and come change it tomorrow." He pulled me in for a hug. "I gotta get to Apollo's; he's cooking."

"He's home tonight?" I asked, worried about whether Hazel knew or not.

"Yea, they switched his schedule back. I'm glad cuz me cooking struggle meals and eating out was killing me."

"OK. Well, call me when you're ready to fix the tire."

Again, he kissed my forehead and waited until I was in my car safely. Immediately, I pulled out my phone to call my sister. She's expressed that she missed Apollo as well, but that uneasy feeling just wouldn't leave her. So, if she was uneasy so the hell was I.

TWENTY-SEVEN

HAZEL

"This place is nice." Majiq admired the restaurant. Along with my sister and parents, Majiq had become my saving grace. Mocha was the only person aware of why I was avoiding Apollo, so I bounced between the houses, claiming to be lonely at home alone, or too drunk to drive home until I knew Apollo had left for his shift. When Cha texted me about Apollo's schedule, I was already aware.

When I left for work that morning, he was getting into his car as well. When I felt as if I'd worn out my welcome at Cha's, I was careful about the times that I exited and entered my home. His overnight schedule allowed me to spend time with my family, go home and leave for work without seeing him. Since that has changed, my overnight bag was already packed and before we came to dinner, I was already at my parent's house waiting for Mocha and Majiq to confirm our dinner plans, and that's where I'll be when we leave here.

"I know. I saw it on one of those DC food pages on Instagram. It's even nicer in person," I explained, sipping my wine.

"Did Mocha say she was going to make it?"

"Yea, she said she had a flat but was on the way." I picked up my phone and checked her location. "Looks like she's almost here."

The waitress came over, ready to take our order. She agreed to come back in ten minutes. That would give Cha time to get settled and look over the menu.

Mocha walked in, sending air kisses to Majiq and me.

"What kind of wine is this?" She lifted the bottle from the ice and read the label. "Shit sounds expensive. I'll take a glass or two. Hell, or three."

"Pierre?" I assumed.

"Of course. Him, among other things." She shook her head, but never made eye contact. Mocha knew that I could see right through her, but I'd never pull a card in front of anyone else. However, she had to know that I was going to ask her how she knew about Apollo's work schedule.

We looked over the menu and ended up ordering four different appetizers, steaks, and shareable sides.

"So, I was thinking, for the events this summer, we can do a car wash or something to raise money for kids in the arts but can't afford the camps. Or maybe even sports camps," I explained my newest ideas.

"I was thinking of going the route of IT classes or maybe science programs," Mocha suggested.

"Of course, you did," I mumbled.

"What is that supposed to mean?" she snapped back.

"Whoa!" Majiq put her hands up, signaling the both of us to stop. "We can do it all. If we think of more innovative ways to raise money, we can make more kids happy. Problem solved. Now, I came to have a drink. We can talk shop later."

I stuffed a piece of steak in my mouth, but damn near choked on it when I saw who walked through the door. Mocha heard familiar voices just as I did. Apollo and Zeus walked into the restaurant with a third person, but it surely wasn't Nyx.

Zeus spotted Cha like he had tunnel vision and approached our table while the other two were seated. Apollo was in my direct line of sight, and his dark eyes felt like they were melting me even across the dimly lit restaurant.

"Hey, I thought you said Apollo was cooking," Mocha said to Zeus, confirming my suspicions.

"I thought he was. I got over there, and he surprised me and Nyx with my pops being home from prison. Pops wanted to come out, so here we are," Zeus explained.

"I would ask where Nyx is, but it may be better that she stays there." Mocha and Nyx were like oil and water.

"Chill on my brother, Mocha." Zeus chuckled a little and turned toward me. "What's up, Hazel?"

"Hey," I greeted him. I liked Zeus when he didn't have my sister fucked up. He seemed like the normal one out of the group and that's a bit farfetched given the fact that Mocha confirmed all three were touched in the head.

"You ladies enjoy your night." He leaned down to kiss Mocha's forehead and went to join his brother and father. Apollo was a spitting image of his father; it was almost uncanny.

I tried to enjoy my dinner, but Apollo's eyes never left me, and the urge I felt to run to him was overwhelming. But I had to ask myself if I'd rather deal with the task of missing him or wonder over and over again why this man was so familiar with my body and even the people around me.

I'd finally gotten in touch with Jordyn, and she sounded like the weight of the world was on her shoulders. She had a stressful job and normally I would tell her she always got through the hell that came with being a detective. But then, she warned me once again to be careful. She didn't mention Apollo but what else would she be warning me about?

"Hazel! Are you listening?" Majiq called out to me.

"I'm sorry. What'd you say?" I cleared my throat and finally pulled my eyes off Apollo.

"I said we should take a girls' trip this summer. It's been a minute."

"I'm down. I can use a change of scenery," I responded, scooping a mouthful of lobster mac into my mouth. Majiq excused herself to go to the restroom and I was left there with Mocha staring at me.

"You don't seem too uncomfortable. She played with her food. I remained quiet. "I know the feeling."

"No, Cha. You don't." I sighed and dropped my fork. "Have you ever felt like someone could see through your soul when you've never given them access?"

"Damn," she said, clenching her chest.

"Exactly. It's like wanting to let someone in and you open the door and they're already standing on the other side. The shit has me so confused."

"Maybe it's the dick." She tried to make light of the situation.

"Can you be serious? Something feels off. However, something about being in the same room with him feels..." I paused. "Right."

"I wish I knew what to tell you, Sissy."

"It's cool. Can we go?"

Mocha nodded. We waited until Majiq returned and asked the waitress for to-go containers and the check. I was relieved and finally was able to breathe regularly when I was on my way back to my parent's house. Apollo didn't make physical contact and I hoped it stayed that way.

"GIRL, get up off my couch and come help me. If you're going to be over here all the time, at least you can be of some use." My mama shook me out of my sleep. "And why don't you just go to your old room?"

"I was too tired when I came in. What do you need help with?" I wiped my eyes and sat up on the couch.

"Go get the crust off your face and meet me in the garage."

I got up, folded up the throw blanket, and straightened up her pillows. I would've felt like I was fifteen all over again, fearing the consequences of Chai coming back inside to her living room being out of order. Once I got myself together, I found my mother in the garage, pulling down all kinds of boxes from the organizer they installed.

"Spring cleaning?" I asked, pulling up a metal chair.

"No. One of your father's lifelong friends passed away and he asked me to look through some pictures." She pulled out a plastic bin and lifted the top. Old Polaroid photos filled the container. "Wow, look! We were so young."

I grabbed the picture my mother held up and smiled at her and my dad on the beach. Their smiles were just as genuine as they were today as he held her from behind.

"When was this?" I asked.

"I had just found out I was pregnant with you." She smiled lovingly.

Showing me more pictures, we laughed at the memories of Cha and me growing up. We had some good times. Especially on family vacations. They'd taken us to Disney World, mountain trips, and even on a cruise. No matter where we went, my little sister was going to find some birds. There were so many pictures of us feeding the birds or with parrots sitting on our arms. Cha was always the outgoing one, and I was the conservative daughter.

We went through the bin, and a photo made my heart drop to my feet. It was a picture of my father and two men that I would never forget the face of. They'd only gotten older.

"Who is this?" I asked, holding the picture up. I knew I wasn't wrong, but I needed confirmation.

"Oh, that's one that he could use. Ace is the one that passed." She pointed to the younger one of the group. "Committed suicide."

Hearing that name confirmed my suspicions. It was Apollo's uncle and father in the picture with my dad. The garage door opened behind us, and my father jogged down the three steps from the house.

"Dad, how do you know these men?" I asked.

"Chai, when I asked you to look for the pictures. I meant alone." He looked at my mother like he couldn't believe what she'd done.

"I didn't think about it, Leo. I got excited about sharing some memories with Hazel and it skipped my mind," she explained.

"What skipped your mind?" I needed answers. This was the second time something had come up about a Tait and the two of them acted weird.

"Nothing, honey." My father put a hand on my shoulder. "These are friends of mine that I used to be close to. Our lives went in different directions, and we aren't as close anymore."

"Is that it?" That was such an open-ended answer.

"That's all you need to know." My father stormed back inside. Only if he knew just how much I needed to know. There were so many puzzle pieces floating around my heart, and it was one solid piece that would fit to make it whole. That piece reveals who Apollo Tait truly was.

"Ma?" I sighed, looking over at my mother with tears burning the rim of my eyelids. Lovingly, she reached up and wiped them.

"I knew something was bothering you when you started staying here frequently. You did the same thing when Quincy died. Neither your father nor I saw this coming, but I can tell you it's going to be all right. Let him love you, Baby Girl." My mother placed all the photos back in the bin and set it back in its place.

Speechless, I sat lost in my thoughts as she walked past me and retreated into the house. What the hell kind of connection did the Taits have to my family for them to be keeping such a secret?

TWENTY-EIGHT
ZEUS

"Good afternoon, Mr. Tait." Ms. Daniel walked past my classroom with an extra hop in her steps. The students were at lunch, and I had my door propped open.

"My brother must be all up in that!" I yelled after her. I didn't give a fuck about being at work anymore after she showed up at my party. I fucked with her about being a cougar every chance I got. I expected her to double back and say something, but Nyx showed up in my doorway instead.

"I sure the fuck am!" he boasted, face stoic as hell.

"Nyx!" I heard Ms. Daniels shriek.

"Didn't you say you had a meeting?" he asked her, letting out a chuckle and entering my class. I let my legs fall from my desk and embraced my brother.

"What time will these lil rascals be back in here?" he asked and sat on the corner of my desk.

"In less than a half an hour," I answered. Look at this shit, though." I tossed the newspaper down on the desk beside him.

"What's this?"

"Nigga, what does it say?" Nyx picked up the newspaper and I watched his eyes hover over the headline for a good thirty seconds before tossing the paper back at me.

"OK?" He shrugged.

"Nigga, fuck is you high or something?" I wondered why it took him so long to read the headline.

"Yea," he confirmed. "They're looking into the explosion. Can't shit trace back to us so, fuck them."

"I know, I was showing your ass as a joke. What are you doing here, anyway? You and Trunch—"

"Zeus!"

"Aight! My bad." I held my hands up in surrender. "You and Ms. Daniels are still going strong, huh?"

"I wouldn't say strong, but we are going." Nyx scratched his head.

"Fuck does that mean?" I questioned.

"It means I'm trying. All that touching and shit is still weird as fuck to me. And she is asking for a lot that a nigga don't know if he's ready to give her," he explained. "The thought of exclusively building something doesn't terrify me, I just don't know if I'm completely capable of giving her everything she's asking for."

"That's what comes with a cougar big dog! She's ready to settle down. And you ain't gon never get used to anybody touching your mean ass so, she gon have to get used to that."

"That's what I'm saying. It is what it is for right now though. I took her to lunch and I'm gonna head over to the mortuary. We got a few bodies that need to be cremated." Nyx stood to dap me up.

"Before you go, you talk to Dad?" I asked, recalling how Nyx just walked the fuck out when Apollo explained how Alonzo got out and Ace's part in it.

"Nope!" he yelled, walking toward the door, throwing a peace sign over his head. As always, talking to Nyx was a struggle. It had become a little easier and I do mean very little, since being with Ms. Daniels.

I organized some classwork from my morning classes and got blank worksheets ready for my afternoon classes. Before I knew it, the bell was ringing, and I had approximately five minutes before my students came scrambling to their seats before the late bell.

"Mr. Tait! Look!" Xavier came running into my class and shoved his phone in my face. I looked quickly before sending him to his correct class. It was a *YouTube* video of a science experiment that had gone wrong. But they made it into a joke in the video where the "scientist" painted his face and lab jacket black when the glass bottle seemingly exploded.

"All right, get to class. You know you don't want Mrs. Frazier sending you down to Ms. Daniels."

Xavier sprinted out into the hallway and still went in the opposite direction of Mrs. Fraizer's class. I shook my head. Xavier reminded me so much of myself at his age. He was so enthused when it came to science, which is why I tried to instill the importance of safety into him. He was a wildcard; however, his video did give me an idea.

It was the end of the school day, and I sat at my desk and Face-Timed Mocha. She was still at work, twisting back and forth in her chair behind her desk.

"Long day?" I inquired.

"Hell yea. Between work meetings and being on the phone with my lawyer all day to iron out the details of this new divorce settlement, I'm swamped. I could use a bubble bath and a glass of wine right about now."

Before I could respond, I heard her office door open. Mocha muted me and looked up. I watched her mouth something, then returned to the phone.

"I have one last meeting baby, I'll call you later." The call ended and I hated that she looked so stressed. I packed up everything I needed from my office and left for the day.

THE KITCHEN ISLAND in front of me consisted of three glass beakers. One was sitting on a heating mantle bubbling from the mixture of compounds inside, and two intentionally sitting away from the heat. Beside the cooled beakers were rocks of sodium that I would need later. The garage door opened and in walks the walking mistake.

"What the fuck are you doing in my house?" Pierre yelled like I was supposed to drop what I was doing and run.

"I just came to have a little chat. This house is nice as fuck, by the way. I didn't have a chance to go inside during my first visit. Have a seat." I motioned toward his dining room table.

"I won't!" I swear I didn't see what Mocha saw in his square ass. "You won't get away with this this time."

He headed toward the door.

"This hollow tip will greet you before you make it to the door. Have a seat." I continued to swirl the beaker around, not making eye contact at all.

"My daughter and her mother will be here any minute."

"See, there was a coincidental accident right outside of the school parking lot. The exit is blocked until I clear it. Have a seat," I repeated. Using my peripheral vision, I saw him slowly approach the table. "Now, to address what you said. I will get away with it. Looks like those doctors were doing pretty well on your skin grafts too."

I noticed his arm looked better than the way I left it.

"If you're here about Mocha, I told you I'm not divorcing her."

"And I told you, you will. One.. way.. or.. the other." Reaching to my side for the pipette, I suctioned up the chemicals and dropped a single drop onto the counter. This time I had to look up to watch his reaction to the drop eating through his granite countertop. "I took it easy on you last time by just burning your skin. Imagine what that will do to your flesh and bones."

"What do you want?" he asked in a trembling whisper.

Reaching behind me, I grabbed the envelopes I found in his office and pulled out the two contracts, then slammed them on the table, along with a pen. "Sign them and date them for yesterday."

"No!" I dropped another drop right beside his arm and it ate through the table. "OK!" He snatched the pen and signed on the line.

Carefully, I placed the papers back in the envelopes and walked back over to the counter. I pushed all three beakers closely together. Using my tweezers, I dropped a large amount of sodium into the second beaker that only contained boiling water and got the fuck out of there. Knowing that the reaction from the sodium and water would be enough to ignite the third beaker, filled to the top with my favorite yellow crystals. If you know, you know.

"Are you going to get this shit out of here?" Pierre panicked behind me.

"No." I slammed the front door and went to take care of my woman.

———

"HEY, WHERE ARE YOU?" I asked Mocha.

"At the light by my place. I have to pee so bad, and the closer I get, the harder it is to hold it."

"OK, well, call me when you get settled." I hung the phone up once she agreed and went to start her bubble bath so that it would be hot. The bathtub caddy sat across it with her strawberries and grapes, two fruits that I knew she ate almost every day.

I heard the door swing open and her heels clicking down the hallway before she busted into the bathroom with her dress already above her hips.

"Pissy ass!" I laughed.

"Oh my God!" she shrieked and held herself.

"Sit yo' ass down before you piss on the floor!"

"Shut up." She breathed as she relieved herself. "I'ma cuss yo' ass out for being in my damn house in a minute."

I laughed and went to make myself comfortable in her bedroom. My dick was at attention just being close to her. After washing her hands, all I heard was, "Oouu grapes!" making me laugh some more.

"Now, how did you get in here?" Mocha moved around the room undressing with a mouth full of grapes.

"I paid Gary to let me in," I mentioned her doorman. "Now go soak and clean that pussy so I can climb up in it?" I said with a low growl.

"Who said you were getting some tonight?"

"You crazy as hell if you think you're about to have my dick in here throbbing all night. After three months, you're riding this dick!" I was serious as fuck, too.

"Yes, Daddy." She giggled and went to bathe.

After a long ass hour, she retreated from the bathroom in a towel, still munching on grapes and a glass of wine in her hand.

"This wine is good. Where'd you get it from?"

"It was something left over from my party. You know since it ended early, there was still a lot of alcohol left. I'll check to see about getting more though." I was eye fucking the shit out of her the entire time I explained.

The seduction in her eyes told me she missed this dick just as much as it missed her. She took another sip of wine and sat on the mantel that sat underneath her mounted TV. Turning to face me, she untied her robe and let it fall to the floor.

"Come here." I eyed her frame like it was my last meal. Mocha crawled up the bed, stopping right above my dick. She tugged at the drawstring of my shorts and took them completely off, having me lift like a bitch. "Sit on it."

Mocha shook her head no. "You always take care of me. Tonight is about you."

My shit was so hard that with any wrong move, I was afraid it was going to shatter. Mocha started with no hands, circling her tongue around the tip of my dick before giving it a slow, warm suck.

"Shit," I let out and dropped my head back onto the pillow. Wasn't no way in hell I would be able to watch her and not shoot a load down her throat before I wanted to. Mocha snaked her tongue down my shaft and deep-throated me until I was covered in her saliva. Her left hand gripped the base of my dick, twisting and stroking while her lips gave my tip extra attention. This was a Mocha I hadn't seen yet but could damn sure get used to.

Looking down, I shuttered like a bitch seeing Mocha please me with her ass in the air, arched perfectly like she couldn't wait for me to slide in. My nut started building with the mouth and twist combo my baby was delivering.

Suddenly, she loosened the grip and ran her tongue down the back of my dick, onto my balls, sucking them with just enough pressure to have my toes curl.

"Fuck!" I moaned. She licked and softly sucked my balls while still stroking my dick, occasionally going to show the tip some love. "Shit, I'm about to nut."

Mocha lifted back up and sucked my shit like her life depended on it. Her tongue work had my shit jerking.

"I'm cummin', Mo."

"Cum!" She moaned, never taking my dick out of her mouth. I shot three months' worth of my seed down her throat and she didn't spit a single kid out.

"Where the fuck did you learn that at?" I asked once I gathered myself. "I know you ain't suck the mistakes dick like that and he still cheated. Ain't no way."

"Shut up and let me know when you're ready for more." Mocha lifted and I could see how wet her pussy was from the front. I was going to take care of all that, but I was damn sure going to let her do her thing for the night. It was my turn in the morning.

"YO' ass always got a hoe bag," Mocha joked as I entered her front area, tying my tie.

"Hell yeah. You never know when you're going to need it. You should just let me leave some things here, therefore; I won't need it."

"You tried that. It's still a no!" She smirked from behind the counter as she prepared her coffee and lunch for the day.

"This is the most I've ever dealt with that word. You lucky I'm in like with your big forehead ass!"

"First, fuck you. Some of the best women come with a big forehead. Second, I know you're used to having your way, Mr. Tait, but we're going to play this a little differently." Mocha tossed me an apple.

A bang at the door made us both look in that direction. I went to open it and smirked at the person on the other side.

"Detective Drescher. What a pleasure seeing you here." I smiled.

"Nothing's pleasant about this visit, Mr. Tait. I would ask why you're here, but I have far more important matters. Where is Mrs. Sapora?" Jordyn Drescher looked like life was whooping her ass. If she was going at these cases like she did my father's, then she definitely looked like what she'd been through.

"Hey, Jordyn, right?" I heard Mocha's heels walk up behind me. "Is my sister, OK?"

"Your sister is fine. This is regarding your husband," Jordyn explained. I knew exactly why she was here, which was why it was a pleasure to see her. However, I was able to contain my smile.

"He's soon to be my ex-husband, so nothing that he's done is my concern. I'll listen, though." Mocha sighed and put all of her weight on her left leg.

"Mrs. Sapora, there was a house fire, and unfortunately, your husband didn't make it."

Mocha stood up straight. Her eyes darted around as she tried to process everything. She hugged herself and rubbed up and down her arms. "And my stepdaughter, Nina?"

"She's safe. She's with her mother."

"Nothing about being with her mother is safe. That bitch probably started the fire! I'm her legal guardian!" Mocha shouted.

"I understand your frustration, go down to the station and present your court order and they will escort you wherever you need to go to pick her up. You'll also need to identify what's left of Mr. Sapora's body within the next few days. It looked as if he tried to run out of the house but got caught in the fire enough to burn him alive." Hazel was clutching her chest as Jordyn spoke, and simply nodded. Jordyn gave Mocha a genuine smile, then shot me a look of death before returning to her vehicle.

"What in the entire fuck!" Mocha paced back and forth with one hand on her hip and the other on her forehead.

"Anything you need from me?" I asked.

"No. I just need time to process things. You can go on to work."

I approached my baby and embraced her, anyway. I caused this moment, and I would be the nigga to help her get through it.

TWENTY-NINE
NYX

If I've ever really wondered why Apollo got so much attention and love from Alonzo, I know why now. Not that I wanted my father's love this way, but letting us know our uncle was a snake and not pulling us in on how to handle it, was fucked up. I didn't appreciate getting news in the same sentence being instructed to cremate what was left of his splattered body. I didn't fuck with my father like that, but Zeus and I would never allow anyone else to.

They thought that I was supposed to sit there and break bread with so much bullshit on the table with our meal. Nah, I passed and let Zeus have that shit.

However, I needed to speak to Apollo about Zeus's ass, which was the reason he was exiting the elevator onto the floor of the morgue.

"This is the quickest I've seen your anger subside." Apollo embraced me.

"It hasn't. You're still fucked up for that shit."

"Come on, Nyx. Even if I would've told y'all, you wouldn't have wanted to get your hands dirty. Especially when it came to Dad. I know the relationship ain't the best, but..."

"And you don't think shit like this has anything to do with that? Maybe if we were waiting for him to arrive instead of being surprised that he was home, I wouldn't be so pissed. You were right for handling Ace, but we should've known something."

"You're right. My bad. Stop storming out like a lil girl though."

"Nigga, fuck you! Lemme show you why you're really here so you can get the hell on." I walked toward the drawers where we stored bodies. Giving the metal handle a hard pull, I let the body slide out and went to the head to pull the sheet back. Apollo took a step closer and let out a hard sigh.

"Zeus?" he asked, looking at the scorched corpse of our brother's girlfriend's husband.

"The cause of death is an explosion caused by chemicals. Zeus is the only logical answer." I closed the drawer back.

"We just told his ass to stop moving without us like this!" he had the nerve to say. I looked up at him and pressed my lips together to let him know his audacity was insane. "Aight, I get it. Damn. Pops wants me to cook dinner tomorrow night, can you bring your ass by and be civilized so we can talk to Zeus?"

"I'll think about it." That was the only answer I could give his ass at the moment. It was time for me to get home. I just wanna sit on the couch and watch a movie with Braiza. I cringed, thinking about how she was going to wanna get a pillow and blanket and get comfortable right on top of me.

Although the thought was cringy, I've started to just let her do her thing. As much as I hated to admit it, I was starting to like it. I couldn't understand how I looked forward to something I hated so much, so I was just letting shit flow. Anyway, I looked down at my watch and noticed that Karmen hadn't shown up. I FaceTimed her since I knew she wouldn't say shit on the phone.

"Where you at? You were supposed to be here twenty minutes ago?" I asked, looking into the phone at her surroundings. Karmen smirked and turned the camera around. "I'ma kill her ass!"

I ended the call and raced outside to the parking lot. I knocked Karmen's phone out of her hand.

"You're just gon stand here and record her?" Braiza's ass was circling my car, piercing my damn tires.

"Stab another one and I'ma break your fucking neck," I growled, standing over her. She was at eye level with the last tire, with the knife hovering over it.

"Oh, like you did Leon?" She stood and eyeballed me.

"Actually, I just choked the life out of his weird ass. But if that's the way you'd like to go, try me."

She dropped the knife.

"Good choice. Get in the car. Now your dumb ass gotta take me home. As a matter of fact, your house is closer, and your reasoning for slashing my tires better be a damn good one." I turned back to face Karmen. "Take your late ass inside."

I picked up the knife Braiza dropped and followed her to her car. By the time I got in the passenger seat, my phone was to my ear.

"Drive," I told her. She had the nerve to sit there, giving me the evil eye. I looked back at her ass while I went through the automated system to get roadside assistance. They took forever and I didn't have the patience to wait. Since Karmen found this shit so amusing, she could meet them outside when they arrived. If Braiza had sliced just one tire, I would've just put a spare on, but nah. She did the most, and I couldn't wait to hear why.

By the time I finally got a human on the phone and the incompetent motherfucker on the phone got my information and dispatched someone, we were turning onto Braiza's street. The entire ride, she kept a mug on her face.

Of course, she slammed the door once she got out and stormed inside. I shook my head and contemplated whether I wanted to go inside or if I needed to call one of my brothers to take me the fuck home. I'd never seen her this angry and all it would take was for her to say the wrong thing and I was going to act a fool.

The more I thought about it, I decided not to ruin the good streak we'd been on. Braiza was pissed about something, and I figured I should just figure the shit out instead of running.

When I got inside, she was inside the kitchen pacing back and forth. Looking past her, I saw she had cooked. I washed my hands and looked at the food inside the pots before engaging. Brai made turkey wings, Mac and cheese, and greens.

"Now, you wanna tell me why we're most likely on somebody's Instagram story right now?" I scooped a spoonful of greens onto my plate.

"No, do you wanna tell me why my doctor has me coming back in there tomorrow?" she asked, venom seeping from her voice.

"Why the fuck would I know that?"

"Any adult knows that when you go to the doctor and they call you to come in about your lab work, something's wrong." I sat at the table with my plate waiting for her to continue because she had me fucked up. It was obvious that she was accusing me of fucking around and giving her some shit. "Helloooo?"

"Braiza, watch your tone. I don't like the emphasis you put on adults. You keep playing this age card and you're the one throwing a tantrum about some dumb shit," I said, sliding the plate away from me. I was starting to lose my appetite.

"Dumb? You're fucking around and bringing me something is dumb?"

"Bitch, I barely like being around you! Why the fuck would I go fuck with somebody at the same time?" I pointed out. "Make that shit make sense, Braiza."

"Bitch? I'ma show you a bitch if I leave that fucking doctor's office with antibiotics."

"I ain't worried about nothing you're talking about! Can I eat in peace now? And yo' ass taking me back to my car in the morning." I pulled my plate back toward me as she stormed off. She locked her bedroom door hard as hell. I ain't give a fuck, all I'ma do is pick the motherfucker, because I'll be damned if I'm sleeping on anybody's couch.

AN AUDIOBOOK PLAYED in the background while I finished stitching up a body for a service this week. I was in my zone when I heard the bell upstairs ring, signaling that someone entered the mortuary. Normally, I would wait until I heard our employee, Ian, greet them and could go back to what I was doing. This time, the bell kept ringing. Groaning, I removed my gloves and sanitized my hands as quickly as I could to get upstairs.

I made a mental note to cuss Ian out for whatever he was doing that made me stop what I was doing to do his fucking job. That was until I saw who was standing in front of the desk ringing the bell.

"She insisted on doing business with you only." Ian proclaimed his innocence.

"Why are you here, Braiza?" I sighed.

She held up a bag of food. "Peace offering?"

"Oh, you must've taken your ass to the doctor. What was it, a yeast infection or something?"

Ian choked on nothing but air and dismissed himself.

"Really, Nyx? Is there somewhere we can go and talk?" I directed her to my office and took a seat.

"So?" I asked, waiting for my apology.

"I'm sorry. I overreacted. I forgot I had some questions about reproduction at my age and the doctor was concerned about my estrogen level. She only wanted to talk about my options for moving forward," Braiza explained.

"Oh yea, just an apology ain't gon cut it. I had to spend money on tires and shit. You're busting that muhfucka open tonight."

"Orrrr..." She stood and walked over to my seat. My dick jumped in my pants. "I can take care of you now to hold you over until tonight."

She was mid-bend when I heard a voice that made my dick go limp immediately.

"Is this what you do in my establishment?" Alonzo stood in the door with a squared-off stance and his hands folded in front of him. He looked like an older Apollo in a suit.

"Oh, I was just bringing him lunch," Braiza said. I could tell she was embarrassed.

"You don't have to explain yourself," I told Braiza. I looked Alonzo up and down. "Is there something I can help you with, father?"

"Oh, Jesus," Braiza whispered and covered her face, even more, embarrassed.

"We need to go over your uncle's memorial arrangements, and this woman needs to excuse herself." Alonzo's voice went an octave lower like it always did when he got upset.

"She ain't gotta do shit. Ace's body has been cremated for weeks now. What is there to plan?" I stood from my desk.

"No Nyx, it's fine. I'll see you tonight." Brai gathered her things and left. Flipping down in my seat, I did my best to remember that the man standing in front of me was my father.

"Now that we're alone, here's a list of the things your grandmother wants at the memorial." The piece of paper Alonzo was holding floated onto the desk. He sat in the extra chair in the room, crossed his legs, and clasped his hands together. "Do you think you can handle that?"

"Do I think I can handle it? Don't come in here like I ain't been the one keeping shit running smoothly in here and on the other side of the business for over seven years. You and Alonzo's mind is so enthralled by the thrill of killing that y'all forget that the intricate part of it all is mine." I snatched the paper up and did my best to focus on the words on the paper. Leaning forward, I tried to play with the lighting in the room to see the letters better.

"Yo' big word using ass can't see now?" Alonzo questioned. I looked up from the paper and almost let loose on his ass. I tossed the paper back at him and retreated to the basement.

"Do the shit yourself, muhfucka!" I heard him threatening me and calling me disrespectful, but he was lucky I ain't put my hands on his ass. These were the reasons I preferred to be and work alone. All his ass had to do was leave the paper with me and go. But nah, he had to sit and question me with shit like he always did.

I pulled out my phone to text Apollo. There was no way in hell I was sitting down to break bread with Alonzo. I let Ian know not to bother me again and retreated to the basement to finish up on the body I was prepping before all this shit.

THIRTY
APOLLO

"What kind of gruesome shit is this?" Gavin rushed to the body laid out in the dining room of the house we were called to. He took over for the victim's wife and continued applying pressure to the wound. I rushed to his side to assist but knew nothing would matter. Observing the wire used to dig into this man's throat, I knew it should have bled him out within minutes. His wife must've just saved his life.

"I came in and found him like this." The wife cried.

"We're going to do all we can for him," I assured her. It was the truth because I knew he would bleed out before we got to the hospital. I wanted to sound enthused when speaking to her, but seeing the bruises on her arm wouldn't let me fake it.

"Apollo, come hold this!" Gavin requested. Standing over the victim's head, I leaned down and grabbed the ripped shirt his wife used to attempt to stop the bleeding. I looked down at him and smiled, making his eyes widen in fear. This wasn't even one of my jobs, but I was going to finish it. While Gavin's back was turned, instead of pushing against the wound, I squeezed it. He gurgled, making Gavin turn to face us.

"We gotta hurry. He's losing too much blood," I said. "I'ma

replace the shirt with gulls, we're gonna keep packing it. Hurry up with that gurney!"

The more Gavin packed, the harder I discreetly tried to squeeze. We lifted him and placed him on the gurney. Gavin hooked him up to the machines and I squeezed again. The sirens went on and we sped off to the hospital.

"His pulse is weakening. Wesley, we're almost there. Hang on," Gavin coached. I kept quiet because Wesley was doing exactly what I needed him to do, die.

By the time we made it to the emergency room entrance, he'd coded. They began working on him and I made a mental note to check in at the end of my shift.

"Fuck!" Gavin shouted.

"What the hell is your problem?"

"There's no way he's going to make it. We've been losing people on too many calls lately. That man had a wife."

"A wife that he was clearly beating on. We can't save them all. Let's go." I hit his shoulder and we were off to another call. On the way to the ambulance, Nyx hit me to let me know he wouldn't be coming over for dinner. I swear it was like pulling teeth when it came to him and my father. I was over it.

I HIT the group chat once I clocked out.

Me: Where y'all at?

Zeus: Football field behind the high school. Nyx here. Nigga looked at the message and tossed his phone. *laughing emoji*

Me: Tell his ass don't be mad at me because he got caught tryna get his dick sucked in front of some corpses.

Nyx: 🖕

Zeus: Hold the fuck up! What? Tell me more cuz this nigga ain't talking.

Me: I'm on the way.

I rode through traffic with my top down. It was a warm spring evening and all I wanted was Hazel riding shotgun. Dismissing the thought, I turned up the music and sang *Chris Brown's Under the Influence*. Singing made me think back to Christmas and the first time I showcased my vocals for Hazel.

She'd been ducking the shit out of me since the spa day a few months ago, and although I knew why, I hated the shit.

Seeing her at the restaurant recently made me practice a restraint I hadn't faced in a very long time. Hazel's eyes locked in on mine and I knew she missed me just as much as I missed her. But I'd gone too far, and now I needed to allow her to be the one to come to me.

I felt bad about tonight's guest, but damn. Something was telling me that my father was getting a kick out of the secrets floating around, but I was ready to have my woman. All of her. I knew that couldn't happen until she got the answers she needed.

"She got you pulling up listening to that sad shit?" Zeus dapped me up, laughing at the fact that I had Lenny Williams's "'Cause I Love You" playing by the time I pulled up to the football field. He and Nyx were tossing the football back and forth with some kids. "Now what's this shit about him getting caught with his dick out?"

"Pops caught Trunch—" Before I could get it out, the football drilled into my side. "Don't get fucked up in front of these kids!"

As expected, Nyx ain't say shit. One of the kids ran over and grabbed the ball so they could continue to toss it.

"Braiza was about to top this nigga off at the mortuary and Pops walked in," I finished. Zeus laughed and I stopped him right in his tracks. "Oh, you ain't off the hook. Nyx got a surprise body at the morgue a couple of days ago."

"Fuck you mean, I ain't off the hook. Alonzo doesn't even scold me about the shit I do. I'm a grown ass man and you're damn sure not about to scold me," Zeus debated.

"We just talked about this shit the first time you burned his ass," I reminded him.

"And that was different. I did the shit so it would easily be ruled as an accident. I ain't need y'all to sign off on shit. Let's not forget the job you took that's probably ruining your life right now."

Zeus recalled the job I'd filled him and Nyx in on recently.

"If you say so, Zeus. So, neither of y'all coming to dinner?" I looked between my little brothers. They both shook their heads. "Y'all better be at this damn service Granny planning for Ace ass. I ain't going through that shit by myself. Y'all ain't gotta respond, I know you hear me."

I stepped off the field and headed home. All I knew was both were going to be front and center if I had to be.

———

"HOW MANY LIVES did you save today, son?" my father asked as I exited my car. He was already in my driveway waiting for me when I got off.

"Plenty," I answered. Alonzo didn't give a damn about my job, he only cared that I kept it to do outside jobs with precision.

Before I clocked out, I checked in with one of the emergency room nurses to see if Wesley had made it or not. He didn't, and I didn't feel bad about it.

"Great. Go get cleaned up, our guest will be here shortly."

I nodded and went to my bedroom. Something told me I needed to find a way to get my mother home soon because if she was here, she would be the one hosting this little dinner. The only person I wanted to come home to after work these days was Hazel. I showered and made my way to the kitchen. Shrimp scampi and salad were requested so I began to prepare everything while my father sat on my patio puffing at a cigar. The doorbell sounded and I stopped peeling my shrimp to go answer.

"Apollo."

"Leo." I shook the hand of Hazel's father. From what my father told me, they've been friends since I was a youngin. Before now, I knew of him, but I only remember meeting him one other time. "It's funny that you live right here. My daughter lives across the street, but I'm sure you knew that."

"I do." His sarcasm didn't go over my head. I'd take it though.

"Leooooo!" my father shouted from behind me. I stepped to the side and watched them greet one another. "I wish it was under different circumstances, but it's good to see you."

"Yeah, man. I couldn't believe it when I heard about Ace." Leo stated. That was my cue to walk away. Alonzo could play the role of a grieving brother and go down memory lane by himself. Fuck, Ace.

Leo joined my father out back and I could hear them laughing and catching up. I was in my zone cutting up the vegetables for the salad when someone started banging my damn door down. Setting the knife down, my chest tightened seeing a raging Hazel at my front door.

"Where is he?" She pushed past me. "Dad!"

She marched through the foyer to my kitchen. All I did was follow like a puppy, excited about her being this close to me again. Upset or not, a nigga would take it.

"Hazel, what are you doing here?" Leo asked stupidly.

"Did you think I wouldn't recognize your car? Tell me why you're here and why it's such a secret that you all know one another!" Hazel's soft brown cheeks were turning a flushing red.

"We can talk about this later, sweet pea." Leo stepped toward her, but she pulled back.

"I don't want to talk later."

I went back to busy myself because the hurt and confusion in her voice almost made me interfere. That was a mistake because now the anger was directed at me.

"Oh, you're just going to tend to your salad, huh?" Hazel's eyes squinted in disbelief. I didn't respond and the next thing I saw was the bowl of lettuce flying off the counter. "Do you hear me now?"

"Hazel, chill."

"Why? So someone can lie to me or divert my attention again?" Hazel stepped closer to me. I looked over at Leo. One may never believe it, but I had heartstrings, and the hurt coming from my baby's voice was tugging at them hard.

"Speak!" Hazel screamed and banged a hard fist into the counter, right into the knife I was using. "Aaarrgghh!"

Hazel gripped her hand, biting her bottom lip in pain.

"Let me see," I told her. Blood was running down her arm, and I needed to see how deep the cut was.

"Don't touch me." Hazel stormed out, leaving the front door open. I watched as she struggled to open her front door and knew that I should grab my medical kit.

"I'm going to check on my daughter," Leo announced.

"I got it. She may need stitches anyway. I'll try to calm her down."

THIRTY-ONE
HAZEL

As if shit wasn't bad enough, the audacity of my father to think that seeing his car parked in front of Apollo's place wouldn't catch my attention. I loved my father and my heart always seemed to skip a fucking beat around Apollo Tait, but I was being left in the dark about something. My mother's words to "let him love you" had been replaying in my head like a broken record since she'd spoken them, but the secrets along with the unexplained familiarity with Apollo made it feel impossible.

I struggled to get inside my place, but when I did, I dropped the keys to the floor and stepped over them. My hand was covered in blood, and the pain caused my fingertips to go numb, but my anger and adrenaline made it tolerable. I burned a hole in the kitchen floor, pacing while dialing Jordyn's number.

I recalled Apollo telling me that Jordyn and his father had a history, so maybe she could enlighten me on where my father fit into all of this. As soon as the phone started to ring, the pain kicked in, making me drop the phone onto the counter.

I hit the kitchen sink faucet and held my hand underneath,

rinsing the blood off. The cut looked too deep, though, and the blood kept gushing. Grabbing the closest kitchen towel to me, I applied pressure to the cut and watched the cloth soak up the blood.

My front door opened, and the sound of heavy footsteps made me tingle from my toes to the top of my head. I knew it was Apollo before he appeared. Still in his shorts and tank, he looked at me with those deep dark eyes and furry eyebrows as he walked closer to me.

"Let me see," he said, reaching out to grab my wrist. My knees trembled, feeling his touch for the first time in months.

"I'm fine," I whispered, trying not to look at him.

"You're not. You need stitches. Keep this here." He placed the towel back onto the cut and went to pull two bar stools over to where I was. Apollo got comfortable on the stool and waited for me to do so as well. He shook his head and chuckled at the stubbornness that I was fighting like hell to maintain.

Apollo cleaned the wound and began fighting through the red mess to stitch me up while singing "Something About Ya" by J. Howell. I looked at him with sadness. To say I'd fallen for Apollo was an understatement. As J. Howell said, he had my heart and won't let go.

"Tell me what's going on, Apollo," I whispered, choking up again. He looked up at me briefly.

"You'll have to ask your pops," he replied.

"I'm not talking about him," I informed him. My voice was shaky, thinking about the moment I was about to address. "In the spa, you realized I was trying to cover myself. You took the sheet and went right to every scar I had as if you knew they were there. How?"

The air was thick as he continued fixing me up.

"Apollo, please," I begged. "I feel so close to you, it's scary. For once in a long time, I didn't have to hide myself because you already knew me. I just don't understand how. My scars, how did you know they were there?"

"Because I killed the nigga that put them there," he confessed, still pulling the needle through my skin. How the fuck did he confess something like that, and make it seem loving.

"Wait, Quincy?"

He nodded without a care in the world.

"I got the call for the job, and—"

"Job?"

"Just listen, Hazel. I got the call, and your pictures around the apartment alone captivated me. It fucked me up to know that someone was violating something so beautiful. I could literally feel your energy through the smile in your photos. After the job, I got curious at work and looked up your name. I saw how bad he'd done you and kept an eye out on you."

"You stalked me?" I called it what it was.

"Nah, I wouldn't call it that until I saw the For Sale sign in the yard across the street and I didn't hesitate to put in a cash offer. Other than that, I would just check on you from a distance from time to time. I was glad to see you move out of that apartment and begin to glow again. Getting rid of Quincy was the right thing. I just didn't know when it would be the best for not only you but me as well."

Apollo looked up and our eyes connected. He finished the last stitch he cleaned around the wound. The sound we heard next made my heart drop.

Beep! Beep! Beep! The sound of someone hanging up on me reminded me I had dialed Jordyn's number.

"Who was on the phone, Hazel?" he asked. Apollo was still calm, but his tone affected me differently this time. It was cold and alarming.

"I, umm," I stuttered. "I forgot that I'd dialed Jordyn when I came inside."

Apollo stood abruptly, knocking the stool over. I jumped to my feet.

"Why'd you call a fucking cop?"

"She's also my friend, Apollo. I needed someone to talk to. This shit has been driving me insane."

"What shit?"

"Being without you," I blurted honestly.

"Yet, you set me up." He walked toward me, backing me into a wall.

"Not intentionally, Apollo. I swear."

Apollo swung and punched the wall near my head, and I immediately broke down. This man had just triggered me so much and he was still the only one I wanted to calm my fears. I watched him turn away from me and rush out into the night.

I held onto the corner of the counter and did my best to not completely lose it. For over a year, my mind had been in a frenzy worrying about how Quincy died. I should be furious about finding out the man that set out to capture my heart had been the one to do so. However, I was relieved. My tears reflected so much at the moment.

My front door opened again. This time I watched my father come inside and wrap me into his arms like I was ten years old again. No words were needed as he held me. My father's love for Cha, my mother, and me was always so strong, which is why I was taken aback by the secrets. Then it hit me. He didn't even ask what I was upset about.

I pulled away from him and searched his eyes. "You knew."

He nodded and let me go. "I hired him, Hazel."

"Why?"

"Hazel, I've raised you and your sister to be strong black women. So, when I thought I saw a bruise you attempted to cover up with makeup, I didn't say anything because I was sure. A few months went by, and I noticed that you'd become distant. I came by your place about a week before Quincy died, do you recall?"

"Yes," I answered.

"Well, your old man was snooping and found medical bills that confirmed my suspicion. I also found powder lead hidden under your cabinet," he said.

"Daddy, I—"

"I know exactly what you were doing, and it made me proud to know you were handling it yourself. But I'm always here to take the burden from you. That's where Apollo came in. Now I didn't know his crazy ass was going to stalk you, but I knew he would get the job done."

Looking at my father was like looking at an entirely different person and I thought back to when Cha mentioned his acting weird when she mentioned Pierre. Little did my father know, Zeus was more impulsive than Apollo. Apollo asked me not to say anything to Cha, but he mentioned the visit Zeus paid Pierre after Cha's miscarriage, so I'm sure he was protecting her.

I heard everything he said, and I had one more honest question. I was in a battle with my head and heart and was unsure of which one to follow. "Can I trust him?"

"With your life, Baby Girl," he answered confidently. "Alonzo and I grew up together, he's like a brother to me. We parted ways because I saw the life he and Ace lived, and it was either stay involved or lose your mother. I wasn't letting Chai's ass go anywhere so I severed ties. You and Apollo were about five the last time you saw one another, but I know Alonzo and Venus raised some crazy, yet good boys."

"Venus? The same Venus that I met?" I questioned, and he even let out a chuckle.

"She's a lot. Always has been. She has good intentions behind her boys, though. You're shocked about Venus, but don't let your mother fool you. She ain't always been that southern belle. But she raised beautiful young ladies. And although Venus has the weirdest way of showing her love, especially for her boys, she'll warm up to you."

"We'll see. I have a lot to process, Daddy. I'll call you tomorrow if you don't mind." I needed to be alone. My dad kissed my forehead and left me to my thoughts.

I found my phone and quickly went to dial Jordyn's number. I needed to know what she heard.

"You've reached Detective Jordyn Drescher. I'm not able to answer the phone." I hung up and called back just to get the voicemail again. I prayed Apollo left this alone. Jordyn's warning now made sense and I hoped Apollo had enough sense to not kill a cop.

THIRTY-TWO
MOCHA

It had been forty-eight hours since Detective Drescher delivered the news of my husband being gone and I'd cut myself off from the world completely. Of course, Zeus broke into my house again when I didn't answer my phone.

"I know damn well you ain't in here pouting about the dead ass mistake!" he shouted from the end of my bed. I was curled up, binging a series I found on Netflix. It took almost two hours to convince him I was just processing everything. *"Oh OK. You got less than twenty-four hours to get your ass up and out of that bed. Your daughter and I need you."*

My heart skipped a beat hearing him include Nina in things moving forward. Zeus knew I filed for custody, and for him to want to be involved with a second thought moved me more than he knew.

Surprisingly, I hadn't shed a single tear over Pierre. There was a relief of not having to deal with what I knew now to be a form of abuse and his cheating. It only stunned me because of Nina. Her father had his flaws, but he was a superhero in her eyes and no matter what she witnessed, she'd never treat him any differently. I knew that this would hit her hard, and I planned to be there every step of the way.

A guard escort led me down to the morgue and who I saw standing over a body shocked me.

"Well, if it isn't my future sister-in-law." Nyx flashed a cheesy smile. The guard left, letting the metal doors swing. I shivered in the cold, dark room. The chill made me reach up and rub my arms. This seemed like the perfect atmosphere for Nyx Tait.

"Oh, now I'm your sister-in-law?" I replied.

"Well, according to a body that recently turned up on my table, you're now a single woman, Chocolate."

"It's Mocha, Jackass! You know what, can I see my husband so I can get out of here?" Nyx aggravated my soul.

He walked over to a drawer and pulled at the handle. For the first time since getting the news, a lump formed in my throat. Nyx pulled back the sheet, revealing his scorched body.

"What happened? I know they said there was a fire, but from what?"

"Chemical burns."

"Chemical burns? What the hell would Pierre be doing with chemicals that could start a fire?" I wondered aloud.

"Fucking with you," he mumbled.

"Excuse me?"

"Nothing. I got some paperwork for you to sign, and you can be on your way." Nyx pulled the sheet back over Pierre's body and slid him back into the dark hole. He sat at a desk and opened a file, holding it close to a light bar that hovered over the desk. He seemed frustrated after about two minutes and slammed the file closed.

"Something wrong?" I asked.

"I printed the wrong paperwork. Give me a second," Nyx responded. Again, I watched as he took his time navigating through the database, maximizing and minimizing the screen multiple times. Then, it hit me. I wasn't an expert, but I made sure to educate myself once my baby girl was diagnosed.

Knowing to let him finish since he was already doing things his way, I allowed my patience to settle in and waited.

"Here it is." I looked up and he was printing out the correct paperwork. I walked over and leaned over his shoulder, grabbing the mouse. "What are you doing?" his grumpy ass asked.

I remained silent as I pulled up computer software. "I may be overstepping, but I think this will help. It has Text-to-Speech, and if you don't want to use that, it also offers different fonts to make things easier."

"You're definitely overstepping."

"It's fine, brother-in-law. You'll thank me later. It helps to open up to the ones closest to you." I squeezed his shoulders and laughed at the sound of him groaning. "I'll take my paperwork now, Ms. Tait."

Nyx looked at me like the little sister that tapped danced on his last nerve.

"That's payback for calling me Chocolate," I said. I knew it was important to let no hints of judgment seep into the space. Even as an adult, I knew Nyx was waiting for it and it wasn't going to happen. He was just like everyone else; he just needed an extra boost to understand things. I instilled that in Nina and wouldn't dare let anyone with similarities feel any different.

"Here man." He handed the papers to me, and I signed them. "Are you using the family mortuary?"

"You know damn well Zeus ain't having that. Plus, I would have to go to war with Pierre's mother to handle the arrangements, and nothing in me is equipped to deal with that woman right now. That'll be the next person you'll hear from as far as the next steps. I'll leave you to it, though. Can you direct me back to the elevator?" I was rubbing my arms again, waiting for Nyx to get up.

"You don't remember how you got down here?"

"Why the fuck are you so damn mean?" I shouted. Nyx and I were back to our normalcy just that fast, hopefully, it came with a newfound respect.

He pushed the double doors open and looked down the hall.

"Once you get to the end, make a right and you'll see the elevator ahead of you."

"Was that so hard?"

"Bye."

Once I was out of the basement, notifications began to come through. One was from my lawyer asking me to stop by. My next stop was supposed to be Penelope's to get Nina, but Angela made things sound urgent.

Entering Angela's office, she wore a smile a mile long.

"Well, that smile is a good sign." I stepped close to her desk, and we shook hands. "Your voicemail had me concerned."

"You shouldn't be concerned at all, Mrs. Sapora. Or should I say, Ms. Cox?" Angela leaned over and set an envelope in front of me. "I guess Mr. Sapora got tired of playing hardball."

Inside the envelope was a signed copy of my original divorce proposal dated the day before he was killed.

"I don't know if you're aware, but Pierre died two days ago. How did you get these?"

Angela's smile fell, expressing that she was just as shocked as I was. "Rio said that a gentleman dropped them off yesterday. They're signed and dated three days ago."

"That's not Rio up front." I pointed out that her normal secretary wasn't present today.

"I know, Shelly is a temp. Rio called off today. I'm sorry for your loss, Mocha. I know things were bad between you and Pierre but all in all, it's still a loss." Angela reached over the desk and grabbed my hand. "Although there is no need for the divorce, the upside is that your custody papers were signed and delivered as well. My counterpart is filing them as we speak."

I was ecstatic about that. Nina deserved to be with a family that loved and cared for her. Neither Penelope nor Ivory could provide her with that. She would stick out like a sore thumb with us, but I know that my family would welcome her with open arms.

"Yes, that is the bright side to everything. Thank you so much for everything, Angela. I'll ensure that you still get paid." I smiled, shook her hand again, and rushed back to my car. *What the hell is going on?* I put my car into park and headed toward Penelope's address, calling Zeus on the way.

"Congratulations are in order. Celebratory dinner tonight, just the three of us?" I could hear Zeus's smile through the phone. I hadn't told him anything, so everything immediately made sense.

"A chemical explosion," I scoffed. "I should've known."

"Yeah, you should've. I didn't kill his ass the first time at your request but the last time I saw a handprint on your arm was enough to send his ass to glory. He must've tried to run if they even had you come to identify his remains. I had enough explosives in that muhfucka to burn his ass to ashes. So, seafood or soul food?"

"I'm really in love with a complete psychopath." I shook my head. "I'll see what Nina wants and if she's in a state to meet you yet. How's work?"

"Ms. Daniels had the nerve to come sit and talk to me during lunch. Talking about her and Nyx are getting serious, and she wants us to at least be professional and cordial." His amusement from earlier was now irritation.

"Well, that's nice of her. What was your response?"

"I asked her ass if she was being respectful when she was about to suck Nyx's dick while he was working."

"Zeus!" I shrieked. None of his damn brothers knew what to say out of their mouths and I don't know why this shit was still shocking.

"What? It was good seeing her embarrassed. But nah, I'm cool with being cool as long as she separates personal from professional. Don't nobody got time for her coming in here pissed at Nyx and taking it out on me or these kids," he explained.

"I understand. She may be a nice woman. Who knows, maybe we can go on a double date or something."

"Yeah, I'll pass."

Zeus acted tough, but ultimately, I would get my way. Just as he got his way with me. We talked for a few minutes until I pulled up at Penelope's. I placed an AirPod in and got out to knock on the door.

"What's taking her so long?" I said out loud. "I should have done what Jordyn suggested and had the police escort me."

"And I told you we don't do twelve 'round these parts. Either she hands her over or I can pay her a visit." If you could hear a shrug through the phone, it would be loud as hell fucking with Zeus right now.

"Wait, I hear the locks."

Penelope opened the door looking every bit of strung out. Her hair was all over her head and what looked like old makeup was caked up on her face. The mascara was running, and it looked as if her skin was cracking. "What are you doing here?"

"Mocha!" Nina attempted to run past Penelope, but she blocked her. Seeing how frightened Nina was didn't call for any words. I immediately hit Penelope in her throat. Her stumbling back holding her throat gave Nina the space to push past her and cling to my legs.

"What's that noise? Mocha, you choked the bitch? What just happened?" Zeus shot off questions in my ear.

"Nah, I hit her ass in her throat." I stood there waiting to strike again but the scary bitch slammed the door.

"Damn, my dick just got hard envisioning it."

I guided Nina to the car and the black and blue bruises that peeked over the rim of the back of her shirt made my heart sink.

"Yeah, well, get ready to nut on yourself then. Whatever the fuck you used to burn the hand Pierre choked me with, I'ma need some of that."

"Say less. Take lil mama home."

THIRTY-THREE
APOLLO

"Check the mail," my father told me over the phone. All that meant was there was a job waiting for me. Checked the burner phone and there was a name and an address texted to me. "This needs to be opened immediately."

"I'm on it."

We ended the call, and I went back to work. Later that night, I went to the address and scoped out the building, its security, and its traffic. Of course, I needed to know my target's schedule as well. After a couple of days, I memorized his routine and that he didn't live alone. I had approximately an hour gap between the time he got home and when his woman arrived. Once I felt everything was mapped out perfectly, I returned to do the job.

I picked the lock with ease, entered the dark apartment, and heard the shower running. Looking around with my flashlight, I got a closer look at the woman he lived with. She was beautiful, and I could feel her strong presence through the picture. Her smile was radiant, and I knew this nigga didn't deserve her. If he did, I wouldn't have been hired to get rid of him.

The shower cut off and I pulled the syringe out of my coat pocket.

Quincy walked out of the room with a towel wrapped around his waist. He got comfortable on the couch and flipped through the tv channels. The light of the TV allowed him to finally notice me in the dark corner.

Quincy jumped up from the couch and tried to rush me. It took seconds to block his punch and have him pinned on the floor face down. Remembering that he was right-handed and would most likely inject himself in the left arm, I bent his right arm back and pinned it against his back with my knee. He put up a fight, but I was finally able to keep his left arm straight and still enough to smoothly inject him with the Fentanyl.

When I was sure that there was no sign of life, I ensured nothing looked out of place and made my exit. On the way to the stairwell, the elevator dinged, and someone stepped out. I dipped into a utility closet and waited for them to pass. I heard a door being unlocked and cracked the door. There she was. As she unlocked the door, I noticed a hospital band from Stanton Memorial. She entered the apartment, and I heard her scream.

Rushing out of the closet, I was hit in the face with her scent. It was so intoxicating. Eau de Parfum by Fenty. If I wasn't trying to get the fuck away from a job, I could stand there and sniff it all night. I made it to the stairwell and out the back of the building.

PRESENT DAY

From that night on, all I could think about was Hazel's smile and scent. Looking at her file at the hospital only made me want to hold her in my arms even more. I checked in on her from a distance about every other month as she seemingly began to heal from that chapter in her life. Each time I saw her over that year, her smile moved further toward her ears, and just like before, it was contagious. She finally moved out of the apartment she resided in with Quincy and into the house across from the one I recently purchased.

Approaching her in the snowstorm was the first time I'd gotten close to Hazel and her energy was just as radiant as I imagined. Now, here we are.

For the last twenty-four hours, I'd been tailing Detective Drescher. What could've been a pivotal or detrimental moment in Hazel and I's relationship took a hard turn toward detrimental the moment I heard her phone beep. I didn't want to believe that Hazel would set me up and I would figure that shit out later. Getting rid of the source was my main priority. Jordyn went back and forth to the precinct and on calls a few times since she left her apartment earlier and now that it was after business hours, she was going right where I predicted.

She jogged up the courthouse steps and looked around. I ducked in the seat of the stolen vehicle I was in and waited until she was let inside the building. I pulled my black hoodie and gloves on, and the fake detailed facial features out before walking around the side of the building to the loading dock. A guard was just putting out a cigarette with his foot as I bent the corner, and I quickly followed him back inside.

He must have felt my presence behind him because he started to turn around. Swiftly, I wrapped my arms around his neck, squeezing until he lost consciousness. He wasn't dead, and I knew I was on a time limit before he woke up. I removed his weapon from its holster and tucked it into my waistband. Then I took his extra magazines and stuffed them in my pocket.

Climbing the stairs two by two, I ran to the fifth floor, hoping that I caught Jordyn in the act. I approached DA Danson's office and caught them in a heated conversation.

"Not this shit again!" Danson shouted. "Were you not present when Apollo Tait locked me in a closet and threatened your life?"

"Of course, I was!" Jordyn shouted back. "But I refuse to think that Ace Tait killed himself and I heard it with my own ears that he killed Quincy Norwood!"

"Evidence! Do you have any of that?" Danson asked.

"No, but I can get it. I just need to know that you're backing me." Jordyn sounded desperate.

"If Tait did murder Ace, you wanna end up like him? Come on, Drescher. You have to make this make sense to me."

I'd heard enough. A gun wasn't my choice of weapon, but with it being two against one and unplanned, I didn't have much of a choice. I used the tip of the guard's gun to push the door open.

"Yes, Detective Drescher, make it make sense." I made my presence known. They were both startled at the sound of my voice. Jordyn squinted, trying to confirm her recognition through my altered facial features. Then, as always, Jordyn tried to harden up.

"The devil always appears when mentioned," she spat in disgust.

"These are her theories, not mine." Danson attempted to cover his ass. I hated a bitch ass nigga, tryna cover their ass after doing some fuck shit. I sent a bullet through his head first, sitting his ass back down in the chair he'd just stood from.

"Justtt the two of ussss," I sang, smirking and looking at Jordyn. Her arm flinched. "Don't go for your weapon so soon. I wanted this to be a little fun."

"You're sick!"

"Maybe a little." I shrugged. "But nah, I did want to have a little fun. However, there's a guard downstairs that will gain consciousness any minute now."

I lifted my weapon and pulled the trigger. I had to respect the fact that she went out harder than the rest of these niggas. Leaving two bodies in a federal building and one being a cop will have my pops on my ass. I couldn't leave potential threats walking freely, though. I went out the same way I came in, and just as I thought, the guard was gone. This place would be swarming with red and blue lights shortly.

HOW WAS SHE THIS RESILIENT? I asked myself as I observed Hazel serve her community with a smile on her face. The news had been covering Drescher and Danson's murders for the last twelve hours and I knew she saw it all. That and the news of her father hiring me to kill her ex would've had the average person cowering away from facing life and the people in it.

But just as she picked herself up after grieving Quincy and healing from his abuse, she was walking around with her chest out. It was part of the reason I loved this woman. That love would always be there, but the answers I got to the questions I had would determine if I could continue to show it.

"Can I talk to you?" I interrupted Hazel's flow of handing out food.

"Can it wait? I need to get through this so that I won't be late for work."

Hazel jumped back in and did her thing. Not wanting to stand around being helpless, I decided to help. Hazel's eyes beamed when she looked over at me, making me feel like I already had the answers to my questions. However, I couldn't allow myself to be blinded. The family business had to continue and although I wouldn't inform Hazel of my jobs, she now knew that they existed. She needed to be trusted with that information.

We finished up and she removed her apron and started cleaning up to leave for work.

"Haze."

"Apollo, I promise I'm not running from you. But I have an early meeting and I have to fight traffic to get across town," she said, moving around to gather her things. "Can we meet up later?"

I nodded and her lil ass lifted with her lips pursed. I kissed her soft lips and watched her walk away from me. I was running late for work myself, but I thought of ways to fit Hazel into my schedule.

"ARE YOU LEAVING US, APOLLO?" Gavin yelled over his shoulder. I parked the ambulance on the corner of the block Hazel worked on, and the crew and I ordered from this soul food place across the street.

"Yea, for a second. My radio is on though. If we don't get a call, I'll meet y'all back here in forty-five minutes."

I took the bags and went to the floor Hazel's firm was on. As always, the place was busy as fuck with people fast walking in every direction and phones blaring. The first bag was for Mocha. The relationship she had with her sister only meant she was feeling a way about me for the past few months as well.

"Peace offering?" I knocked on her door and held the bag up.

"Oohh, is that Fred's?" She jumped up and grabbed the bag.

"Yep, seafood free."

"Shut up." She snatched the bag and looked inside. "And the only peace offering we need is you making things right with my sister. If she's happy, then we're fine."

"Understood," I agreed and headed toward Hazel's office. Per usual, she was on the phone.

"Kira let me call you back. My man brought me Fred's." She hung the phone up and snatched the bag, just like Mocha.

"Your man, huh?" I chuckled and closed her office door. "That's not your conscience speaking, is it?"

"I didn't do anything wrong, Apollo." She set the bag on her desk and faced me with her arms folded. "I called a friend and forgot that she was on the phone because my hand was throbbing with pain. The situation looks fucked up, but it isn't what it seems. It doesn't matter now though, does it?"

Hazel cocked her head to the side, and I knew she was referring to Jordyn's execution as they were calling it on the news.

"Does that bother you?" I asked.

"A little." Hazel walked toward me. I don't even think she meant to be seductive with it but my dick hardened. "But not enough to let you walk away from me again. I can't go through that kind of hurt and confusion again."

I couldn't contain myself any longer. I gripped the back of her neck and kissed her. I missed her lips, her taste, and her scent. Hazel surprised me when she went for my belt buckle. I led her over to the couch, carefully taking my radio off in case of a call and letting my pants fall around my ankles. Laying Hazel down on the couch, I took in how the sun hit her skin, and how it allowed me to drown in the deepness of her brown eyes.

Hazel pulled at my shirt, bringing me down to kiss her again. I lifted her skirt, pulling the leg on the outside of the couch, out of her thong. I slid into her opening, and it still felt like heaven. I was deep inside her walls and looked down at her.

"How do I really know you're OK about Quincy?" I had to ask.

"Because I tried to kill the bastard myself. Now, fuck me."

My dick jerked at her confession, and I tried to carve out her lining. Holding her free leg in the cuff of my arm, I gripped her ass from underneath and gave her long strokes, grinding against her love button every time.

"I love you, Apollo." She gasped. I guess that button really did work.

"I love you, too, Fat Girl." The sound of her juices and our sloppy kisses filled the air. "Cum for me, baby."

I wouldn't be able to stay in there too much longer, especially not with her contracting her pussy around my shit.

"Cum with me."

Shit, she ain't have to tell me twice, and I wasn't pulling out. She was stuck with a Tait, and if I had my way, she was going to birth one too. Our orgasms came almost simultaneously, and we laid there breathing heavily.

"Move, I gotta get up. I can't believe you came in me." She pushed against my chest.

"Nah, let that shit marinate." I smiled.

"Apollo!"

"My name always sounds good, rolling off your lips. Round two?" I was joking but was also serious.

"No, we both have to get back to work." She pushed at my chest again. This time I got up. Hazel pulled some wipes out of the drawer of her desk and tossed them to me. We cleaned up a little and got dressed.

"I'll be back." Hazel walked out of her office looking around all suspicious and shit. I sat and opened my container of food. I had about fifteen minutes left to get something on my stomach.

"I guess we're all at peace now, huh?" Mocha's ass was standing in the doorway with a smirk on her face.

"Yup," I confirmed.

"Nasty asses!"

THIRTY-FOUR
BRAIZA

I should've been aggravated at my man throwing his feet up on my desk and all over my files, instead, I admired how handsome he was. Nyx wore a light blue button-up and some navy blue slacks. His locs were freshly twisted and those eyebrows were thick and wild.

Since Valentine's Day, I hadn't completely broken his wall down, but I got enough bricks removed for me to see that Nyx was who I wanted. I was also assured that this is what he wanted too. He was making himself comfortable in my office, which only meant he had something on his mind.

"What is it?" I asked.

"Huh?" He pretended not to know what I was talking about.

"Anytime you come in here and make yourself at home, you have something to get off your chest."

"You don't know me," he debated with a sexy smile.

"I do. And although I enjoy every moment of your company, I have things to do. What is it?" I pressed.

"She ain't got shit to do!" Randi shouted from the front of the office.

"Mind your business!" I shouted back. Randi didn't respond

immediately, but I heard the keys that he kept attached to his belt loop coming our way.

"You must be Nyx." Randi extended his hand and Nyx slapped it instead of shaking it. "Yea, you're right. His ass is mean."

Nyx looked my way, and I dropped my head, rubbing my neck.

"You have been in here talking about me?" Nyx asked.

"Huh?" I responded.

"Yea, she's been talking about you. And obviously, most of it is true. Has she been riding that dick like I told her to?" Randi's ass always did too much.

"Randi! Back to work!" I shouted. He sashayed out of the office and Nyx's eyes were still on me.

"We're going to talk about that later," he said. "But I wanted to ask you to come to my Uncle Ace's memorial with me. It's about to be a full-blown production with all the theatrics about to take place and I need someone to keep me from losing it."

"I'm happy to come and support you. But you can't lean on your brothers?" I questioned.

"Them niggas will be a part of the theatrics. Apollo acting like he gives a fuck, and Zeus will act a fool over the fake shit before I will."

"And you're OK with me being so close to your family at such a time?" I wondered. Nyx nodded. "OK."

"I've been thinking since you brought up the reproduction shit. I realized that you never talk about your family. What's up with them?" he inquired.

"The only family that I have just walked his crazy ass out of here. I grew up in the system and Randi is the closest thing to family I have. Which is why I chose this career. It's a struggle with these badass kids, but I want these kids to feel like they have someone even when they don't have it at home," I expressed.

"You sound like Zeus." He smirked in admiration a little.

"Yeah, we bump heads because of his tactics but I admire the relationships he builds with these students."

"He aight when he wanna be." He talked about his brother.

"You mentioned that you've been thinking about the baby conversation. Did you ever want kids?" I asked.

"Nah, not really. Never thought about falling in love either, so I guess one lil jit wouldn't hurt."

Nyx had my heart beating a million miles a minute. Just a few months ago, this man wouldn't even touch me intimately. Hearing him speak of a future together had me holding back tears. Randi knocking on the door was the lifeline I needed to not cry in this man's face.

"Yes?" I called out, giving him the OK to enter.

"Trevor and Cameron's parents are here to meet about yesterday's fight," he announced.

"I'll be right out." I turned my attention back to Nyx. "Can we talk more about this later?"

"I don't know. It's shit like this that has me second-guessing shit. I'm the parent that will fuck shit up behind my jit. I'm not sure the world wants that." He let his feet hit the ground and stood. "I'll hit you up later."

I watched him leave and was disappointed that I didn't get a hug. I know his breaking out of his comfort zone was going to be a work in progress, but I'd yet to know what his lips felt like. Therefore, I always looked forward to the physical moments I do rarely get. Shaking it off, I went back to handling business.

"GIRL, don't slow creep in here. Join the team. You're Braiza, right?" a beautiful woman with soft brown skin asked. I nodded, trying to place where I'd seen her before. "I'm Mocha. Zeus's woman. Come on."

She grabbed my arm and sat me in a row of seats beside a woman that looked just like her.

"This is Hazel. She's with Apollo. Seems like they all dragged us in here. It's been a shit show already."

I shook Hazel's hand and looked around for Nyx. He was running the show, so he had to leave a few hours earlier than me. We spotted one another at the same time. He was standing over by a projector and motioned for me to come over.

"Hey," I greeted sweetly. Fear of rejection made me not want to reach out to embrace him. Thankfully, he slid his hand around my waist and pulled me close. I held onto him like it would be the last time. "You gon be OK over there with the women?"

"Yea, they seem nice," I replied, looking back over at Mocha and Hazel.

"They are. Mocha's mouth gets out of hand but she's growing on me." I saw something in him brighten up when he spoke of Mocha. Not in an attracted; I should be worried kind of way, though.

"She must match your smart-ass mouth then," I joked.

"Whatever. Let me finish making sure these things are working so we can get this over with," he said. I turned to go back to my seat and a loud scream made me jump out of my skin. "See. This is the shit I was talking about."

Nyx groaned and his face crumbled into a mug. The man he called his father at our improper run-in, walked in with an older lady holding onto him.

"Not my booyyy!" she yelled. Then sobbed loudly. I hurried to sit back down. Mocha and Hazel wore the same looks as I did. They must have known their men were also on the verge of losing their shit.

The service was filled with Nyx's grandmother yelling without letting anyone say anything. No one could get through their acknowledgments, nor could the pastor get through the eulogy. Nyx even cut the slide show short. His father looked back at him, and I palmed my head when Nyx shot him the finger.

"Let's wrap this up!" Nyx yelled. This man walked up to the table where an urn was sitting and grabbed it. His ass grabbed the top of the urn and the bottom fell to the floor, spilling the ashes everywhere.

Mocha, Hazel, and I gasped with our hands over our mouths.

"What have you done?" His grandmother fell to her knees, yelling.

"Hold on, I can fix it!" Nyx held up a church finger, walked to the back, and went inside a door. He returned with a vacuum cleaner and hit the power button with his foot. Everyone sat in shock as the loud machine picked up the ashes.

He disappeared with the vacuum and came back holding the clear suction container. He grabbed the picture that sat on the stand and handed both the container and picture to his grandmother and walked out.

We all continued to sit there, silent. I was slightly embarrassed. Apollo and Zeus sat front row laughing their asses off while their grandmother told their father to get Nyx. Suddenly, the lights went off except for the ones in the back of the room.

"Wrap it up!" Nyx yelled again, his voice in the distance.

"Y'all heard the man." Zeus laughed and came and held his hand out for Mocha.

"That is not funny!" Mocha shook her head and took her man's hand.

"What's up, Ms. Daniels?" Zeus spoke.

"Braiza will do just fine. Hi, Zeus. Your brother should be ashamed of himself, and you should be too for laughing," I replied.

"Girl, welcome to Death Row." Hazel slid past me and went to Apollo. Pulling out my phone, I texted Nyx to see where he was. He told me he was out front, so I started that way. It had begun to drizzle, and Nyx was hitting a blunt under the tree

"What was that about?" I asked. "And do you have to smoke that thing?"

"If you want me to attempt to go to the repast, yeah, I need to smoke." He looked down at me.

"I thought the point of me being here was for you not to act like that?" I reminded him.

"Me too. It ain't work."

"Obviously," I scoffed. "We can ride together to the repast, and you can just bring me back to my car afterward."

He nodded, and although I hated the smell of the blunt, I stood there beside him. Nyx took his jacket off and put it around my shoulders, following up with his arm. He pulled me closer, and I felt his lips on my forehead. My entire body shuttered, and my eyes closed slowly, letting the silent tears fall.

"Wipe your eyes, man. I ain't bring you here for that soft shit," Nyx spoke, before inhaling the last of his blunt. He tossed it and grabbed my hand and walked toward his truck. "Let's go."

My heart was so full at what was supposed to be a sad time for his family. One that I was learning wasn't your typical family. Regardless, I'd bask in this moment.

THIRTY-FIVE
ZEUS

"Now you know Nyx was wrong as hell!" Mocha looked over at me as we walked into the repast. I hadn't been able to stop laughing. I'm talking stomach was hurting and tears rolled down my face laughing.

"Nah, Granny wrong as fuck for waiting all this time to have this memorial for her rat ass son and still act a fool. And Alonzo is even more wrong for making us sit through this shit!" I rebutted.

"How the hell are you a teacher, making up words and shit?"

"I can do that." I chuckled. "Hazel, funny as shit, welcoming *Braiza* to Death Row. That's what y'all think about us? I'm telling both of 'em."

"Yep. We've learned the hard way that when you're stuck loving a Tait, you're stuck loving a Tait," she explained.

"As long as y'all know." I gripped the back of her neck and kissed her before we went to take our seats with my brothers and their women. Before we sat down, Mocha took me to the end of the table where an older woman was sitting and talking to an older man. She was pretty as fuck and looked just like Mocha and Hazel.

"Ma, Dad, this is Zeus," she introduced me.

"We know exactly who this is," her father replied. "Take care of my daughter, young man. Y'all aren't the only ones in the business."

I'd heard of the old timer through Apollo, so I knew that he knew of us. His warning was loud and clear, but not loud enough for me to give a fuck though. I didn't care who he was. Respect is returned when given.

"She's in good hands. Keep the threats to yaself," I responded and stood with my shoulders squared,

The man chuckled. "Just like your damn father. I can respect it."

I nodded and Mocha and I took our seats.

"Did you check on Nina?" I asked.

"Yea. She and Majiq were coloring about an hour ago."

"I can't wait to meet her," I said.

"You think it's time?" Mocha inquired. "I mean, I've only had her for a week."

"I've always given you your space to do what you need to, but I'm going to be around. I don't see why we should prolong it," I expressed.

"Can I think about it?"

"Of course. But I'm still meeting her today."

"Zeusss!" Mocha whined. "That's not letting me think about it."

"You can think about it all you want. The only conclusion you need to come up with is how to explain to Baby Girl that this." I waved around the room. "Will also be a part of her new family."

Mocha wanted to protest and the next voice I heard made her body clinch, which didn't help me at all at the moment.

"Sorry, I'm late. My flight was delayed." My mother strutted into the room. Mocha, Hazel, and even their mother groaned. I shook my head, knowing that this had the potential to go from bad to worse. Still, I got up to greet my mother.

"Hey, Ma."

"Hey, son. I see you're still playing mistress." She looked down at Mocha.

"Hello, Venus." Mocha's mother stood. "You got something you need to get off your chest regarding my daughter and her relationship?"

"Which one?" Venus spat back, and I knew I needed to intervene.

"There is only one! Ma, you gotta chill." I looked back at Mrs. Cox and let her know I had it. "We've talked about this already. You're going to respect my woman. Her circumstances ain't ya business. Just respect that your son is happy and has his shit handled."

"Talk to your mother like that again and I'ma handle yo' ass!" Alonzo barked from across the room. My assumption was Apollo kept everyone in the dark about Alonzo's release because my mother looked as if she'd seen a ghost.

She ran to him, and it was mind-blowing how he took her in with open arms. Apollo was right about Venus getting the fuck out of dodge when Alonzo got sentenced. But I guess love was a motherfucker. I let them have their moment because I wasn't about to be in here going toe to toe with Alonzo.

Sitting back down, I heard Mrs. Cox down there mumbling about whooping my mama's sage-toting ass. Mr. Cox told her to calm down and I turned to Mocha. She was looking at me like I was crazy.

"What?" I asked.

"You expect me to tell Nina she's about to be family with that?" she questioned.

"Nah, not immediately. Venus has to grow on you. I'ma check you like I check her though. That's still my mama."

"You ain't checking shit!" Mocha looked me up and down and then leaned in to whisper something to Hazel. I mushed her upside her head, resulting in a playful pushing match.

"Don't be talking shit about me."

My cousin Karmen walked in and flopped down at the table, making my granny startup. "Where have you been? You are walking around careless like your daddy ain't just been killed!"

"It's about time!" Karmen said, making my family's head snap in her direction. Her ass hadn't spoken a word in years, we'd forgotten how her voice sounded. That's why she and Nyx got along so well. "Granny, you know all the shiesty shit he was into. I'm surprised this ain't happened sooner."

I leaned in so my brothers could hear me. "Aye, Nyx, point me to the utility closet and I can make a spill that will clear this muhfucka out in three minutes!"

I thought this was going to end up in a shouting match, but all Granny did was start crying and shit again to deflect from Karmen's words.

"No need. I'm out," Nyx said. "I'll make sure Ian cleans up and shit. Karmen, you should've brought your mute ass in here sooner."

"Say no more." We all stood and said our goodbyes, even with Granny in the background wailing.

"WHAT'S UP MAJIQ?" I greeted as Mocha and I walked into Mocha's place.

"Hey, y'all. Nina's in her room. She ate and had a bath."

"Thank you." Mocha hugged Majiq and once she left, I followed Mocha down the hall to the room, she turned into Nina's. Nina was on the floor playing with dolls.

"Hey, Bird!" Mocha's smile touched her ears.

"Cha!" Nina ran into Mocha's arms.

Mocha sat her down and bent down to Nina's eye level. "I want you to meet someone. This is Zeus. Zeus is very special to me and will be around a lot. Is that OK?"

Nina nodded and looked up at me with innocent eyes. I, too, squatted to her eye level. I began to say something to her, but she wrapped her little arms around my neck so quickly, all I could do was embrace her back. The happy moment was short-lived when she flinched at me touching her back.

"What hurts?" I pulled Nina back to look her in her eyes.

She looked to the floor. "Just my back."

I looked over at Mocha, who had tears building. "Cha and I are going to make sure no one hurt you again. OK?"

"Yes," she whispered, still looking at the floor.

"Pick up your toys and I'll be back to tuck you in." Mocha lifted Nina's head when she spoke to her, and those blue eyes lit back up. This time, I followed Mocha to her bedroom. She began moving around the room, picking up clothes I knew she threw around the room getting ready this morning. Standing at her dresser, folding clothes and shoving them into the drawers, I caught the gloss of her eyes in her reflection.

I wrapped my arms around her from behind. Normally, I would be able to feel her relax in my arms, but she covered her face, crumbled, and let out a muffled sob.

"Mocha, what's wrong, baby?" I turned her around, pulling her hands away from her face.

"Nothing now." She shrugged. I looked into her eyes, confused. "Since the day I left Pierre, I hadn't shed a tear. I was so determined to be the strong, independent woman chasing her dreams that I blocked out everything else. I didn't even let you explain when it came to Tina because I was building a wall, and I felt so alone within those three months.

"My family was right by my side, but my grind mode was activated and my end goal was all I saw. Then Pierre's death, and now Nina being abused by that bitch that birthed her. I still have not allowed myself to shed one tear.

"Just hearing you tell Nina that she's safe, also made me feel the safest I've felt in a long time and these emotions hit me like a tsunami."

"Y'all both are safe, and you don't ever have to carry a load alone again. I don't give a fuck how light or heavy it is," I assured her, kissing her salty tears away. "Get Nina ready for bed and I'll be back."

"Where are you going?"

"I have an experiment to finish up."

IT DIDN'T SURPRISE me that the doors were unlocked. I walked right in, seeing if an alarm would sound in any way. Swirling the chemicals around in the pipette, I slowly walked toward the sound of the television. The blue light lit up the walls in the dark area, and as I walked in, I saw Penelope sleeping with her arm thrown behind the back of the couch. A near-empty bottle of Casamigos sat on the table.

Lifting what had become one of my favorite compounds, I poured it directly on the hand that hung off the couch.

"Arrrgggggggghhh!" Penelope jumped out of her sleep, screaming in agony, holding up the hand that now had the skeleton of her hand showing.

"Shut the fuck yo' before I pour this shit down your esophagus," I said calmly. It had been a long day and I just needed to get my point across.

Penelope bit her bottom lip to stop yelling and her breathing was so hard it sounded like she was growling. I looked over her appearance and my lip twisted up in disgust.

"This is a long way from the way you looked, holding on to my girlfriend's mistake that night at the play. You gotta tighten up. Eww."

"Fuck you!" she spat.

"No thanks. You look like you need a bath." I walked around the couch to stand over her. "Yea, you definitely stink. Anyway, I'm here because a child left out of here a few days ago with black and blue bruises."

Penelope's eyes were on me as I spoke, but as soon as I mentioned Nina, they rolled to the back of her head. I tilted my glass beaker that she hadn't even noticed was hovering over her hands. I emptied the glass, watching as she screamed and shriveled up while the chemical ate through her flesh and bones.

"I bet you won't put your hands on anyone else, huh?" I laughed. "Oh damn, you can't! Now, use your elbows to call for help. My brother works at the hospital, so if I get wind of any authorities snooping around, I'll burn your ass alive! Got it?"

Penelope nodded and I left. Giving my brothers a call in the group FaceTime while driving back to Mocha's.

"Ain't y'all niggas had enough for the day?" Nyx groaned, answering the phone.

Apollo laughed. "What's up?"

"I'm just calling to let y'all know I just burned a bitch hands off since y'all so adamant on me updating y'all on shit like that." I shrugged.

"And you chose to call after you did the shit? That makes really good sense, Zeus," Apollo sighed.

"When should I expect the body?" Nyx asked.

"Oh, this one is for Apollo little brother," I explained, and Nyx left the call.

"Mean ass." I chuckled.

"You should have seen that one coming. But what's up?" Apollo asked.

"Pierre's baby mama. I burned the bitch hands off. I couldn't kill her so close to Pierre's death without it looking suspicious. I see you're not working, so put in a call to let you know if twelve is snooping around when she goes in."

"Aight."

We ended the call, and I went to slide into bed with my woman. This thing with Nina is new to a nigga but I loved kids and since I wasn't letting Mocha go again, that meant I wasn't letting Nina go either.

THIRTY-SIX
NYX

It was taking everything I had not to explode as I watched Braiza ride my dick reverse cowgirl. That kickboxing shit kept her fine ass in shape and the view was amazing. Her ass jiggled while she bounced and rotated on her dick. Yep, at this point, this shit was hers.

Her thick, black hair went further down her back and I noticed that she'd thrown her head back. I knew why when her walls clenched around my dick.

"Mm hm, cum on this dick." I smacked her ass and locked my lips, watching her cream. Braiza slowed down, trying to catch her breath from her orgasm. "Nah, keep riding."

I smacked her ass again, gripping and holding on to the left cheek.

"Shit, I'm cumming, Brai!" Braiza tried to lift but I held onto her waist for dear life. She was going to catch all this nut. Thrusting my hips upward, I released all in her.

Once I let her go, Braiza leaned forward onto my shins with my dick still jerking inside of her. Brai looked over her shoulder. "I can't believe you did that. Are you feeling, OK?"

I tapped her side, telling her to lift. "Yea, I'm straight, come here."

I hated that she still got surprised when I did shit like this, but I get it. I normally hated to cuddle after sex but fuck it, I was in love now. Braiza snuggled against me and interlaced our fingers.

"I guess it's safe to talk baby names since you're shooting up the club," Braiza said.

It had been almost a year since we'd been dealing with one another, and she hadn't ever made me laugh that hard.

"Don't say that shit no more." I laughed.

"Ain't that what y'all say? I ain't that damn old!" She hit my chest.

"Nah, but as you can see, I wouldn't mind starting to try so it wouldn't hurt to hear what you have in mind. Don't be coming up with weird shit, either." I looked down at her and she was smiling like a Cheshire Cat.

"I was thinking a Jr. maybe?" She peeked up at me.

"My daughter is going to be my Jr."

"Huh?"

"It's not conventional, but I get enough shit about being named after a goddess, I ain't putting my son through that. So, Nyx, if it's a girl, and we can look up the list of the Greek gods for the boy's name," I explained.

"That works." Braiza lay there, tracing my tattoos for a second, and suddenly got excited. "Oh! I forgot to tell you about this book I started."

"I haven't even gotten through the last one."

"I know, but I just want you to see what's next." Braiza rolled out of bed and went to grab a book out of her bag. "It's something new I tried. I think it would be considered paranormal."

"OK, send me the audiobook link. I'll read it next," I told her.

"Read the back first to see if it may be something you'll like." She flipped the book over and handed it to me. I leaned over into the light to see if I could get through the first few sentences to make her feel better but the font on the book was weird as hell.

I began to get frustrated, and Mocha's words played in my head. Shit, I was thinking about building my life with Braiza, which meant that I trusted her. *Right?* I went back and forth with myself for a second and then tossed the book onto the bed.

"So?" She grinned, waiting to hear my thoughts.

"I, um, I couldn't read it."

"Why?"

"I'm dyslexic, Braiza. It would take me forever to try to get through that synopsis." I sighed and looked away. Her soft hand cupped my chin and made me look at her.

"I swear I told Randi that something about you was special. I just couldn't put my finger on it." She looked at me with admiration and I was confused.

"Special?"

"Yes, special. You're one of the smartest people I know, Nyx. Dyslexia only means you have to work a little harder to process things. You have a career and run a successful business, and you worked hard to get there without giving up. Give yourself some credit!"

I cupped her face the same way she cupped mine while pouring into a nigga. Pulling her close, I parted my lips and covered hers. She was hesitant but engaged fully in a slow, sensual kiss. She tasted good as hell while she moaned against my mouth. My dick was back at full attention.

"Damn, that was worth the wait," she panted.

"I love yo' old ass." I expressed my gratitude for her response to my confession.

"I love you, too." Braiza kissed me again and climbed back on my dick. If she didn't end up pregnant that night, I would for sure have to go make sure my soldiers were intact.

THIRTY-SEVEN
HAZEL

"Where you going?" Apollo grabbed me as I tried to roll out of bed.

"I've gotta be to work in an hour. I have to get up," I replied. Groaning, Apollo let go of my arm. He'd been here since his family showed their entire ass at his uncle's memorial and the nights had been full of talking and nasty ass sex. I quivered just thinking about the shit he did to me. *Nope. Go get your ass in the shower, Hazel.*

I washed my body and heard Apollo enter the bathroom. The toilet seat lifted and the sound of him peeing made me cringe. I didn't care how much I had told him I hated it, he still did it.

"What are you going to do with your day off?" I asked, deciding not to even repeat myself.

"I actually have to teach a first aid class in a little while. I can stop by for lunch if you want."

"I'm taking Cha somewhere around that time. I'll just text you when I get off." I rinsed the soap off my body. I stepped out of the shower and wrapped myself up in a towel.

"Yo' ass gon be late." Apollo shook his head.

"I'll need to leave in the next twenty minutes, that's enough for me to do my hair and get dressed."

"Yeah, right," he debated. I rolled my eyes and went to my closet. I decided to just do a ponytail and a simple orange blouse with gray slacks. A simple eyebrow fill-in and lipstick look would have to work for the day. I rocked my feet into my heels and busted out laughing at Apollo waiting at the front door with my purse in his hand.

"It's been twenty-three minutes." He looked at his watch.

"Shut up!" We laughed as I locked my house up. "You go wash your ass and don't be late for that class while you're worried about me."

Apollo leaned down and kissed my lips. "I'm always on time, baby. Text me later."

"YOU'RE LATE!" Mr. Jenkins yelled. He sped past the elevator just as I was getting off.

"I know! I'll be in your office in ten."

Dropping the files and my purse on my desk, I bit into the donut that I was hanging between my fingertips with the coffee cup I also held with three fingers.

"They say black folk always stop for something to eat even when you're late." Mocha stood in my doorway shaking her head. "Mr. Jenkins has been poking his head in your window for ten minutes."

"I know. I have to present these presentations for his ten o'clock meeting," I said in between bites.

"Good luck. He just dropped a pile on my desk, too. Ever since we knocked Daija's account out of the park, he's been drowning me with accounts like hers." She sighed.

"Tell me about it." I organized the files I needed and stuffed the donut down my throat. I guzzled some coffee to wash it down and got to work. "Don't make plans for lunch, I want to take you somewhere."

"You ain't gotta tell me twice. I love being treated."

"Hush and pull my door closed please." I raced to Mr. Jenkins's office.

"What do you have?" He got right to it once I walked in. You would think that with the amount of money I was bringing in, he would cut me a little slack. Hell nah. Mr. Jenkins was still an old grump when he wanted to be.

Twenty minutes later, I walked out of his office, having to come up with something new within the next two hours. I was up for the task, but the way Mr. Jenkins had just dismissed me made me feel even better about my plan behind Mocha and I's lunch day.

———

"WHERE ARE WE? I'M HUNGRY!" Mocha whined.

"You're going to eat. I want to show you something first." I hit the elevator button and pressed the number three. The doors opened to a vacant space with large windows. I stepped off and smiled, doing a 360 turn with my hands out. "What do you think?"

Mocha stepped out slowly with a confused look on her face. "What do I think about what?"

"The space. What do you think about this being the office for our very own marketing firm?" I clasped my fists over my mouth with excitement.

"You're serious sissy?" Cha began to beam.

"Yes! Think about it. We're making so much money for someone else. With our skills and your social media presence, we could do this." I watched Cha looking around, nodding her head. "You in?"

"Hell yeah!" she said and jumped right into my arms. I let her do it and she was looking at me as if she wanted to cry but was still smiling.

"What is it?" I asked.

"I'm proud of us," she exclaimed. "Haze, you're glowing. I haven't seen you this happy in a long time. Even when I didn't know the totality of what you were battling, watching you heal from Quincy's death looked good on you. But this is a different kind of glow."

"I am happy, Cha. Like, happy without worrying about if I killed

Quincy or not. I'll tell you about that later. But I can honestly say the same about you."

"Yeah." She exhaled in relief. "The last six months have been crazy. I want to say things feel back to normal, but you know just as I do that being with a Tait is in no way, shape, or form normal. But things feel right."

"Trust me, I know!" We laughed and hugged one another again. "OK, let's get something to eat and call this real estate agent to make an offer."

———

I GOT off earlier than expected, and when I pulled into my driveway, I saw Apollo hadn't made it home yet. I knew it wouldn't be long since he thought I would be getting off work soon, so I decided to make my baby dinner. He always cooked for me, and I'd yet return the gesture.

I wasn't a chef, but I watched my mother in the kitchen all my life. Thinking about the conversation I had with Mocha earlier, I smiled again. Apollo and I were finally through that awkward stage with all our chips on the table and were finally able to just enjoy the dating stage and one another.

Two hours later, I wrapped the plates up in foil and put on something comfortable to walk across the street to surprise my man. I rang the doorbell and Apollo showed up shirtless with some gray sweat shorts on. My mouth watered, making me look forward to dessert.

"I cooked for you." I held the plates up.

"Ooh, shit." He kind of blushed, taking the plates out of my hands. "Sit down, I'll get us drinks."

Apollo returned to the table, set the drinks down, and handed me a utensil.

"How was the class?" I unwrapped my plate, revealing the smothered chicken over rice.

"It was good." Apollo mixed his gravy into the rice. "I didn't have a class full of amateurs, so it went fast."

He took a fork full of rice and chewed it a little before spitting it in his napkin.

"Hazel, I love you, baby. But leave the cooking to me." He got up and threw the entire plate in the trash. My jaw was on the floor as he came back to the table and drank his entire glass of juice.

"It is not that bad!" I pouted.

"Fat Girl, that gravy tastes like flour and the rice is crunchy as shit! Go put some clothes on, I'll take us out."

Leaving the plate there, I got up and stormed out of the house, calling my mother and Mocha on FaceTime to tell them what had just happened.

"He's right, Hazel." My mother took Apollo's side. "I hoped you would finally get it right, but you can't cook no gravy."

Mocha was in tears, laughing at the entire scenario. I hung up on their asses too.

"I can cook," I mumbled to myself, changing out of my leggings and tank and into a pair of jeans and a t-shirt. I sat at my vanity and quickly brushed over my ponytail. Before I got up, something caught my attention. It was the pair of infinity earrings Apollo got me on our first date. I put them on, and my mood changed.

Locking back up, Apollo was waiting for me by his car. He opened my door for me and didn't even notice the earrings until he got in the driver's seat.

"Forever love, huh?" He flashed that sexy ass smile. "Wit'cho non-cooking ass."

I pushed his shoulder playfully. "Whatever."

"It's OK, Fat Girl. I have forever to teach you."

THIRTY-EIGHT
MOCHA

"What are you in here smiling about?" Zeus walked into my soon-to-be old office and asked. I turned the screen around and showed him. "That's dope. Y'all ain't have to do that."

"I wanted to." I blushed. I'd convinced Hazel to put on a summer charity event that would cater to academics within the camps. The main one is Zeus's science camp. "The event is in a couple of weeks so the donations should hit right on time. So, get to planning."

"Thank you, love." Zeus came around my desk and kissed me. We talked more about what he wanted to do with the kids when Hazel came knocking on my door, holding her phone with an attitude. "What my brother do now?"

"Fuck you!" Apollo's voice blared from the phone. Zeus and I laughed as Hazel turned down the volume on her phone.

"Apollo wants everyone to come over for a cookout this weekend," she huffed.

"OK. What's the attitude?" I questioned.

"I told his ass to just text y'all and he threatened not to give me any dick for the rest of the week if I ain't walk in here to tell y'all." Hazel rolled her eyes.

"Y'all childish as hell," I laughed, making Hazel stomp back toward her office.

"Calling somebody childish when I know for a fact your ass would have a fit if I held out," Zeus pointed out.

"You ain't that stupid to threaten me though. Now get back to work. I know you missed me and all but you ain't have to drive across town for a kiss!" I playfully shooed him away.

"The school is five minutes from here." Zeus pressed his lips together and jerked his neck back. "You've got your face buried so deep into your computer; you missed this bag sitting behind it."

He lifted the bag and opened the bag and the smell of Caribbean food hit me.

"You and your brother sure do know the way to a woman's heart." I snatched the bag.

"Greedy ass. I love you."

"I love you, too." Zeus kissed my forehead and left. I watched his tall, fine ass walk to the elevator. I couldn't wait to mount his ass later.

———

IT WAS Memorial Day and Apollo had been raving about this cookout all week. Claiming that we hadn't had real barbeque until we had his. So, here we were. There was pulled pork, ribs, brisket, chicken, hot dogs, and burgers. He agreed to let my mother do the sides as long as Hazel didn't touch shit.

Music blasted in his backyard, and surprisingly, our families were getting along. Even my mother and Venus peacefully caught up while Nina sat in her lap.

I was nervous about everyone accepting my baby, but they welcomed her with open arms, and I was glad. Both Zeus and I agreed he was burning shit down if they didn't.

"How are you guys adjusting?" Hazel asked. She, Braiza, and I were sitting at one of the umbrella-covered tables Apollo had out back. Despite all the craziness, Braiza seemed to adjust well.

"Better than I thought. I felt like I would have had to ease them both into being around each other, but shit, they excluded me half the time. Zeus even learned how to help her with her schoolwork so now I have to force my way in." I sounded jealous but I couldn't be happier.

"He's so good with kids. Don't worry, I get jealous of how the kids stick to him too," Braiza said. "It's almost summer and all they're running around screaming about is Mr. Tait's science camp."

"Yea, he's a natural outside of being naturally crazy." I looked across the yard, spotting Zeus blow up some slip and slides. "See. I wonder who talked him into that."

"Bird, you wanna help me with the water hose?" Zeus yelled and Nina flew off my mother's lap like a true bird. Ten minutes later and the music was turned down. "Aight, come on y'all! We're doing a relay race. Men versus women. You gotta slide down, take a shot, and run back to tag the next person. Bird gets to go by herself and sip her juice."

"I'm down. What are we betting?" I made the game a little more exciting.

"Winners get an unbothered night at the strip club," Zeus's father said. "I haven't been out since I came home. I'm due for some fun with my sons."

Everyone heard Nyx groan and ignored him. The women agreed and lined up once Zeus had the shots set up. Nina went first and took a drink of her Caprisun, then ran back to tag me in. Zeus and I took off running and slid down the slip-and-slide. He got ahead of me because my ass flopped too damn hard and knocked the wind out of me. That fucked up the entire rotation and resulted in the men dapping each other up.

We ate, listened to music, and danced until the men said that they were going to get dressed. We put what was left of the food up and cleaned Apollo's house.

"What do you think they're doing?" Braiza asked while we were all sitting around having some girl talk.

"I don't know. But we're not going to wait around wondering," Venus said, puffing a blunt.

"Venus, no." My mother shook her head.

"Come on, Chai. Let's have some fun for old-time sake." Venus nudged her.

"Somebody wanna fill us in?" I inquired and was sorry I ever asked.

An hour later, we were all meeting back up in front of the club my mother saw that the men were at. She was the only one that had her man's location. Venus handed us all costume wigs and we were dressed our sexiest as we walked in the club.

Standing near the entrance, we scanned the area to find the men.

"There they are." Braiza pointed at the guys, and I quickly lowered her arm. They had their own section and each man was getting a lap dance, except for Nyx. "What are we about to do?"

"Follow my lead," Venus said. "The dancers usually wait until the song changes to move along." The song ended and my mother was on Venus's heel approaching the section.

"Come on." I grabbed the girl's arms and tugged them in that direction. My mother and Venus went straight to their men and started dancing with their backs facing them. Hazel and I followed suit and as I was dancing, I noticed Braiza stayed outside of the section. Zeus slapped my ass a few times as I ground on him to "Body Party" by Ciara. I locked eyes with Braiza and used my head to nod toward Nyx, whose face was still buried in his phone.

That was a mistake because as soon as she attempted to dance on him, it blew our whole cover. His mean ass pushed her away from him so hard she flew forward.

"Damn, Nyx!" She screamed so loud we didn't have to struggle to hear her over the music. She pulled her wig off and faced him. Suddenly, I was jerked around, and my wig was snatched off as well. With the exception of Braiza, me and the rest of the women were laughing so hard looking at our men's faces. They couldn't do shit but laugh as well.

"Bring y'all asses on!" my father barked, still laughing. We all got outside, and Zeus asked us whose idea this was. Everyone pointed to Venus and Alonzo just shook his head. We walked through the parking lot talking shit and Braiza was still upset, looking at the strawberry-looking burn on her knee from falling.

"Y'all are crazy. I don't know if I can do this if this is what I'll have to endure." She shook her head. We all looked around like she had lost her mind.

"Girl, welcome to Death Row!" we all said in unison.

Even Nyx had to laugh. "Get yo' ass in the car. You ain't going nowhere."

THE END

WANT TO BE A PART OF THE GRAND PENZ FAMILY?

To submit your manuscript to Grand Penz Publications, please send the first three chapters and synopsis to info@grandpenz.com

Made in the USA
Middletown, DE
05 July 2023